Dead
of
November

A Novel of
Lake Superior

Craig A. Brockman

Address all inquiries to:
Craig A. Brockman
8770 Hawthorne Dr.
Tecumseh, MI 49286
CraigABrockman.com
craig@craigabrockman.com

ISBN: 978-0-578-62353-5
Library of Congress Control Number: 2019920424

Editor: Tyler Tichelaar, Superior Book Productions
Cover Art and Maps: Craig Brockman
Cover and Interior Layout: Larry Alexander, Superior Book Productions

Printed in the United States of America

To Sal

Contents

Akudo: It Creeps from the Water (Ojibwe)

The loon keens while lost in gray, wandering on still water. Silent Manitou; wraiths cloaked in ragged plumes of fog, transparent against the rock, sweep across damp sand. Enfolded by the green black limbs of spruce and hemlock...they vanish. From shore, the gentle waves whisper incantations to these spirits.

The warbling call echoes off cliffs and forests, over beaches and grass, onto stones and fallen birches, and back over infinite water. In boundless depths, leviathan phantoms glide in darkness over bones and ballast.

We come back. We always come back.

PROLOGUE

THEY STEPPED ALONG THE NARROW path between blueberry bushes and wintergreen, under the deep shadow of whispering white pine, and onto the dazzling wide beach rimming the bay. Like players, they walked from the wings of a darkened theater onto a bright stage as broad as the world.

The kids rushed ahead, casting aside sand and towels, and plowed into the water while Uncle Matt emerged a few steps behind, lugging a chair and a duffel bag. They would need few props today.

The Shallows near Naomikong Point is one of the secret, warm beaches hidden in the bays and hollows of Lake Superior. Locals find a little tropical escape there on those rare eighty-degree days in August. Today, they had the whole beach to themselves, except for a woman who sat on a rock a hundred yards or more from shore. In eerie silhouette, it was hard to tell whether she was facing them or looking toward the vastness of the bay.

Offshore, a sand bar occasionally develops. On those days, they would wade through hip-deep water and float a plastic cooler out there for the day. Today, their uncle decided to stay near the shore with the three children. Thunderstorms threatened, and a tall, dark cloud bank, already building behind them, loomed from the northwest.

In Michigan's Upper Peninsula, known most places as the U.P., a warm day often ends in rough weather as the damp onshore breezes, having traversed hundreds of miles of churning, freshwater sea, carry abundant moisture over warm land and whip it into towering storms.

Matt kept an eye on the line of clouds, the restless whitecaps far out in the bay, and the lady on the rock. Strange that she was here alone. No other cars were in the parking lot. Matt thought it was probably just a seasonal resident who'd walked from those summer homes a mile or so up the beach. She sat on the largest of the eight or ten rocks scattered offshore that ranged in size from an old trunk to an overturned skiff.

The kids swam and played. They slithered on their bellies, sleek as otters, until Uncle Matt, one of those rare freshwater killer whales, with white paunch and tanned arms, grabbed their feet and hauled them back into deeper water. It was a perfect day.

The woman was still on the rock. She hadn't moved. Matt asked the older nephew, Todd, "Has she even looked around since we got here?"

"Nope," Todd said. Together, they watched her across the water. The boy could sense that something about her was not quite right. But after all, she was an adult, and at eleven years old, Todd thought most adults were weird.

When thunder rumbled, Uncle Matt decided it was time to gather up the kids, and of course, they whined as they reluctantly collected their stuff. A branch of lightning sketched across the sky, and the concussion of thunder was loud enough to convince them.

With truck doors open, Matt made the kids wipe their feet as they threw their things in back. He looked again at the woman on the rock. There was a distant flash, and after only seconds, thunder. She was in danger. He had to say something or do something.

Choppy waves began pushing offshore ahead of the storm, making it urgent that he get her attention.

Matt stepped into the water, up to his ankles, and shuffled out a couple of steps. He felt awkward. He was not a complete novice at rescue, but in the volunteer fire department, he didn't have to work alone. He wasn't sure what to do now, and he certainly did not want to put the kids in danger.

"Hell-o! Are you okay?"

Nothing. *God, this is stupid.*

He looked at the kids, then back to her. *What is she doing out there?*

"Stay by the truck!" he shouted to them. *No matter what happens,* he thought to himself.

Matt only had seconds to weigh his options and make a decision. Back and forth he rationalized. If he just drove away, he didn't want to hear tomorrow about a lady who got struck by lightning at The Shallows, but he risked stranding the kids if *he* got struck. But then he continued to argue with himself. *The storm wasn't overhead, just close.* He could be out there in two minutes. Calling 911 would take too long and the storm would be here by then. *How often do one of these rocks get struck? They've been here for centuries. This is ridiculous! It's dangerous!* He wondered if she could be having a seizure or some kind of diabetic crisis. *What the hell is she doing?*

"Hell-o! Hey! Do you need help?" The woman was motionless.

Matt stood with fists pressed into his hips, elbows angled outward, and nervously pivoted left and right, looking across darkening water to the waves far out in the bay, still tipped by sunlight. He glanced back along the infinite arch of trees and beach that disappeared north and south as though there might be someone else who would come to the rescue.

He finally sighed, and stepped farther into the water, hesitated, then started forward again, wallowing deeper as quickly as he could. Soon, he was up to his hips. The water had been perfectly clear earlier, but now it was murky—in fact, filthier than he'd ever seen it. He couldn't even see his knees in this cloudy mess, and the waves were getting bigger and more restless.

Matt was more than halfway out there. Another rumble, but still distant enough, he thought.

As he waded nearer, he could see by her figure that she was younger than he'd thought. It was that modest, old-fashioned, black one-piece suit with the little skirt and full back that made her look much older. The suit looked like something his mother might have worn—or his grandmother, and for an instant, he thought it almost comical, except that it was worn and dirty.

He was close to her. The water smelled bad; he looked around in the darkened murk, fearful of brushing against a dead salmon—or something worse. *Damn! Come on, lady!* The strangeness was palpable, and he couldn't control his rising panic.

"Hey! Come *on*! Are you okay?" No response. Loud, seismic thunder. *Damn it!*

Matt stopped behind her, and reached cautiously. But just before his fingers touched her gray, mottled shoulder, her head quickly swiveled.

The last thing he heard was his own screaming babble. "Oh, n-no! N-no! God, N-no!"

CHAPTER 1

INDIANA

THERE IS NO PLACE so cold and deep as grief, and no water wide and clear enough to wash away the stain of regret. Many carry grief day after day and year after year until the burden feels lighter, not by its diminishing weight, but by their increasing strength. Grief is abiding, tenacious, and raw. Some can keep it dammed up for months; some can even freeze it for a lifetime, but a few choose simply to conceal it beneath the pain and grief of others.

§ § §

When a session approached grief or loss, Adam Knowles could drift and daydream in a world of his own hurt. He would have to force himself back to the discussion. This situation was not always therapeutic for a psychologist, but his clients considered him compassionate and engaged, and for the most part, he truly was.

This counseling session had been silent for several minutes. Adam continued to stare patiently while waiting for his client to speak when she was ready.

Finally, "I can't forget her scream. It just sticks in my head." Carol swept a tissue from the box, dabbed her face, and then twisted the Kleenex in her hands. She spoke in a soft accent, typical for her Southern Indiana roots. Her hair was dark brown, straight, and pushed back with simple barrettes above her ears. Grief had vandalized a handsome face.

"I can't sleep because I hear it over and over and over. That was my daughter finding her baby dead in my house. I'd only laid her down an hour earlier, and when Kaylee came home, she found her. Dead."

Adam maintained silence but scratched his left knee, tousled the thick black hair above his right ear, and adjusted his black frame glasses.

She took a deep breath. "I can't sleep, and then I'm exhausted all day at work. And this with everything else going on." She made the briefest eye contact and looked down at her hands holding the tissue.

"Did Dr. Patrell prescribe anything for you?" Adam rubbed the stubble on his chin, part of a short goatee connected to a thin mustache.

"Yeah, Ambien didn't work, and now he gave me Restoril, and that seems to work okay, but I have to take two, and then I feel like crap the next day."

"Carol, you know I can't prescribe because I'm not a psychiatrist, but I can write a note to Dr. Patrell if you'd like."

"No thanks, Dr. Knowles. I think I can make the Restoril work and try to catch up on sleep on the weekend. It's actually a little better."

"Good. Good. This has been devastating for you to say the least. Unbelievable. But you're making progress. Think of where you were last month before you went back to work. You were paralyzed."

"I know." The tiniest smile at the corner of her mouth erased much of the ravage that had been sketched by pain.

"How's Kaylee doing?"

She sighed, then looked up. "She's actually doing pretty well—considering." She nodded. "They really helped at school, and she has a good counselor."

"Good. I'm really glad to hear it. She's been through so much in her life. I'm glad she got help when she did," he said, then waited a beat to give her more time. "Anything else you need to talk about?"

"No. Thanks again. I have to say you've really been a help. I even recommended you to somebody at work. 'Just go see Dr. Knowles,' is what I told them."

"Oh, now I have a reputation to live up to." Adam raised his eyebrows and smiled while he tilted his head. His narrow face and ragged hair looked comical. "But call me Adam. Please." Despite his PsyD degree, he was not comfortable accepting the mantle of doctor. He felt unworthy, as though somewhere along his wayward path he'd lost claim to that title.

She smiled and reached out to shake his hand. "Thanks, Adam. I am better. Much better."

"Great. How about I see you again in two weeks? I'll send a note to Patrell, and you can just let me know if you want me to mention the sleep thing, or you can call him."

"No, I can call him myself if I need to."

He laughed. "Whoa. Look at you taking charge! I like it. My work is going to be done here pretty soon, I think."

She acknowledged the humor with a quick nod and a dry grin. "Yup. I have to take control sooner or later, I guess." They stood and he opened the office door. She walked to the front desk.

He leaned out to the receptionist. "Jean, could you schedule Carol back in two weeks?" Jean nodded and smiled at Carol.

"Bye, Carol." He raised his hand.

Adam went back in his office and sat at the desk. He keyed in a few notes on his laptop, reached for the bottle of hand disinfectant, rubbed his hands, looked around his desk, and picked up a folder.

Other than the laptop and a couple of folders, little else was on his desk. No photos or mementos, nothing hanging on the walls or sitting around the office except for one large framed photo of Iroquois Point Lighthouse that hung across from his desk. On the floor under the photo was a cardboard box scrawled *Office*, as though the photo could easily slide off the wall into the box and be ready for leaving.

Jean walked in and delivered a handful of reports and other mail. She was an attractive woman on the heavy side of middle age, but she moved deftly. Her positive attitude kept things running smoothly. They had an easy working relationship, a similar sense of humor, and a heart for caring service to their clients. Adam had met her husband and kids on occasion, but he had avoided most of her invitations to socialize in the couple of years he had been filling in at the clinic. He was still temporary.

Jean laid down the stack of papers. "Here's a call from somebody you used to work with." She tapped the top of the pile. "He said it wasn't urgent, but if you could get back today or tomorrow. And Burroughs canceled for this afternoon—again." She paused, smiling. "I put in Dean Trippet. He called yesterday and wanted to get moved up because he's going away next week."

Adam waited before responding, staring at the note on top of the pile.

"Oh, yeah." He shook his head. "I'll call Sandy Burroughs and make sure everything is okay. Wasn't she going to talk to DSS or a social worker or someone anyway?"

"Yeah, I think so, but she said she had to take her mother to an appointment or something."

"Yeah...right." He was still distracted by the note Jean had delivered.

"I'm going to run home for lunch, if that's okay. Be back at one," she said as she walked toward the door.

"No, problem. But you're fired." He smiled picking up the note from the pile of papers.

"Great. Now I can get unemployment. Maybe I need to talk to someone. Know any good psychologists?"

"You're funny."

"Later."

The yellow note on top of the pile would have to be from his former supervisor and mentor, Ron Jarvin. Even though it had been a few years since Adam had had contact with him, he knew what Ron probably wanted. He set the note aside without reading it—but it was right there.

A few of the other reports required him to sign off. One over here, another done and put over there in the basket. The mail could wait. *But what did Ron really want?*

Adam had worked with Ron for several years at County Behavioral Health in Sault Sainte Marie. It had been his first job after getting out of school and was not an easy place to start a career. At CBH, you dealt with everyone who walked in the door. And the snow, darkness, and alcohol were not only his clients' problems; they eventually became his problems, too.

When the job came up in Fort Wayne, it was time to make the leap and leave Sault Sainte Marie. Actually, if he were honest with himself, the job he had left had little to do with it. It was only after the tragedy with his wife, Julie, and then losing track of his best friend and co-worker, Cam, that he had decided to leave. He had needed Cam, but he had not been there. Any grief or remorse had been stuffed into a memory, the lid forced down, and stacked with all the other excuses for why he had moved to Indiana.

Adam finally picked up the note. He was caught off guard by the sense of dread he felt trying to decide whether to call the number now or to put it off until he got home tonight. Maybe Ron just had a simple question about a client. What if it was a lawsuit or something else that had gone bad?

He knew the dread he felt was really about Julie. It was hard to open this wound again. But it was also about Cam. Why was he suddenly feeling this ominous cloud? Arguing with himself, he thought maybe Ron was just going to be in the area and wanted to say *hi* or just wanted a job reference for someone.

There was always a glimmering in the back of his mind that someday Ron would call on him to fulfill the offer Adam had made before he left; that if Ron ever needed extra help for a couple of weeks at the agency, he could call. He'd thought that after two or three years, Ron would forget about it, but Adam still felt a commitment to Ron—and, somehow, to all the unfinished, stowed away remorse he had left up there.

It haunted him: his inability to come to grips with Julie's death and his failure to reach out to his best friend, Cam. He could not admit those things to himself.

Adam stared at the yellow note for a long while as memories of a former life welled up inside. Gradually, he saw only the yellow of the paper. The old reels in his mind whirred away, the light flickering on, and the film clicking as the rerun of this horror film played.

Adam had lived with vivid dreams most of his life and had *night terrors* as a child. The dreams were mostly of familiar things, not always terrifying. Over the years, a few of these rather mundane dreams would serve to find lost items or to solve unanswered questions for those around him. Later, the dreams became more frightening. A few dreams actually predicted events or untangled a tough problem for someone. Those dreams seemed to come from somewhere else, tapping into a deeper vein of fear and mystery. Adam was not fond of the dreams, and he tried to avoid mentioning them to friends or even to those involved in the dreams. He saw them simply as *his* dreams: sometimes accurate, sometimes distorted. They were his private world.

There was that time when one of his dreams escaped his private world. Adam had been mortified. It created a sensation at the agency in Sault Sainte Marie where he had worked.

The Reilly family had thought they were visited by the ghosts of relatives. They also believed these relatives were trying to tell them something, but it was never clear. Only Adam seemed to listen to the family, and not discount their story like so many others. Even though it was a tragic situation, they were ultimately able to receive comfort.

One family member, a daughter, had gone missing several years before and was presumed to have been murdered. While he was working with the family, Adam had a dream one night where he saw the girl's ghost standing on Miner's Castle overlooking Lake Superior near Munising. He recognized her from a wallet photo her dad had shown him. She smiled, held up a funny stuffed moose, waved, and was gone. He never would have told the family because it seemed so strange that he would dream about her.

The stuffed moose seemed so odd, and at the same time, so relevant. It turned out that the moose was the key. When, in conversation, Adam happened to share the dream with her father, the father was stunned. The moose was her favorite stuffed animal, and it had been left near her bed when she went missing. It had actually disappeared on the night of Adam's dream. The family thought it had simply been mislaid. Ultimately, the family interpreted the dream as confirmation that she was, unfortunately, dead. Sadly, her body was found not far from the parking lot at Miner's Castle the following spring. Further evidence eventually led to the capture of her killer.

Somehow, the story of his dream got out and Adam was embarrassed. However, Ron, his supervisor, was enthralled when he learned about the episode. He praised Adam's insight in helping this family resolve a painful crisis. Many on staff at the agency were uncomfortable with this *hocus-pocus*––including Cam. The town's rumor mill cranked at full speed and made Adam a minor celebrity for a month or two.

The dreams were more likely to occur when he was tired, stressed, or at some critical stage in his life. He felt tired as he sat in his office, and after getting this note, he sensed he was once more at a turning point. In recent years, the dreams were rare. He had not had one in months, but now he could feel something happening. When the dreams were about to occur, there was often a familiar, copper taste and he could smell what he would only describe as rain or fresh air. He sensed those now. Over the years, he had discovered it was possible to step away from the dreams or stop them, but he was drowsy, the office was quiet, and he found it hard to resist.

The movie reel rolled and clicked. Sand and sun and a stiff onshore breeze swept away the walls and windows of his office, and the top of his desk drifted away paper by paper.

Julie was next to him on the blanket again. He felt the sand, whipped by the wind, sting his ankles and legs. The sun was strong, and whitecaps from far out in the bay chased each other all the way to the shore. Adam and Julie sat close so they could hear what was said, but they also sat close just to be near.

"You're burning," he said. "Your skin looks red."

She reached into the bag and handed him the sunscreen. "Do you mind? Besides, that's racist. Native people don't burn, and I don't appreciate being called a redskin."

He smiled. "I don't mind. Hey, you're only half Ojibwe; it's the other side that's burning." He snatched the bottle and squirted a puddle of cream into the palm of his hand until the stream made a loud, squishy fart sound. He laughed.

"Excuse you," she said.

"It's the beer. Pew! Stuff smells like coconuts."

"Not like any coconut I ever smelled. Besides, all the beer you've had would probably just blow your ass off."

"It wasn't me; I swear. And I've only had one, uh—six pack."

"I'll let it go this time."

"You'll let one go?" He snorted at the stupid joke. He spread the cream thick on her shoulders and back. Her skin felt like warm velvet. He swept slower across her upper back, then lower. "I'm afraid you'll have to take this off in order for me to do a proper job of it."

She smiled; her eyes closed, enjoying the sensation. "You'll have to wait to do a proper job of it." Along the deserted beach, she turned to see a family playing at the edge of the water about a half mile away. She took the bottle, and finished her arms and legs. She pushed him away, stood up, and smoothed the lotion on her stomach and the backs of her legs. He watched every move. She sauntered toward the water, her suit riding lower than she would have allowed if anyone else had been around. She was taut and had maintained the gymnast's body she'd had in school. Her dark skin and hair were ravishing when contrasted with the white suit. She stopped to take in the blue-green water, slashed by whitecaps. He admired the brilliance of the shore with the gleaming sand, the white waves, and her silhouette against the water. Even with the wind off the big lake, it was splendidly warm. She looked back, and mouthed as she pointed, "I'm going in."

"Be careful!" he shouted.

She didn't hear him above the roar as another stiff gust blew sand across his legs. Fortunately, the wind was out of the northwest, which seemed to keep those nasty stable flies from chewing at their shins on this warm day.

She picked up one of the inner tubes that lay on the sand while he emptied his beer and lay back. *Glorious*, he thought. *Perfect day.*

She looked over the surf a while longer, turned, threw the tube back on shore, skipped into the water up to her knees, and dove headlong into a big wave.

He lay there a long while, the waves, wind, sun, and beer kneading his mind into a happy mush. He was thinking of almost nothing. Slowly, the heat convinced him he needed another beer, and it was probably time to grab the other tube and follow her into the lake. He propped himself up on one elbow and reached over with his other hand to lift a beer from the cooler. Looking around, he snapped open the can and pushed his sunglasses up on his nose. He sat up so he could look over the waves to find where she was floating. He couldn't see her. He waited to see if she would bob up somewhere. She did not.

Slowly, he stood and surveyed the water. Their little world of blanket, cooler, towels, and sand was shrinking around his ankles as the great water seemed to swell with intimidation. It was the big waves obscuring his view, he convinced himself. He looked far out where whitecaps gamboled like lambs and then near the shore where waves crashed like rams. On the beach were two tubes––she wasn't even in a tube, he realized. He spun to see where the beach met the wall of birch and spruce thirty yards from the shore. Panic simmered: She must have come out of the water and gone into the woods.

"Jules?!"

Quickly, he walked a short way along the beach and looked across the water again, then searched the sand for footprints. Turning, he tramped up the slope of the beach to the trees. He looked side to side to see around the trunks and into the shadowed depths. "Julie? Jules!" He spun and looked over the water and called for her the last time, "JULIE!"

Then a voice. Her voice? He wasn't certain. The voice was emphatic, but not frantic or imploring, "Come back, Adam. Help. Come back!"

The reels clattered to a stop, and he found himself flailing in darkness.

§ § §

The rattling of a lock and opening door in the waiting room roused Adam. He was leaning back with the chair pushed away from the desk, his head back, his elbows bent outward with fingers entwined over his eyes. His legs were out, heels on the floor.

"I'm back!" Jean called pleasantly from the waiting room. Her keys clattered onto her desk, and he heard her sharp steps coming toward his door. He sat up suddenly and shuffled some papers, slid a chart in front of him, and was reaching across the desk for a pen when she leaned against the doorframe. She said nothing. Her face changed from a smile to that same look of pity and confusion he'd seen before.

She sighed. "Adam, are you okay?"

He leaned back in his chair again, looked down, and took a deep breath. "You know, it was just that call from Ron Jarvin—that guy from up north. It sort of brings a lot of stuff back to mind." He tapped a pen on the desk. "I'm pretty sure I know what he wants, and I just don't know if I'm ready to...."

"Are you sure that's what he wants? Maybe it's something else." She waited. "Do you *have* to call him back? I didn't promise anything; I just took the message."

"Yeah, I know. I'll think about it and maybe call him tonight."

"Are you okay? I can't cancel your one o'clock, but I could probably take care of the rest of your schedule."

"No, I think it's okay. Thanks, Jean; don't worry."

"Just let me know." She looked down at him for a while, slid a couple of envelopes onto the desk, and walked out.

Adam sat with hands folded between his knees and stared at the little dark square of floor between his feet and under the desk. It was unusual, even for him, to have such a vivid dream in the middle of the day.

He shrugged, shook it off, and was about to reach for the mail on the desk when an object on the floor next to the desk's leg caught his attention. He stared—confused. Leaning forward, he picked up a smooth gray stone—a beach stone—cold and wet. A circle of water where it had been darkened the drab, blue carpet.

§ § §

In his apartment, with walls as bare as his office, Adam sat on his gray, scratchy sofa, pondering the yellow note. He had forced himself to push through the afternoon schedule with half his mind intent on listening to clients and making recommendations while the other half was somewhere else. It was no longer difficult to function this way. Autopilot was default. He was compassionate, competent, thorough, but still distracted.

Half of his mind *was* somewhere else. It was with Julie. And since coming back to his apartment, he had let himself sink into deep, painful memories. He always tried to avoid this place—a land of echoes, faded photos, and grief.

Her body was never recovered. That compounded the uncertainty and hopelessness. He had never found...*closure*. God, he hated that word. He vowed he would never use that word with his clients. Who ever finds closure? Who ever *wants* to find closure? It's like closing the lid on a casket.

Grief and regret can be entombed or laid in an urn at the back of a closet, but they still molder and rustle like the decaying and crispy bones they are.

He would be satisfied if he could just find peace.

After having that vivid dream in the office, he was empty. Something was wrong with that dream, with everything, and he could not put a finger on what it was. He had missed something, but he could not figure out what it was.

Despite his efforts, Adam could not put Julie out of his mind. She had been life itself to him. He'd had few relationships before her, and after turning thirty, he was wondering if he would ever find that One Certain Love. But when she came along, it was like turning on a light. It was light itself. She filled him up with her happiness and crazy insights and her intensity: laser-focused. Her laughter—just hearing her laugh on the phone or when she made fun of his attempts at being the handyman or tech genius—made everything right. God, *everything* was right when he was with her! Not perfect, but everything was right. Now everything was not right.

He ran his hand through his hair, then steeled himself to set aside his thoughts and make the call. He snatched his phone quickly, as though it were about to jump away. He punched in the number. It rang only once before Ron Jarvin picked up.

"Adam! I'm glad you called."

"Hi, Ron."

"Well, it's been.... How've you been?"

"Okay. Yeah, I've been good. How've you been, Ron?" This felt awkward.

"Swamped. It's a mess."

"I figured. I mean, I wondered if maybe that's why you called. Is this a good time for me to call?"

"Oh sure. You already guessed. You're not going to wait for me to butter you up, stroke your sense of guilt or ego in order to get you back here? You went right to—"

"Hey, you started it!" They laughed. "Sorry, Ron; I.... You can understand it wasn't easy for me to call you back," Adam said.

"I know; I know," Ron stumbled. "I'm sorry, but I just had to reach out. I didn't mean to open any old wounds, but it didn't do any good for me to sit here and wonder if I should call or not. I just bit the bullet and picked up the phone this morning. I don't mean to be trite, but it was hard for me, too.... To call you I mean. I really hope you're okay with me reaching out to you."

Adam stared at the stubbly green carpet in his living room, his left hand tucked under his right arm against his side and his legs crossed. "No, no, it's all right. I'm really glad to hear from you. Honestly, I was thinking of calling you for a long time. I'm glad you called; it's good to hear your voice." He scratched his head and looked at his watch.

The line was quiet. Adam could hear Ron inhale. "Adam, you said when you left I could call if we got in a jam, so I just had to give it a try. So now that the door is open, I guess I'll barge right through."

"Yeah, that door is open." Adam smiled and the tension left his voice.

"Good; I feel better." Ron laughed. "Adam, it's been hell. Insane. County Behavioral Health lost its contract with North Shore Counseling. We couldn't afford it anymore, and you remember, we shared Cam Jourdain with North Shore. He sort of took a header off the cliff of sanity and is now somewhere up by Grand Marais or Vermillion in a cabin or some shack, and no one's heard from him in a year."

The line was silent. "You still there, Adam?" Ron paused. "I know you and Cam were close. I wasn't sure if you were still, uh, friends or had contact."

Adam sighed. "He was in a free fall when I left three years ago. I don't know anything about him. Is he still alive, for Chrissakes?"

"Yeah, one of the counselors from the tribe said that a former client knew about him, but I guess Cam still doesn't want to talk to anybody."

"Jeez. He was a great therapist. Really connected with people. Probably too much, sometimes."

"Definitely too much." Silence. Ron continued, "So—"

"So," Adam interrupted, "I'm fairly committed here. I'm not swamped, but I've got a good setup and it pays the bills. I've got an agreement with one of the hospitals, so I have good control of my hours. Being an independent contractor allows me," *an escape hatch, he* thought, "some flexibility."

"I know it's a lot to ask, and you know I wouldn't have called except that you said when you left that I could always look you up if I needed help. We're really swamped. It's really tough to get anybody to come up here even as *locum tenens*. We need someone who understands our clients."

"Ron, I knew it would only be a matter of time before you called. And honestly, somewhere deep down I probably hoped you would, or that I would at least have a chance to open this avenue again. It's weird because I just had a dream today about..." *Stupid*. He hesitated, "about being up there."

"Sure. I have to say, as long as we're having this little session here––and I'm sorry for playing therapist––but I've thought about you a lot, and I guess I had a hunch, *hope* may be a better word, that you were ready to come back."

Ron waited for a response, but Adam said nothing, so he continued, "Yeah, I've thought about your dreams, too, since you've been away and...there are some things I want, well, I *need* to run by you. If you decide you don't want to fill in at the clinic for us, that's fine, but I'd still like you to come up for a visit. We have a lot to talk about, and I miss ya."

"Yup, I know, and," Adam shook his head, "bringing up the dream thing feels a bit weird. I wish I hadn't. But anyway." He paused a long time until Ron nearly interrupted again to ask if Adam were still there. "Well," Adam continued, "maybe I can help you out. I just need to think it all through some more. And I would need to make some arrangements here, that's all." He ran his hand through his hair. "Let me think about it."

"I'm really glad to hear you'll think about it. I have a place for you to stay if you decide to come. Sorry if I'm moving too fast. Really, this is up to you," Ron said.

"No, that's okay; it all enters into my decision," Adam replied.

"Did you know Maggie Stewart from the B&B by the locks?" Ron asked. "She contracts with us for accommodations sometimes, and

I'm pretty sure you could stay there if you do decide. It's off-season and all. Anyway, it'd make sort of a soft landing for you."

"Sounds like you put some thought into this."

"I really don't want you to come up here with any false assumptions, Adam, because there is some strange stuff going on, and I only feel comfortable discussing it face to face. It will be clearer when you get here why Maggie is a good fit."

Adam was silent as he tumbled the beach stone in his fingers. "I don't know what you mean by weird stuff. Now I'm curious. Anyway, something is telling me I need to come back," he said, then scrambled. "I mean I, uh, I have to get back up there some time."

The wall had been breached and the past was rushing into the present. They continued the conversation for another half hour. Adam knew Ron probably had more in mind. Why else would he mention the dreams again? Ron was one of the few people Adam had shared his dreams with because Ron always seemed fascinated by them.

Adam hung up and sat on the couch a long time. His apartment, his work, and his life in Fort Wayne began to peel away. His thumb gently rubbed circles over the cool gray stone as though it were the back of her hand.

He fell back into memories of her. One of the first times they had been alone, he had reached out and held her hand as they stepped out of the birch grove and onto the beach. It had been disguised as chivalry, but she had not let go as they walked the beach, swinging their shoes at their sides. Her hand so warm and small and.... *No. Put it away.* He swallowed. His throat ached and tears welled. God, how he missed her, and how desperately he needed to work through this grief. It was time. He had to go back: walk the beach, slip into the deep woods, hear the silence, and find his way again.

As memories came winding through the fog and he allowed them to emerge, he had the nagging feeling that something was not right.

He had been haunted by suppressed memories. But this afternoon, dreaming about that terrible day, he was haunted by something more. Something was missing: out of place. He was not seeing it. A festering thorn was working its way to the surface.

Figure it out. Go back and retrieve those memories of Julie and make sense of this. Find peace.

He curled one hand in the other on his lap and sighed definitively.

Then find Cam.

CHAPTER 2

THE CABIN

I cannot find myself in your eyes.
I cannot see the soul of your shadow.
I will wash this stain of regret
In the depths of...

H E TAPPED THE STUB OF pencil on the rough plank table. *What rhymes with shadow?*

I cannot see the soul of your shadow.
I cannot find myself in your eyes.
I will wash my stain of regret
In the wide, clear...

— *Cam Jourdain*

Crap. He scribbled his name a few times: Cam Jourdain, Cameron Jourdain, Cameron James Jourdain. He set down the pencil, leaned back, and looked at the rafters. With a sigh, he ran his hands through his long, black hair and rubbed his eyes. In ragged socks, he shuffled across the pine floor, picked up the fire iron, opened the whining stove door, and poked at the blackened logs until he coaxed a ribbon of flame. Straightening, he pressed his hands into his lower back, scratched his beard, and yawned. At the table, he turned up the wick on the lantern as the log cabin's dark walls absorbed the light and responded with silence. Dead silence. He brooded over the table. Clear blue eyes, wide lips, and broad features had aged beyond mid-thirties, and his large frame had dwindled after a year in the wild. He stood, flipped the latch on the heavy door, and stepped into darkness outside the cabin.

Cam stood on the wooden landing, allowing his vision to adjust until he could see starlight twinkle through black branches. Fifty yards away, the lakeshore glistened and the water whispered. He stepped back inside the door and slid into his boots. The door clunked shut, and his untied boots clumped down two steps to the ground and along the path that wound to the shore. The way was lit by an inch of new snow that crunched underfoot. He paused on the edge of the broad beach. Despite the night's encircling silence, the lake seethed, and reflected stars danced on its surface. Somewhere down the beach, a pack of coyotes yammered; then it was quiet again all along the shore and into the forest. The lake's motion was mesmerizing. At the edge of his awareness came the gentle *thump, thump, thump* of a freighter far out on the lake, and he could barely make out the lights of the passing ship on the dark horizon.

Cam turned back to the cabin and was about to step off the path to relieve himself when a puff of onshore breeze disturbed the stillness, pushed past him, and rustled dead weeds along the trail. The lower spruce bows dipped and waved, and the fresh snow hissed. He heard a creaking and looked up toward the cabin, where a sliver of light from inside the cabin shone along the edge of the opening door.

"Weird."

He saw no one and heard nothing more. He walked back up the steps and pushed the door farther open. The inside of the cabin was as he'd left it. *Didn't close it tight, again,* he thought. The door rattled as he shut it behind him, but he turned and pushed again just to be sure it was closed. It had been another long, boring day. He was tired and ready to turn in.

He rustled around the cabin to complete his usual evening routine. He had to stow food and clean up the dishes to foil the mice. This late in the season, there was not much threat of insects. Fortunately, brushing his teeth was one habit he had not surrendered, only because he could not afford a toothache or broken filling while stuck out here.

With flashlight in hand, Cam left the cabin for the outhouse, and when he finished, he re-latched the door. He kicked off his boots, picked up the lantern from the table, and set it next to the bed. As he turned some fresh logs with the poker, sparks flared like angry hornets. Jeans and flannel shirt were hung over the chair, and he slid under the covers in long underwear. From his vantage point in bed, he surveyed his small space again, then reached over and turned off the lantern.

§ § §

At the edge of a dream, floating near wakefulness, Cam was in a village or an encampment, with the smell of smoked fish hanging near a smudge. Sticks clattered and voices laughed as children scuffled. Graceful bodies cast shadows on tree trunks. He lifted from sleep by degrees and became aware of his cabin again. The fire in the stove had died to an orange glow—just enough for him to make out the room's interior.

Cam turned on his side, facing the room, thinking he was still dreaming, and saw a young Native man, adolescent age, sitting on the floor near the stove. His back was against the log wall, his left leg outstretched on the floor, and his right arm rested across his other knee, which was pulled up near his chest. He was looking into the glowing fire with an expression serene beyond youth. Over his left ear, two feathers fanned downward from a tuft of fur and touched his shoulder. The young man's left hand rested on the floor and loosely held a gracefully curved, decorated wooden shaft, about as long as his forearm. The end was carved into an oval, the size of a large egg: *an Iroquois war club*, Cam thought. The young man's leather leggings were stained and worn, and his moccasins were crudely stitched.

After a short time, the young man turned slowly away from the fire and met Cam's gaze with a simple grin. Slowly, he stood, took in the room around him, and started to walk toward the door. Then, as if in a moment of confusion, he looked around, turned in the opposite direction away from the lake, and without slowing his pace, walked through the wall and disappeared. Cam blinked slowly, but convinced it had been a dream, he was soon back asleep.

Hours later, lost in an addled nightmare of sharp edges and heavy fog, Cam heard a hoarse moaning that carried him to the surface of waking. He had not yet opened his eyes. This raspy whine continued until he was brought fully awake by the hammering rattle of the two small windows on each end of the cabin. Morning gray outlined the stove, table, shelves, and the rest of the clutter that made up his small world. The moaning swelled, as did the rattle. He realized something brutal was blowing in off the lake, and the ticking and hissing at the windows suggested snow and sleet.

The cabin had grown frigid; Cam tried to sink deeper into layers of blanket so only the top of his head was exposed as he peered out under the covers' edge. He had not prepared for an early storm, and the thought of exposing himself to a cold cabin, stoking the stove, checking the water and, worst of all, spending the day trapped in this damn cabin again, was more than he cared to deal with.

With a sigh, Cam threw back the covers and sat at the edge of the bed, then stood quickly and slipped into cold jeans and shirt. A hooded sweatshirt from the bench near the bed was pulled over his head, and he considered wearing the gloves on the shelf, but decided against it. A broken-down pair of sneakers slumped near the door. He tiptoed over to slip them on. Another gust moaned at the door, and the windows played a flourish. Through frosted glass, he could see the tall spruce trees, with limbs waving like angry giants, drowning in a hazy surf of wind and snow.

Cam shuffled back to the stove and opened the door. Far away, the wind's metallic sigh keened in the flue like a dirge from another dimension. He stirred the blinking coals, added a few slivers of kindling, and the updraft soon ignited a small flame. With sticks and a couple of smaller logs, the hungry flames leapt into a crackling fire. He swung the latch shut on the glass and iron door, then slid a chair closer to spread his hands in the traditional pose of a man seeking warmth from a meager flame.

Something changed in the storm; the ticking sleet subsided, and waves of fine, cold flakes lashed the cabin. During heavy gusts, tiny frozen flecks forced their way through cracks under windows and around the door. Finding the calm of the room, they slowed and settled like dust. Cam's attention was held by this gentle cascade, and his mind was blank as he awaited warmth. A crystalline draft was swirling. It flowed and fell in the icy air around the door. The room was not warm enough to thaw the fine snow dust that seeped and shifted in gossamer shapes as it drifted to the floor. Another gust rattled the windows and sprayed another glittering shower. The dance and drift were captivating, and he imagined forms in the sifting snow as it blended with the cabin's background shapes: feathers, swans, and dandelion fuzz.

Cam shook his head as the images became more distinct and static. He was about to stand and find something to stuff in the crack along the doorjamb when a strong burst sent a cloud of snow into the room. He paused and sat back in his seat as he thought he saw something forming in the pattern of drifting snow. Glinting and blurry at first, then fading, now returning, sparkling around the edges—a shoulder, a mitten, maybe a large fur hat. Indistinct and imaginary, the shape of a man was forming. Suddenly, crackling into focus, a ragged figure, heavily clothed and covered in snow, stood in the room. Cam covered his eyes with his hand, then rubbed his face, and looked up again.

At first, the figure of the man seemed solid and whole; then it shimmered and blurred again, as though finding focus. The image appeared near in the room, then far, approaching and receding. Was the figure moving into the room, or was the cabin moving toward him? Cam was as fascinated with his own calm objectivity as he was with the apparition forming in front of him. To get a broader view, he slid off his chair, sidled across the floor to the wall behind him, and leaned back near the stove where the Native youth had sat hours earlier.

These experiences were not entirely foreign to Cam. The dream or vision of the Iroquois warrior and this man materializing by the door were not his first encounters. These, whatever they were, were becoming more frequent. Seeing two in one day was very strange. In Cam's mind, they could only be testimony to a creeping insanity or some lingering flashbacks that were the wages of the mental torment and regret that had brought him to this cabin and this lost place in life.

The man had formed completely and was bent slightly forward as though ducking under a low ceiling as he looked side to side, not engaging with anything in the cabin, but looking beyond the bed, the table, and Cam. He wore a fur coat neatly trimmed, and over his left shoulder was slung a canvas bag. Ice had formed on his beard and the brim of his fur hat. There was a tired desperation in his search. He approached the stove and moved to a spot a few feet to the left of the fire. Lifting the bag off his shoulder, he removed a heavy, leather mitten from his hand and spread a callused palm toward heat that was apparently somewhere other than the crackling cabin stove. His form shimmered, receded, and broke up like a weak video stream, and Cam once more had difficulty determining whether the apparition had entered the cabin or the room had been relocated elsewhere. It was unsettling. Not only was the strangeness of seeing an old woodsman appear in the cabin unsettling, but so were the alterations in time and perspective he was experiencing. *Why should it matter?* he wondered. *None of it was real.*

Psychotic.

The dimensional distortion faded and the image of the man emerged clearly in view again. The woodsman was down on one knee, hunched over, and reaching into his bag. He withdrew a chunk of something that looked like grizzled, dried meat; he bit off a piece and chewed thoughtfully as he looked around. He put the chunk between his teeth, fastened the bag, lifted it onto his shoulder, wiggled his hand into the leather mitt, and stood. With the large mittens, he brushed and smoothed his coat, adjusted the bag, took the meat out of his mouth, and turned to look north toward the lake. He shrugged, turned the other way, and walked south through the wall, out of the cabin, and away from the lake.

Cam sat next to the stove a long while with his elbows on his knees and his face in his hands. Except for the tick and sizzle of the stove, the room was quiet. The light through the window was milky and pure. Outside, the day was slipping into silence. The storm had died, and Cam had no idea how long he had been sitting there since the dream or specter that wavered between time and reality had played its scene and departed.

"I'm not crazy," he said to himself. "I *know* crazy; I'm *not* crazy." He rested his chin in his hands and looked around the cabin. "Then why the hell am I talking to myself?" He got up slowly, put a log in the stove, shuffled to the bed, lay on his back, and pulled up the covers.

I can't stand it here. Escaping to the cabin was supposed to quiet the demons, but now, for the last few weeks, he'd been seeing ghosts, of all things. He had been doing better—at least he was no longer hearing voices or crawling with spiders—but now he was apparently hallucinating. He knew the jargon, and had sat on the other side of the couch, so he tried to be objective about his looming mental instability. He had concluded that his searing psychosis was probably the result of a brain cooked with weed, booze, and coke, and seasoned with the deep trauma of the past few years—the loss and regret.

I can't stand it here. For the first time, he was ready to think about that twisting path, that painful series of events he would have to face in order to crawl back to a life. *Is this the bottom?* he wondered.

§ § §

The rest of the day was spent in the typical routine of tending the fire, reading, writing, pacing the cabin, and fussing with frayed clothes and cracked dishes, all the while feeling more bored and mind-numb.

By mid-afternoon, Cam was down to staring at a blank wall, daydreaming. He loved the serpentine curves of adjoining logs at the corners of the room that looked like massive fingers enfolding him.

He heard a rhythmic knocking, not on the cabin door, but near. Somewhere outside. The sound had probably been going on for some time, but he had been too distracted in his musing.

There it was again. A steady knocking. Cam stood to look out the side window toward the direction of the noise. It stopped. The outhouse stood in that direction, forty feet from the house, but it was not in view from the window. The sound had to be coming from out there. It wouldn't be the first time he'd forgotten to turn the hasp that locked the door. But there was no wind to stir it.

Anyway, he needed to use the outhouse, and he wanted an excuse to get outside and see what the storm had left. So he pulled on boots and coat and cracked open the door. Crystal snow had packed around the doorframe, and much of it cascaded into the room. He scuffed as much of it as he could back over the threshold.

The tapping was definitely coming from the outhouse. Cam grabbed his shotgun, checked the chamber, and shuffled out the door. The weather was warmer; the snow wasn't deep, only a few inches, but it was wet and heavy; sprayed on the cabin and trees like fake Christmas snow, thick and even. The tired boughs of spruce trees rested on the ground and transformed the forest into a maze of pathways. The outhouse door tap-tapped four or five times. Someone or something was in there.

Cam had built the outhouse during the first couple of weeks he'd moved into the cabin. More than an outhouse, it was large enough to serve as a shed. It had been a chicken coop at a farm near Newberry before he had torn it down and rebuilt it here. Regulations would never allow someone to have an outhouse this close to the lake, he figured, but he'd dug a deep hole, covered the toilet seat with a plank, and hung tools around to make it look like a tool shed—even though it still smelled very much like an outhouse. *It's the U.P.,* he thought. *Who cares?*

A sad whimpering came from the shed—faint, tremulous, and high-pitched. The door rapped against the jamb. "Are you okay?" he asked flatly when he neared the building. Cam felt foolish saying anything. "Who are you?" *It's just an outhouse in the woods, after all,* he thought. *What could it be?* But with everything else happening, it could be anything.

"Hey! Is everything okay? What are you doing here?" It was quiet. No response. No tapping and no whimpering. He knocked firmly on the door. Something scrabbled inside; tools rattled on the wall. The whining returned, anxious and wavering.

The door was hinged so that it opened outward. Cam carefully turned the handle, easing the door open a crack. He could see that the plank had been knocked crooked off the toilet seat. Through the hole under the toilet seat, a light was coming from the back of the building. Whatever it was, it had pried off the siding and come up through the hole. But he still didn't know what he was dealing with.

He stepped to the other side of the door. In one swift movement, he pulled the door all the way open, stepped away, and brought up the shotgun. Nothing.

Leaning forward, he peered around the edge, looking at the plank wedged awkwardly across the seat. The floor was scattered with tools and torn paper. He heard the whimpering before he saw where it came from; sad, worried eyes, a trembling snout, a broad back, and a tail covered with hundreds of vicious spines. A porcupine. *Just a damn porcupine.*

Wedged in the corner, clinging to the tool rack, the animal looked over its shoulder with an anxious expression that bordered on embarrassment. Distraught and humiliated, it whined in regret.

Cam shook his head and chuckled. The porcupine frowned. It had forced its way in, but the plank had fallen back over the hole and become wedged so that it couldn't get out. The animal was probably looking for old tool handles to chew to get the salt that accumulates from years of sweat. Or it could be looking to eat rubber or resin or anything else that might be available in an old building. Cam stepped back, leaving the door open. Finally, the creature got up the courage to slink down and venture out.

He watched it totter away through the snow. Here was an animal trapped by its own foolishness, he thought. It ambled away sluggishly; no hurry. It didn't have to hurry. It didn't have to be brave, smart, or brutal. It was covered in viciously effective needles that kept everyone away. And, like Cam, it didn't even know it.

§ § §

The cabin's interior was as boring as it had been before Cam went outside. He put a few sticks on the fire, and snacked on some stale crackers. Eventually, he crawled back into bed with a book and tried to read until he lay dozing in the fading afternoon light. The stove snapped, and an occasional breeze returned to moan through the flue.

A drop of water struck Cam's cheek. He wiped it away and rubbed his hand on the rough blanket, but he noticed that the blanket had damp spots. The roof had not leaked, but he remembered seeing condensation on the roof boards on cold days last winter when he had tried to dry his clothes indoors. There were no wet clothes in here now, but snow had blown in earlier and eventually evaporated in the dry cabin. The possibility also existed that as the cabin warmed, the snow on the roof would melt, and under the right conditions, could wick under a shingle or around flashings and seep in.

Another drop hit Cam's forehead and he heard another fall onto the blanket. "Damn." He did not like to think about repairing a roof this late in the season.

He snapped the edge of the blanket, turned on his side, slid over a couple of inches, and pulled the blanket over his head to give himself just a couple of minutes before he had to move the bed and get a kettle to put under the leak.

Cam sniffed. *What is that smell?* Like fish—dead fish. He flipped up the blanket and looked over at his smelly old shoes, then slowly around the cabin, but he still felt too lazy to investigate. He rolled on his back again and looked up above the rafters where the ceiling boards lay in near darkness. He tried to find the leak's source. Over time, he had memorized all the patterns in the wood grain as, hour after hour, he had lain daydreaming or untying twisted thoughts; trees and sunsets or animals and faces were all spread across the ceiling, and they were all familiar. Some changed, but most were always the same. A favorite turtle with a cartoon face was low near the wall, and the face of a bearded Santa with no eyes was by the center beam. Stretching between two rafters, he often imagined the silhouette of a woman with her arm draped casually over her hip.

His attention focused directly above, Cam noticed a form he had not seen before, possibly formed by a leak in the roof. Something was emerging from the patterns of wood grain and knotty planks. He squeezed his eyes between index finger and thumb and shook his head. There was something gray and undulating, forming...a face. It was distinctly a face, but strangely torn or deformed. Cam swallowed and frowned, squinting his eyes to see. Farther across the ceiling boards, a hand formed out of the dark, and then another on the other side. More drops of water struck his forehead and spotted the blankets.

"Not real!" he whispered. The image floated against the ceiling above the rafters. Changing.

Cam's breathing quickened as a rush of putrid odor forced him to gulp and hold his breath. The face, gashed from the right eye through the nose and upper lip, leered from the wooden pattern. The top half of the face was almost displaced from the bottom and the edges of flesh hung gray and withered, the eyes scummed over. The body emerged and separated from the wooden ceiling, floating, and slowly, slowly sinking. The smell drenched the room and caused him to gag.

Gray rags covered the body and moved wave-like with the rotted fingers and bare feet.

Cam heard himself yelling as though outside himself. "No! No! Damn it! Stop!"

He thrashed, threw off the stench-soaked blankets, and rolled away across the floor. Kneeling on hands and knees, he vomited, dry-heaved. The horror lowered from the ceiling, arms flailing in slow motion, downward to the bed until it sank through the mattress and down through the floor. Cam rolled on his back and screamed at the ceiling, "Dammit! It's enough!"

The other ghosts were only hallucinations or dreams without sound, smell, or sense of presence. This was entirely different.

Lying on the floor, Cam took several more deep breaths as his pounding heart slowed. He tucked his hands behind his head and looked out the small window to the gently swaying branches. He was beginning to see that he had to find the way out. He *had* to find a way. There was no alternative. He knew he would need help. He knew Ron would be there if he needed him. It was time to reach out. It was time to leave.

The dark wet patch on the blanket shrank rapidly and vanished along with the rotten, fishy smell.

CHAPTER 3

THE DRIVE

Through Northern Indiana to Southern Michigan, the brown fields and gray, spindly fence rows turned past the car window on a monotonous carousel. On this lonely freeway, scattered traffic proceeded north, changing position in a slow minuet; move out, pass around, move back in.

Looking for excuses to delay his departure, Adam had left Fort Wayne later than planned. Driving for nearly two hours lost in thought and with a measure of dread, he knew he was headed back to face something he dearly wanted to avoid, but had acquired the resolve to face.

It had taken only two weeks to wrap things up in Fort Wayne. Putting his practice on hold had been easy: a phone call to the agency, follow-up arranged for critical clients, and a bouquet of flowers for Jean. She knew he wouldn't be back. He tried to reassure her he would, but he really didn't know. His apartment could be sub-leased for the remainder of the year. Three boxes had been left in the basement while the rest of his possessions fit into a backpack, duffel bag, garment bag, and black plastic bag that sat in the backseat.

Adam glanced at his face in the rearview mirror. He looked gaunt, and the angle of the reflection caught the few gray strands at his temple. *They'll think I look older. Too much gray for thirty-six.* He didn't know why he'd started the full, stubbly beard after he got the call from Ron, but it also showed flecks of gray on his cheeks. It darkened his Levantine features even more. *Aladdin*, he thought, remembering how embarrassed he had been when a teacher tried to get him to play the role in middle school. Being on stage was the last place he had wanted to be.

He suppressed other subconscious voices, probably those of his parents, that said he should be doing better at his age. *He had his reasons,* he countered.

His thoughts stayed with his parents. He had no regret that he would not be seeing them this time. Now he would have an excuse for not coming home for Thanksgiving. They would probably be as relieved as he was.

They had adopted him as an infant when they were in their thirties. Adam was certain they would have been happier without him. He thought of them now as one person—a single statue poured from iron and bronze. Like two trees growing together as they aged, branches intertwining, embracing in fear, not in love. Their intertwined limbs provided support for harsh times, but left them always competing for light and attention. They were stunted, not strong; indistinguishable, instead of unified.

They were never harsh, and they were meticulous in caring for him. He was grateful for that, of course, but it always made him feel as though he was their obligation and never their passion: a pet.

Where did he come from? That was a question an adopted kid should be able to ask. But it was never discussed. Not with them. It had made him lonely. He was sure it was part of why he had chosen to be a psychologist. He wanted to understand people. He wanted to understand the passion and intensity others seemed to share. His life with his parents had been unruffled and bland. Conflict was avoided, issues were sorted out, and calm was given precedence over real peace. He wanted to hear of real conflict, so he found it in the lives of others: his clients.

But as Adam aged, his dreams provided that source of conflict he craved. "I've never thought of that before," he whispered to himself. His dreams were an area of self-diagnosis he'd never really explored. As he pondered this, he noticed that the car was growing cold. He turned on the heat, checked his gauges, and scratched above his brow, trying to recall his train of thought.

Dreams were the other reason he had become a psychologist, he remembered. As a child, he had started having vivid dreams, and his parents were so worried over this departure from their bland plane of existence that they knew something must be wrong with him. They would look at each other worriedly when he tried to tell them about a premonition he might have been given in a dream. They invariably explained away or compartmentalized these as *coincidences* if the premonition turned out to be true.

They took him to a therapist: Sarah Brighton, MSW. Three tidy visits and she assured his parents he was a normal twelve year old and his dreams were not a sign of psychosis or schizoaffective disorder—a term his mother threw around incessantly until he finally told her he was about to go Norman Bates on her if she used it around him or anyone else one more time. That seemed to whip her into states of anxiety and confusion to such a degree that she short-circuited, shut down, and withdrew from him. Forever.

He was, after all, just a normal kid with some fantastic dreams. *Thank you, Sarah Brighton*, he smiled to himself. Sarah Brighton,

MSW, listened and laughed and cared. He hadn't known people like that were in the world, and he wanted to be like that. Not like his parents. He wanted to continue seeing her after those three visits, but his parents had all they needed: an outside source who could assure them their kid was not going to destroy their safe world.

A deer hit by a semi-truck lay twisted on the shoulder of the freeway. A broad splash of blood trailed to a mass of protruding bones and scattered intestines. Two teenage girls in a compact car glided by the carnage in giddy conversation. The girl on the passenger side turned her head to track the trail of gore as they passed him. Unfazed, she never changed her expression or stopped talking.

Gross, Adam thought, and looked away from the carcass. He realized he had been driving all this while without listening to the radio or connecting his phone. He clicked on the radio and scanned for a station.

After a while, a local forecast described a cold front moving through with high winds and snow squalls. Adam realized he had not bothered to check the weather before he left—a mistake when heading up north in November. The forecast soon became reality.

He was midway through Michigan, where T-Rex oil pumps dipped and fed on fossil fuels within earshot of the swoosh and drone of sprawling wind farms.

Wind bullied the car and a charcoal cloud bank stretched northeast to southwest across the seamless gray. Hung beneath the looming clouds were ragged sheets of gray and white cascading to the ground. Adam watched nervously as the stately wind turbines, blades flailing, were overtaken and engulfed in the approaching maelstrom. His hands tensed on the steering wheel.

A massive wall of cloud and snow leaned forward and dropped a curtain across the road, sending slithering, white snow devils under the tires. A set of headlights glared halfway into his lane as a van plowed through the median. Instinctive reaction caused him to swerve toward the shoulder, and by the time he had wavered back on course, the white had closed all around.

For seconds at a time, Adam could not even see the front of the car. Brief flashes of pavement covered in twisting snow emerged long enough for him to see the center line or glimpse the fog line on the right.

Adam checked his lights, turned on wipers, and coasted into oblivion. If he slowed too much or stopped, he could be hit from behind. If he pulled off the highway, he would not see if another car was on the shoulder or where the ditch was. His eyes jittered from windshield to rearview mirror and back again.

Ahead, Adam saw a brief view of red taillights that became brighter as brakes were applied. His foot swept to the pedal, and he was about to brake hard when the lights careened off, bounced violently, and disappeared into a steep ditch.

"Dumb ass," he muttered.

Another two minutes seemed like hours, and the possibility of ditching was imminent. The car rocked with the force of the wind, and ribs of drifting snow were forming across the highway. The deeper Adam went into the storm, the darker it became. Whether he flipped his lights on bright or dimmed them didn't matter; no one could see more than a couple of feet ahead or behind.

Headlights appeared in his lane and swung quickly left, bringing the tail of an out-of-control car sliding into his lane. Adam cranked it wildly to the right, and his front tire dropped off the edge of the pavement. When he turned left to get back in his lane, the front tire ramped back on the highway, sending him into a sideways spin. He was broadside on the highway and still sliding, waiting for the impact of a truck or anything barreling through the whiteout. He twisted the steering wheel right and overcorrected. He gasped as a set of taillights passed inches to his left, scarcely missing a car parked foolishly on the left shoulder. He straightened out, pulled back into the right lane, and slowed down.

Adam's world shrunk to small and terrifying—from the front of his hood to the back window. He was trapped. The chance of colliding with someone or getting hit from behind seemed inevitable. *Ditch it! You're lost either way.*

The wind chanced a brief opening, and Adam could see a light that seemed faraway, set along the side of the road ahead. It was dimly visible through wavering sheets of snow—a porch light or window, but strangely out of place so near the highway. If he ditched it here, he could take his chances, run to the house, or whatever it was, and ask for help until the storm blew over, then get the car towed.

Through the blizzard, a brief corridor opened again. Adam sucked in his breath at the sight of a woman silhouetted near the distant light, a young woman, the side of her face and hair against a fur-lined parka. "Jules?" Incredulous. *Stupid,* he thought, immediately shaking his head. The ravaging stress was getting to him. She was gone.

Adam cranked the wheel toward the light, bracing for the bounce and impact he would feel as he crashed into the ditch. But it never came. As he kept plowing ahead, the side of the road opened into an expanse of blazing lights—neon, fluorescent, incandescent lights over large windows, and gas pumps that had all been cloaked in the deep blizzard, making them look small and distant. It was a modern-day oasis appearing out of the clouds.

The illuminated snow thrashed around the station. Adam rolled ahead to park directly in front of tall windows where he could see a small, middle-aged lady with a long dark ponytail, streaked with gray, standing behind a counter. She was talking to two men in jeans and flannel shirts, oblivious to the chaos raging outside. There was no woman in a parka.

§ § §

Adam sat dazed in the car for five minutes. Emerging slowly, he crunched through snow to the door dressed in sneakers, jeans, and sleeves rolled up on an untucked shirt.

The woman turned her head and started to speak in a smoky voice with a slight Southern accent that was not entirely out of place. "Dude, you look like you saw a—"

"Looks like you saw a freakin'—blizzard!" the older of the two men interrupted. He had a thin, graying beard and a too-tight knit cap. Further north, they would call it a *chook* or *toque*, to be proper. His voice was high and excited. His lower lip protruded from a wad of snuff.

The three laughed.

The other guy was younger, with a thicker dark beard and a too-tall baseball cap. In a pinched voice, he said, "We didn't think we'd see anybody else stagger in, but it's a good thing you did, dressed like that an' all, an' besides—"

"You wouldn't've lasted a hot second out there if you'da ditched it. Not dressed like 'at," the older guy cut in again.

Adam mussed his hair and gave a weary smile. "Yeah, I wasn't; I mean, I don't know what the hell to do. There's no way to go back out in that stuff, and," he turned and stared out the window, "I think they'll have to clear the highway of cars...and maybe some bodies, too. Jeez," he nodded, "that was insane!" He couldn't help but look toward the back of the store where tall glass doors framed frozen pizzas and sandwiches wrapped in plastic. There was no woman in a parka there, either. He couldn't ask them; it was too crazy. But what the hell?

"Hey, I thought I saw someone in a parka standing outside before I pulled in here. It was hard to see."

This brought laughter. Graybeard was first to respond.

"Sometimes these squalls can blow in an *es-skee-mo*, but that hasn't happened in about eight years."

"It's the venison jerky that brings 'em in," the younger guy nodded, straight-faced.

The lady smiled. Adam's hands were still shaking, but this little gathering of good-humored survivors was therapy, and they helped calm his nerves. Out the window, the snow was relentless. Remarkably, another car pulled in by the gas pumps.

The woman behind the counter raised an e-cig to her lips, and by her voice, her vaping must have been preceded by a few decades of real cigarettes.

"Do you need a place to stay?" she offered, and "smoky couch" popped into his head for some reason.

"I'll have to see how long this storm lasts, I guess," Adam said. "I was trying to drive through to the Soo, but I'm pretty sure—"

"The Big Mac is closed and Mackinaw City is probably filling up," the old guy freely interrupted again. Adam was back among people who knew that Sault Sainte Marie is usually called *The Soo*, the Mackinac Bridge is sometimes called *Big Mac*, but usually just *The Bridge*, and there is no place called *Mack-i-nack* anything. It's always pronounced *Mack-i-naw*.

"There's the motel in the back," the woman said in her throaty voice.

Adam looked at her as though her suggestion was a joke.

He laughed, "Yeah, that would be nice if—"

"Or you kin shack with us, or I'm sure Ruthy here would have ya," Graybeard brayed. "Hee, hee, hee." He was on a roll.

"Buzz is gettin' snow blind or snow crazy or something as he, once again, goes *way* over the line." She shook her head.

The younger guy nodded as though Buzz was doing fine.

"I'm serious," she added. "There's a motel back there with eight rooms. I have three open."

"No sh.... Uh, I mean, amazing!" Adam thought for a while, and looked out the window again, shaking his head slowly. He was both appalled at the weather and amazed at his--luck. "Yeah, there's no way I'm going back out there in this stuff."

§ § §

The windshield was covered in snow and more was falling. After a couple of quick swipes with a bare hand, Adam dropped into the seat and drove slowly, tires crunching, to the motel behind the gas station. The low building was adrift in snow. He squinted to find the door marked 3, parked the car, and grabbed his phone, backpack, and duffel bag. He hustled up to the door. The key dangled on a red plastic fob that was also marked with a 3, and it worked the deadbolt on the hollow-core door.

The double bed took up most of the room, and a nightstand was wedged near the bed with a lamp that turned on when he flipped the switch next to the door. An old tube TV sat on the low dresser with a smudged remote control on top. An electric baseboard heater warmed a room that smelled like basement and soapy disinfectant. *Thank God. It will do.*

Adam slipped out of wet shoes, set them on a rug near the door, pulled a crumpled jacket out of the backpack, and hung it on hooks. He hoisted the duffel bag on the bed, zipped it open to retrieve his overnight pack, and rustled around for something to sleep in. After using the bathroom, he mechanically washed his face and arranged his toothbrush and razor near the sink. With both hands resting on the sides of the sink, he stared into the mirror and said to himself, "You made it."

Adam checked his phone and realized only nine hours ago he was in his apartment in Indiana. There were no messages. He knew there wouldn't be.

The bed creaked as Adam lay down, and he arched his back to pull out a corner of sheet stuck under him, and tugged it back over. *I should let someone know where I am.* He glanced at his phone on the nightstand. *Who cares?* He fumbled to find the switch and turned out the light.

With eyes closed, Adam saw only snow washing over the hood of the car as he drove through the tunnel of light. He remembered the rumble of the car, the shaking gusts. Graybeard and Buzz were in his thoughts. *An' you kin shack with us, eh? Or Ruthie, here. Do ya need a place to stay?* He was very tired.

A coppery taste and vague smell of rain slid past his senses like highway warning signs seen too late. On the edge of consciousness, Adam realized he was entering a dream—a deep, strange dream that was sweeping him far away. He was so tired....

Snow blew over the hood like waves over the bow of a boat. Water and foam roiled in front of him, and soon the windshield was no longer sloped away but upright and near his face. The wipers continued their rhythm, but not from above the car's dash; they extended from the top of the glass in front of him. Waves bucked and swayed with the slapping wipers as an engine droned in the background, mingled with the smell of diesel exhaust and cold water.

"Do ya need a place to stay?" Adam heard a man's voice through the clamor, but he was not sure if he understood what had been said. Louder, the voice repeated, "I *said*, do ya need a place to *stay*?"

Adam turned to see a stout man at the wheel in a cramped pilot's house on a fishing boat. Now there was a fish smell, too.

The man had both hands on the wheel and looked into the wash on the windshield. Adam knew the man, a Native fisherman, from somewhere, but he couldn't place him. The man smiled, the corner of his mouth pushing into his plump cheek, and he went on to his next question without waiting for Adam to answer.

"What d'ya know 'bout this lake?" The man turned his round face and looked Adam in the eye, still smiling. His hairline receded to a wispy stand on top with gray and black tangles on the side.

The man looked back into the spray on the windshield and spoke above the noise. "Three hun'red an' fifty miles long and a hun'red and sixty wide, thirteen hundred feet deep, thirty-two thousand square miles in area, the biggest in the world." He wiped the windshield with his gloved hand. "More coastline than the states of Florida and Maine combined. It takes a hun'red an' ninety years for water to cycle through it out the Saint Mary's River." He smiled, turned to Adam, and winked. "Wik-ee-pedia." He reached over into a greasy bag and pulled out a cold piece of fried fish. With raised eyebrows, he offered it to Adam.

"Whitefish from last night. Caught it yesterday."

"No, thanks." Adam had to repeat it louder over the noise of the boat. "No, thanks!" He turned and looked warily through the windshield.

"There's some cold Buds in the tank." The man pointed with his lips.

"No, I'm fine." The boat bounced hard. "I'm fine!" Another bounce. They were both talking loudly now as Adam asked, "Where are we going? I, uh, I don't think I remember your name. I'm sorry. You look familiar. Where am I, uh, are we?" He vaguely surmised it must be a dream. Maybe brought on by the stress of the day. He really didn't want to believe he was starting to have these dreams this often again.

The man smiled and nodded. "The name will come to ya." He turned to look straight at Adam. "Even though we never actually met."

The man turned back, and there was a pause as they both watched the water through the windows and wipers.

"Call me Skipper," the man said as he laughed with a high-pitched "Tee hee!" and chomped on fried fish.

Adam took a startled breath. Julie's father was called Skipper.

The man looked forward, nodding and grinning.

Gradually, spray over the bow subsided; the boat slowed and the bucking stopped. Skipper looked ahead while munching on another piece of fish, crumbles on his lips and shirt.

"Yah, jeez, I miss this stuff." He looked at the fish in one hand while he deftly throttled down and turned the wheel to the left with the other. Adam leaned into the turn as the engine burbled to silence. The lake was suddenly still under a bright, blue sky. Adam looked around in wonder.

"Here she is." Skipper turned to leave the cabin for the back of the boat, hesitated, reached back for the greasy bag, and shambled out the door. On the deck, he lifted a broad lid, reached into the cooler, and snapped a beer can from a six-pack.

"Got a coupla PBRs in here yet from when I was over in Ashland." He looked at Adam hopefully.

"How often do you get to drink PBR in a dream?" Adam muttered to himself. "Sure; why not?" He leaned over and Skipper handed him the cold, dripping can. He popped it with a hiss and took three gulps. *I must be dreaming. This stuff tastes amazing.* He took another pull.

"Jeez, slow down. I only have about another twelve in 'ere," Skipper chuckled.

They had suddenly steered from night into day. Adam gazed over blue-green water and up at warm blue sky as a pair of eagles circled high and slow far off the stern. He took a deep breath and let it out slowly.

"I guess you're supposed to be Julie's dad? I only saw you in a couple of pictures and, so, I hate to say it, but I thought you were lost out here and never recovered, just like your, uh, daughter. Is there something you want to tell me?" *Jeez, that sounds silly—clinical. And in a dream, no less.*

The man looked serene as he followed Adam's gaze over the water. They stood silent a long while.

"Never lost. I always knew where I was. We was never lost." He paused, wiped his brow with his forearm holding the can of beer. His expression changed. "Ha! I once was lost and I've seen some, but now I'm found, I've seen it all!" He toasted his beer to the waters. "Hoo-o we-e-e! My wife was the religious one an' she used to say something like that, but it went a little different."

Skipper lifted his foot, wedged it on the side of the boat, and rested his forearm across his knee, while looking out over the lake. "Yup. This lake's alive. It sings and shimmers from Duluth to Thunder Bay, from the Grand Marais on the west shore to the Grand Marais in the U.P. What lake has *two* places called 'Great Swamp'? The wind blows from the caves in Pictured Rocks across to Agawa Rock, and it shudders the trunks of great black spruce on the northern shore. A lonely waverin' sort a' call that reaches all the way down to the deepest dark. Castle Danger to Castle Rock and from Chequamegon Forest to Tahquamenon Falls. This lake is alive. And, no, that's not from yer Wik-ee-pedia. I seen it." He set his beer can on the gunwale and rolled up the paper bag of fish. "By God, it's alive."

Adam longed to ask him about Julie, but he realized, again, that it was a dream and the man would only give him the answer Adam wanted. He would ask anyway. He barely noticed that the boat had begun gently rocking on easy waves. The man was silent and stared peacefully toward the horizon.

"Skipper?" Adam began.

The man picked up his beer and drank, then held the can nestled against his chest. "The winds! Jeez, such winds. Starting in the west at Duluth-Superior, it squeezes through thirty miles of straits between Isle Royale and the Keweenaw. About the time those breezes get going, an ol' Alberta Clipper sweeps down through Nipigon Bay and Slate Islands and slams everything to smithereens in the east, tearing up ships and shore along the way. West to east, wave after wave, like a big weaving machine. Um, what's that called?"

"A loom?"

"Yeah, like in a loom."

Adam was about to interrupt the man again, but Skipper continued. It's *my* dream, Adam thought.

"Sometimes the wind can pour in from the south and bring those nasty flies that look like plain ol' house flies. Some call 'em black flies, but they're stable flies, and I always thought they must've come from hell. Well, now I know. Ha! They do!"

Skipper laughed heartily, stopped suddenly, waited, then glanced over the side of the boat. He looked sideways at Adam, raised his eyebrows, and tilted his head expectantly toward the lake.

Adam hesitated, then looked out across the water. After a while he could hear distant whispering, and a sad, high-pitched moaning; it carried on a light breeze that was scattering tiny ripples on the surface. The sound swelled imperceptibly, followed by a sudden flurry around the boat. The water was writhing, and Adam realized the surface was teaming with fish that seemed frantic to escape the deep. The ripples were growing into waves, even though there was only a breeze. Thick, black clouds erased the blue from the sky, and he could hear the sudden rumble of distant thunder.

Skipper spoke over the tumult. "It's alive, eh? But now it's angry. Angry! And something's got it all riled up. Ya know? An' we're all leavin'. No one can stay no more. We are *all* leaving!" He looked grim as his hands gripped the rail.

The water had become murky and churning. Fish leaped out of the lake, trying desperately to escape to the air. Adam looked around frantically from Skipper to the roiling clouds, then down to the water. The whispering and moaning were all around them. The boat began moving in a serpentine current that turned inward as they slowly circled under lowering black clouds. Skipper began to laugh hysterically as the boat moved faster. As it leaned starboard, Adam saw a great bowl forming in the middle of the flow. The pace quickened. Skipper fell silent as voices wailed from out of the water and across the lake. Beyond the current, great bubbles of sulfuric, putrid gases burst to the surface.

Adam felt the wind against his face and could feel the force as the boat accelerated. The bowl deepened, leaning them into the vortex. Faster. He grabbed the gunwale; they began to roll.

Lightning struck. And again. Gaunt faces and scrabbling white limbs were visible under the water—writhing and struggling against the current and against one another. Hundreds, thousands of emaciated, blanched bodies were clawing and scrambling, their faces masks of panic and fear as they raked each other.

Adam looked at Skipper, who was staring wide-eyed, mouth gaping at the underwater bedlam and deepening whirlpool.

Pistons of lightning were striking the lake. Rolling bodies covered the surface. Ragged arms and rotted legs flailed from the gray-brown water. Adam no longer saw the smiling, round face of his father-in-law, but a face bloated and white, pocked with decay, dead fish eyes, the lips pulled back from his teeth, "WE-ARE-ALL-LEAVING!"

The boat heaved slowly into the whirlpool, turning onto its side; then it was swept under the struggling mass of carrion stew that surrounded it. A moldering hand reached Adam's shoulder and squeezed as it pulled him down.

CHAPTER 4

THE WALK

T HE EAVE DRIPPED STEADILY FROM the cabin's melting cover. Transient November snow can be lovely; bare branches are traced in white on oak and beech trees that still carry dead leaves and are hung in delicate icing, all set in foggy dampness. From sagging limbs, cedars shed bright orange needles that appear to illumine the murky shadows under tented boughs. But November snow can also be a sinister reminder to anyone foolish enough to face the inevitably harsh winter unprepared.

After the previous day's torment, Cam had spent the night curled on a rug by the stove, covered by a coat, with a dusty cushion under his head. At first light, he sat up on the cabin floor, leaning against the wall with the cushion at his back while he removed the broken lace from his left boot. Not a strap or string was left in the cabin to make another lace, so he had to add another knot until he could get to town. The chair by the table had become as uncomfortable as straight-back, chiseled stone, so most of the time, he sat on the floor or lay on the bed.

The snow and approaching winter were on his mind, and he was thinking about leaving the cabin––a lot. But he could not overcome the simmering anxiety that came with thoughts of returning to his former life. Especially now.

Until the past few weeks, there had been a process, a determined path, that seemed to be leading him toward healing. He had been close to finding clarity for the first time in years when all this had started happening: *Ghosts? Hallucinations? Psychosis? What the hell?*

Today, his plan was to hike to the overlook and try to make a decision. He needed to get out of the cabin and get a change of scenery for a day. He looked up from his boot to see the early morning sun had found a rare path through the trees and into the east window. A spotlight fell on both the common and the forgotten in the dark cabin. He stopped his boot lace repair to admire the milkweed pod stuck in a wine bottle that glowed green on the small, white, chipped dresser. On the floor was an empty blue bong that had not been used since he got here; for a while, it had become home to some very mellow bait minnows. Near the stove hung a jumble of pots, pans, and utensils, and a lower shelf held a few dishes and a silverware tray. Writing things were scattered on the table, along with pocket contents and two knives. The light was adequate to brighten the rafters where snowshoes, skis, and poles were stored. But he looked away quickly, not wanting to see the boards on the ceiling or to remember the horror that had lowered itself from there the day before.

Under the shelf on the north wall were four pegs that held shirts and coats like a row of headless guards by the door. The floor was scattered with socks, wood scraps, bark from the stove, and three dusty rugs. Broken-down sneakers were still by the door.

In time, the ray of sunlight moved slowly down the wall and toward the floor, but he looked above the white dresser where a shelf held about a dozen books with rocks for bookends. Three white, ceramic canisters labeled Flour, Sugar, and Coffee contained bills, shot-gun shells, and––a folded piece of white, lined paper. He blinked. His lips were a tight, thin line.

The stovepipe sizzled where a drop had worked around the flashing.

"I'll have to fix that," he said. The lace broke again as he was stitching it through the boot. "Shit!"

§ § §

About fifty yards behind the cabin, a two-track road ran east and west to the bluff. In winter, Cam's pickup truck was parked out by the road so he didn't have to shovel the narrow driveway back to the cabin on those very rare occasions when he had to drive to Paradise to get supplies. The prior winter, he could only get out if someone happened by with a plow on their way to hunt or cut wood.

Last winter, he often had to trudge out to the road to start the truck. If he didn't let the engine run once in a while, he was afraid it would not start when he needed it. He even went out at night a couple of times when it got below zero. A spare battery was kept in the cabin, and a few times during the season, he kept the truck running long enough to completely charge one battery, if it got low; then he would change it out so he would always have a fresh battery. It was a little obsessive, he thought, but he was afraid to lose his only tether to the outside world. And he sort of loved that rusty, old truck.

The day was warming, so the path out to the two-track was thawing, and his truck was still parked near the cabin because he hadn't expected the early snow. Someone, probably deer hunters, had sloshed by with a four-wheeler. That would make the hike up to the bluff a little easier.

The walk became more difficult after Cam left the road and wound up to the bluff. He could have continued to follow the road to where it circles back around to the bluff, but the old trail through the woods was shorter, and he liked walking the deeply furrowed path where leather boots and moccasins had tread for more than a thousand years.

Cam fell into a rhythm as he walked. He forced himself to think about his struggle. His decision was either to get out of the cabin now before another brutal winter came rumbling in or to accept the challenge of staying: killing enough game, cutting enough wood, checking the roof, stocking up supplies, and all the general repairs. He still had about $2,200 left of the $3,500 he had started with, but he knew that, even if he lived off rice, beans, fish, and venison, he would not have enough money to make it until spring. He was damn-sure getting tired of the food, and he was definitely getting bored in the cabin.

Cam brooded over his situation. These apparitions put a new wrinkle in things. Did he really need to get out of here and get some serious help?

Progress had been made. He was beginning to deal with the worst of his emotional turmoil: the loss of his two best friends; Julie to drowning and Adam to grief. There was the possibility he could get back to the real world, try to get traction, and start a life again. He had quit drinking and smoking weed the first month after he had banished himself to the cabin, so he felt good about those accomplishments. Did he have the courage to call Ron to see if there was any way he could get some help easing back into a better existence than the stinking cabin?

What would he tell Ron? That he was having hallucinations? Seeing ghosts? Cam certainly thought, based on his experience as a therapist, that he might have developed a case of PTSD that could display this degree of pathology arising from his loss and from--he would not go there. Not yet.

Maybe these hallucinations were flashbacks from the two times he'd messed with those magic mushrooms. That was the only time he had done hallucinogens in the past few years, and he had never enjoyed it. And there was that week or two somewhere when he was doing Ecstasy.

And he sure as hell didn't believe in ghosts.

As an agnostic, Cam did not think he believed in spirits or an afterlife. *I don't know.* He hadn't thought seriously about an afterlife since he was a kid. He was raised Catholic, but religion just seemed like too much work. A farce. *If Jesus died to take care of sins, then why do I have to spend the rest of my life doing stuff to get rid of them?* It's all gibberish. Then the standard dismissal: Christians are just hypocrites. As a therapist, he'd seen what people of faith were really like behind closed doors.

Yeah, clients would talk about their faith, but it meant nothing to him. *Ron believed. At least he used to. Ron wasn't a hypocrite like them. Ron wasn't shy or afraid to talk about his faith. It was something natural for him.* Cam scratched his head, then pulled his hat down farther. Ron had been a Jesuit brother for a few years. Cam smiled as he remembered the saying: *You never discover that someone is a Jesuit because they will always tell you.* This was not true for Ron. He could never boast or act self-righteous. Cam had known Ron for years before finding out Ron had gone to the seminary to become a priest. Adam had told him.

Adam was on the fence when it came to the supernatural. At least that's what he had told Cam. The whole discussion had come up when they were dealing with the Reilly family at the agency. The family was certain they were being visited by lost relatives, and it was tearing them apart. It became a point of contention among the staff. Adam had been convinced that a whole family couldn't be nuts. They were actually seeing something, he believed. Cam was quite convinced the whole family was, in fact, as crazy as a nest of snakes. Adam would not let it go, and Ron seemed to side with Adam, or at least wanted to give Adam room to work it out with the family. Cam could never see it. If there were souls on the other side, at least one of them would have contacted him by now. One soul, for sure, he thought.

Probably what bothered Cam most was that, somehow, the whole thing got worked out after Adam had a weird dream that offered comfort to the Reilly family. Cam could not fathom it. He was even a little concerned about Adam's mental state. Cam had a chance to discuss it with Julie, but she seemed unconcerned. She didn't necessarily think it unusual for Adam to have such an experience, so Cam became exasperated and stopped talking about it.

Cam suddenly snapped out of his thoughts when he saw someone far ahead on the trail. The person was at least a hundred yards ahead, motionless and situated a couple of feet above the trail. Cam thought it must be a hunter on a deer stand. *Why would an idiot build a stand right in the middle of this trail?* The figure was perfectly still, facing him, and appeared to be frozen in mid-stride. Suddenly, like turning on a switch, the person started walking in place and lowered to the path. He had been hovering above the path; now he was on the path and heading toward Cam. The man was so far away that it was difficult for Cam to figure out exactly what was happening. Cam continued to walk slowly. The other man approached at full stride, as though he clearly had somewhere to go.

In a minute, the man was coming nearer to Cam, but the trail was silent under the man's tall, leather boots, which were laced over thick wool pants. He wore a long coat and a muskrat hat with ear flaps pulled down. The rest of his head was mostly shaggy hair and whiskers. Over one shoulder hung a ragged canvas bag stenciled *U.S.*, and a smaller leather sack was slung over his other shoulder.

"How ya doin'?" Cam offered.

The man was looking intently down the trail, so it was hard to read any expression on the vacant features. But at the last second, his hairy cheeks slightly rounded with the shadow of a smile, and he gave a little wink as he passed on down the trail. He seemed like a caricature of some old miner or mountain man. Cam laughed to himself. He didn't recall ever seeing anyone like him around here before, but the guy looked like he knew where he was going, and Cam figured he was either poaching or just another hermit who had wandered out of his territory.

When Cam got to where the man had been standing, he stopped. There was nothing there; no structure, no rock, no log that the man could have been standing on. The trail was lined with gray trunks of maple and beech, and overhead the stark branches rustled and clicked in a sudden breeze. He looked back and saw only one set of tracks on an empty trail. Looking up through bare branches, he whispered, "No more." He had made his decision.

CHAPTER 5

SAINTE MARIE INN

ADAM AWOKE GASPING AND CLAWING at sheets, surfacing from a dream, drowning in a whirlpool of corpses. Sunlight cut through a slit in the curtains. He sat up, breathing heavily, and looked around, suddenly reminded of where he was by the musty smell in the room. At the same instant that he saw 10:07 AM on the clock radio, there came a knock at the door.

"Housekeeping."

Wide-eyed, Adam rumpled his hair. "W-wait. Sorry. I, uh, I'll be out in a minute."

There was no reply. The cart trundled away down the sidewalk. He rolled onto his back and pressed the heels of his hands to his forehead. The memory of the dream on Skipper's boat washed over him. "Jeez," he murmured.

He showered, dressed quickly, and stuffed things into his bag. The TV mumbled in the background. He looked up in time to see a local report of the blizzard: snow-covered cars and jackknifed trucks. Banners and crawlers that reported closings and hazards obscured much of the screen. While holding a T-shirt in one hand and reaching for socks on the bed with the other, he froze. On the screen was a distant shot of two men in EMT uniforms, surrounded by the stubble of a snowy cornfield. The men looked down at a snowdrift as they talked solemnly. The scene jostled as the camera operator drew near and stopped for a closeup. A pair of sneakers, toes down, protruded from the end of the snowdrift. The only words Adam heard were the reporter's voiceover: "So far, there are at least three dead and two persons still missing...." Adam thought of the cars veering off the road and wondered how many dying stragglers, lost in snowy blackness, he had driven past. He wondered how close he had come to lying beneath a snowdrift in a cornfield.

Adam shook his head, finished packing, checked his phone to see if the Mackinac Bridge was open, and then picked up his stuff and left.

On new snow, the sun was blinding. A pickup truck with a snowplow was rumbling through the lot, clearing drifts, but the sidewalk outside the room had been under the eave, and it was clear, scraped, and salted. His car was covered in snow. Fortunately, the vehicle next to his had already left so he was able to step to his car to get the door open. It started. The car whirred while he got out to brush a hole in the back window and wipe most of the snow off the windshield. He kicked down the mound of snow behind the car that had been left by the plow and then got in.

The car eased out. Adam pulled up to the pumps at the front of the store, topped off the tank, then pulled near the big windows of the convenience store again.

"G'mornin', sunshine," Ruthy greeted him as he entered the store, e-cig at her lips.

"Don't you ever get to go home?" Adam smiled and stamped his feet.

"Ah, jeez. Double shift again. Janey couldn't make it down her road, so hopefully she'll get here to cover tonight." She took a long drag and watched Adam as he walked to the coffee machine. "You gonna make it to the Soo, ya think?"

"I hope so." He topped off a second cup and rustled around in the doughnut case. "It looks like the bridge should be open." With two doughnuts balanced across two cups of coffee, he had to step gingerly to the counter.

"Yeah, the bridge is open. Just sloppy out there." She grinned. "You want a cupholder for that?"

"Yeah, sure. Thanks." He slid cash onto the counter. "By the way, thanks for getting me in here last night. I think it saved my life."

She smiled. "Someone saved your life, anyways. You got here at a good time. I saw on the news that it got pretty nasty out there." She took a drag and looked up at the TV. "Real bad."

Adam stared at the coffee on the counter while he thought again of the snowdrift with the sneakers sticking out and mumbled, "Yeah, nasty." He looked up at her. "Thank you. I hope you get home tonight and don't have to do a triple shift."

"Yup. You, too." She held her e-cig between her fingers, angled near a smile. "I mean, hope you get home, too."

§ § §

Ice and snow had turned to slush on I-75. By the time Adam was near the bridge, the snow had melted, leaving only wet highway.

The Mackinac Bridge was spectacular: a five-mile ribbon of highway laid over a green metal span nearly two hundred feet above water with towers to the sky. Below, extending from horizon to horizon, the broad, sparkling Straits of Mackinac lay iridescent blue-green. To the east, far in the distance, Mackinac Island sat round and gray, except for a white dash across its southern shore: the long and stately Grand Hotel.

It is not entirely fairytale that somewhere is a highway in the sky that stretches over great waters to some forgotten land. On certain foggy days, crossing The Bridge can be a magical experience; the road climbs out of the mist into clear sky overhead, like a highway floating on clouds.

Until the middle of the twentieth century, Michigan's Upper Peninsula was a forgotten land isolated from the world like Prince Edward Island or Cape Breton Island. Some would say it has not changed much since then, and that the people and culture remain intertwined. Nowhere have European and Native peoples lived side by side for a longer time, generation after generation. Anyone, Native or European, whose family had lived in the U.P. for more than a few generations was sure to be biracial from somewhere in the family tree. Whether it was the early settlers who were Finnish and Cornish miners in the western U.P., or the French trappers and British soldiers in the east, intermarriage with the Ojibwe and Potawatomi throughout the region had been common.

After 1958, when the bridge was opened, the culture evolved slowly, while in some remote areas, things stayed the same. Into the twenty-first century, a few *Yoopers*, because of wariness or simply indifference, still have not ventured over the bridge.

At the midpoint of the bridge heading north, the highway tilts downward and a sense of quiet relief and decompression sets in for the traveler. An audible sigh. Adam enjoyed a feeling of escape whenever he crossed The Bridge. He always felt like he was entering a different world, a new country.

§ § §

Adam paid the toll and continued north. After he crossed the bridge and descended to U.P.'s south shore, the scenery became rugged and rocky with pointed balsams and black spruce standing like pickets along the highway. After thirty miles, the landscape opened up, across flat and grassy farmland, winding to Sault Sainte Marie.

Adam had turned off the car stereo at the tollbooth and did not bother to turn it on again. His mind meandered, and back up here again, his thoughts naturally trailed off to Julie.

He remembered Julie LaFave; the sad, tearful, Native woman he had met in counseling after her father had gone missing on the lake. She had been Cam's friend since childhood. When Cam came to Adam and described Julie's situation, Adam was eager to help out in any way he could.

A chemistry, at least a friendship, had developed during those sessions, but it was kept in check by a professional distance. After a brief course of therapy, Julie was doing well, and they did not meet again until much later, thanks once more, to Cam. When they met again, she seemed like a different person. Adam had never gotten to see much of her bright, happy attitude and nimble wit while she was in therapy. Getting to know her again was easy. She was quick to draw him in with a joke or let him in on any one of her twisted, hilarious insights. As the relationship quickly progressed, they would talk for hours. Laughter had never felt so good, and no one had ever made him feel like this. Getting to know Cam, and now Julie, was helping him evolve into a different person.

It didn't matter what they talked about or how long they were talking, it all seemed relevant when she was there. Adam loved looking at her mouth—her lips, her sideways smile—and hearing that tiny hint of a lisp when she was tired.

They were happy. But in that last year, things began to change. Not terrible, just different. It was still not in his character to talk about it—he didn't want to analyze her, and he was hoping it would pass. He thought she was just experiencing stress from work. The physical therapy facility where she worked was always understaffed. Maybe it was a little anxiety because she was becoming a thirty-something. It all seemed completely inconsequential--to him.

They were pretty sure they wanted to have kids someday, but during that last year, she never talked about that, either, so he didn't bring it up. Maybe he should have. As he drove and sank deeper in thought, he realized there may have been other things he should have talked about but never did. Did she expect him to counsel her about something, or did she think he should know what she needed without saying it? He put it away. Again.

He arrived at the inn at dusk.

Horizontally, the snow lay white, and vertically, the gray trees and older homes on the block enfolded Sainte Marie Inn. The only angles that contrasted with this grid were on the inn, which was still rimmed with snow from the previous day's blizzard. Two towers rose from the sprawling house, one at the corner and one in the center. Dormers receded into darkness on four or more roof lines that swept in several directions. The broad, dark porch wrapped the east side and came around the front to brow the windows like sleepy eyes. Behind the inn, mostly hidden from the street, was a long, hulking, brick structure, two stories high, with tall arched windows. It was older, more decrepit, and seemed awkwardly attached to the back of the main building.

The inn appeared lifted from a Victorian Christmas card. He sat in his car a long time. The inn had been familiar to him, but he'd only driven by when he was near the locks. He'd never looked closely at the place.

A light went on next to the door, and the sleeping porch awoke. A figure behind the door's frosted glass rocked slowly and moved away.

Adam carried his duffel bag up to the door and rang the bell, even though he knew whoever was inside was aware of his arrival. The bell clattered loudly inside. He waited. The door clicked with a warm, metallic sound and opened slowly. His host peered silently around the door. A short, rounded, gray lady, with a pleasant face smiled up at him and eased the door wider. She wore a too-big sweater, a dress that came just below the knees, and sturdy brown shoes.

"You're Dr. Knowles, I suppose. I'm Maggie Stewart." She had a Scottish accent. Her smile broadened as she offered her hand. Despite her pleasant greeting, he could not help but detect a tired sadness to her demeanor.

"Yes, but please, call me Adam. I'm really glad to be here. I hope I'm not too late for you. I had quite a trip."

"No, no, not exactly a flurry of activity here. I got your text," she said, maintaining the smile and looking over her right shoulder down the long, empty hall behind her. "You got my reply, didn't you? I never know with the coverage I have here."

"I did." He raised his eyes to look around her and down the hall. The smell was musty and splendid, touched with scented candles and old cigars and a lingering hint of dampness that the best old houses acquire.

Her face brightened as she saw him taking in the scene. "You've never been here?"

"No, I used to drive by a lot. Who doesn't know the Sainte Marie Inn? It's beautiful. I'm glad I could stay here."

"You're here for a reason, then." Her words hung a few seconds.

"Yeah, I...."

"I mean, Ron arranged everything," she continued. "He thought you needed something more than a hotel. Come in and put your bag down."

He nodded and half-smiled while looking for a place to set down his bag.

"Oh, just set that down anywhere. The butler will get it. Ha!" Her laughter was full and pleasant now. "Come on. I'll show you around."

Adam set down the bag and followed her down the hall. She took a few steps, then turned to face him. "I'm sorry; I know you must've had a terrible trip yesterday, getting caught in that squall. Do you want to just go straight to your room and collapse? I wouldn't mind a bit if you did."

"Oh, no, I'm fine today. Thanks for asking. It was really bad, but somehow I made it through," Adam said. "I'd love to see the place."

She smiled. "You know, I just have to say before we go any further, there *is* a reason you're here."

Adam raised his eyebrows.

"I've been doing this for thirty years, and I'm pretty straight with people. I have to be. I've discovered that it's best to start off on an even keel." Maggie took a deep breath, then continued. "I'm here alone, it's November, and knowing Ron, he knows I'm alone. And I know about who you are and everything." She smiled. "Not everything, but you know what I mean. I know why he wanted you to stay here, to ease back into the Soo."

Adam laughed warily. "I'm not sure about all that, but I, well, I guess that's a good beginning." He shrugged. "You'll have to tell me more."

"Yes, I hope we will have time to talk. I think we will have lots to talk about, but being a shrink and all, I'm sure you'll be just like our friend Ron—trying to pry all the little beetles and crickets out of my addled brain."

Adam smiled and nodded as she continued down the hall.

The low light in the hall came mostly from an open door, far at the end. Two or three yellowish wall sconces were lit, but barely illuminated the tall coved ceiling, crisscrossed with plaster moldings. Shards of patterned plaster were missing in places. The walls were painted mossy green, but small gray patches were visible where it had flaked near the top. Despite the wear, the dark emerald was vibrant against cherry woodwork that surrounded every door and trimmed the hallway.

"It's so old, and so hard to keep it all up since Mr. Stewart—I mean, my husband, Leslie—died." Maggie motioned to the first room on the right as they left the foyer area. "This is the sitting room. They used to call it a drawing room or reception room, but I suppose that room across the hall would be considered the reception room now. But I never use that room."

She led him into the large, lowly lit, sitting room with coffered ceilings, and walls of recessed walnut panels that reflected the orange glimmer from the fireplace. Tiffany style lamps sat on low tables on each side of the mantel. A large couch was set between two stuffed chairs facing the fire. Midnight blue, velvet pillows flanked the ends of the couch, enhancing the muted hues of antique rugs. A painting of a ship was propped on the mantel with a glass net float on one side and a lantern on the other. Lighthouse paintings hung on each side of the fireplace.

"You mean it's all right to use this room?" he asked.

"Of course. It seems some of the guests never leave this room!"

"I can see why."

Maggie turned left toward tall, leaded glass pocket doors that she slid open and walked through into the room that adjoined the sitting room.

"This is the library. You're welcome to use it if you find anything you're interested in, but I keep my desk and computer in here for doing my office work." She pointed at a neat, low desk against the wall near the doors. On the desk was a keyboard, an older monitor, a few papers and pens, and a green lamp.

Adam looked up at the bookshelves lining the walls.

"Most of these are old collections and such that Mr. Stewart kept, but you're free to browse if you happen to like reading old books. Lord knows Ron digs through them every time he's here. I suppose he still has a bunch of 'em at his place." Maggie walked to a bookshelf on her right. "I keep some newer stuff here. I don't go for the horror stuff, ya know, or all that violence, but I like the mysteries, and I have a lot of historical novels if you're interested."

"Thanks. I hope I have time to look at them."

"I'll show you the rest of the place."

They went out of the library and back into the hall.

"There's a bathroom over here, and on this side is the big dining room," Maggie said as they walked over floorboards that squeaked in a random musical tempo. She pointed out the wide, ornately trimmed stairway across from the dining room that swept around into darkness. "You can use this main stairway, but I'll show you the servants' stairs. They're at the end of the hall by the kitchen, and they go right up near your room."

Adam stopped and looked into the shadows at the top of the wide stairway before continuing down the hall.

"This smaller room here on the left is a breakfast room between the kitchen and dining room, and it's usually where we have breakfast when there are more guests." She laced her fingers in front of her waist and turned to look back around at the formal dining room. Tall built-in cherry cabinets with glass doors stood against the wall, and a heavy, round oak table spread with a lace cloth anchored the room. In the table's center was an elaborate model of a schooner made entirely of glass with wispy sails. The polished oak floors shown in the low light. A separate glass cabinet held ornate dishes and glassware. "We rent out the big dining room a couple of times a year for business meetings and so forth, and I cook a Thanksgiving dinner for a few folks every year," she said to Adam as she reached in and clicked off the light. "You're welcome to join us, of course; I don't know what your plans will be."

"Thanks. That's really nice. I guess I haven't thought about it." Actually, he had thought about it, and he was still hoping that coming up here was the excuse he needed for not going back to his parents.

"And here's the kitchen. Not much, but you're welcome to use it. And, of course, you clean up after yourself."

"No butler?" He smiled.

"No butler!" Maggie laughed, and pushed his shoulder. "You catch on right quick." He smiled at her way of rolling the *R* to make her point.

Maggie opened the refrigerator door. "I leave this shelf open for guests if you want to keep anything in here." She closed the door and turned to him with hands on her hips. "Breakfast is usually at eight or there'bouts. I do a load or two of wash on Mondays and Thursdays, but you're free to use the washer and dryer in the back room whenever you want. I'm not sure what your schedule will be." She looked at him levelly and smiled. "Any questions?"

"No, this is great. When I'm working, I usually just have coffee for breakfast and maybe toast or cereal if I have time. I'll get fat if I eat breakfast every day before work." He grinned.

"Oh, that wouldn't hurt ya. But no problem. You can always pack something. I have sandwich bags and such in there," she said, pointing at the kitchen. "I'll show you upstairs to your room if you want to go back and grab your bag--unless you want to come back down later and get it."

"No, I can take it now." Adam went back down the hall along the creaking floor and past the dark stairway, looking sideways at darkened rooms where a few beams of street light filtered through lace curtains and glinted off glass and silver. He stopped to look in the sitting room where the dwindling fire and low lamps cast shadows across the panels into dim corners. He wasn't sure if sitting in here alone would make him feel uneasy or if it might just be delicious. He picked up his bag and returned down the hall to where Maggie waited in the kitchen.

"Like I said, there's the big stairs that you passed down there, if you want to use them, but it's easier to use the servants' stairs if you're here by the kitchen." A small cove rose up two steps to a small landing, then turned right up narrow steps.

Just before stepping onto the cove's bottom step, Adam looked to his right toward a short, dark hallway with a massive arched door that exited on the left.

"Oh, that goes to the old brick infirmary," said Maggie. "When the house was built, the hospital from the fort was still here so, for some reason, they attached the house to it. I guess they had plans to make some sort of sanitarium or something. We've never used it, and it's sat here all these years. But we still have to maintain the dang thing. It's locked." She turned. The conversation was finished.

The second floor was like the first, with the same tattered green paint and cherry woodwork, but the hall was much narrower and darker than the one below. Maggie pointed to the left at the top of the stairs toward a short hallway with four doors that were formerly servants' quarters. She stepped up to the first one on the left.

Opening the door, she turned to Adam. "I know this one is at the back of the house, but it's a little bigger, and it's close to the kitchen, so I thought it might work better for you if you're going to be here for a while. I can show you some other rooms, but the front rooms I keep for short stays, and I have a couple coming in before the holidays." She pointed down the short hallway. "There are two other rooms down there, and that over there is the shared bathroom for those two rooms." She stepped away from the door to his room and made a quick nod, inviting him to look in.

Adam leaned into the surprisingly large room. It had a small, separate bathroom. "Perfect. This is really nice." The furniture was old, but fit the house, and the room had a TV and small desk. *Better than my old apartment*, he thought.

"I stay up on the third floor if you ever need anything," said Maggie, "and you can text or call me."

"There's *another* floor?"

"Actually, it's a half floor with the sloping ceilings and such, but it works well, and climbing all these stairs is my exercise." She laughed. "I turn in early. Just lock the door up front when you go out. Turn the deadbolt." She paused with her finger on her lips. "I can't think of anything else. Any questions?" Her eyes widened, "Och! I almost forgot. Here's the key for your room and one for the front door."

Adam took the gold fob with two keys. "Thank you so much. No questions right now. I just have to get a couple of things from the car," he said.

Outside, it was turning colder. Adam hurried to the car, reached in, and pulled out his pack, garment bag, and plastic bag. He stood looking toward the house. The sitting room window was to the right of the door and faced the porch. A dying fire caused shapes to flow across the curtains until a figure's shadow moved in front of the window. It moved slowly away and then appeared in the window again. He thought it must be Maggie tending the fire before she went to bed.

Adam closed the car door, locked it, and went back in the house. As he stood in the entry, he realized he'd left a file with employment information in the car. He dropped his bags on the floor in the hall and went back to the car. When he returned to the house, he stepped through the front door and noticed his garment bag had been picked up and hung on a hook near the door.

"Thanks, Maggie. I'll take the bag up to my room!" he called toward the sitting room as he turned the deadbolt to lock the door. He took the bag off the hook, picked up his pack, and stepped to the door of the sitting room. There was no one there. The fire was only a few glowing coals. The library through the glass pocket doors was dark.

Adam left the sitting room and, as he was going down the hall, he heard the broad staircase creak. He kept walking and glanced up the darkened stairs as he passed.

"Goodnight, Mrs. Stewart!" he called.

There was no response, so he continued down the hall, but just as he passed the kitchen and was about to step into the cove that led to the servants' stairs, he heard a woman's voice far away behind him on the stairs.

"Goodnight, Adam."

CHAPTER 6

MORNING INN

L IKE RISING FROM A GRAVE, Adam awoke to brilliant light washing the room. Lying on his back, he breathed slowly. Dreams from his first night at the inn were jumbled and meaningless, none of them vivid or prescient. Mundane. He was grateful for that. The clock radio by the bed said 8:00 AM, but it seemed much later.

Hushed voices from downstairs funneled up the servants' stairs, indistinct and garbled as they echoed in the big house. The smell of coffee and bacon was probably what woke him.

Sitting on the edge of the bed, Adam ruffled his hair. A bow window framed by red curtains comprised much of the wall, and it shone with a flood of white sunshine. Four shimmering, red-and-yellow, stained-glass panels crowned the top.

Adam shuffled to the window. The facade of the time-washed infirmary loomed on the right, set with three arched windows on each floor. They had neither curtains nor shutters. The sun was shining fully on the building, but it did not penetrate the empty glass sockets. He could see nothing inside the building.

In the mirror above the pedestal sink, he scratched his stubbly beard. *This looks a bit much,* he thought, and quickly lathered up and shaved, leaving a short mustache and goatee. He brushed his hair and pulled on socks, jeans, and a T-shirt. The door eased open with a groan, which caused the distant conversation to stop. After he stood quietly for a few seconds, the conversation resumed: Maggie's Scottish accent and another man's voice.

The steps were polished and slippery in socks. A small whine from the third riser caused the conversation to stop again briefly. The silence drew out until it was awkward to wait any longer. It was still unclear where the conversation was coming from. He wondered if he should continue downstairs, but it would not be polite to wait too long for breakfast.

At the bottom of the steps, Adam angled past the kitchen and headed for the little breakfast room between the dining room and kitchen. No one was there. In the elegant little room's center was a table set for four, surrounded by bulky chairs with leather seats that seemed out of place. A towering buffet was stacked with serving dishes, seen through glass doors. Lace curtains filtered bright sun into the room and highlighted a window seat with a blue cushion below two tall windows.

"Adam?" A male voice came from the kitchen. "Adam, we're in the kitchen."

He hadn't bothered to look in the kitchen as he'd hurried by. Entering the door, he was dazzled by a room filled with wavering reflections from glass doors on cabinets that reached to high ceilings, shiny black countertops, and stainless-steel appliances. A white antique stove sat in front of a brick chimney. Washed in light, Ron and Maggie sat at a mid-century dining table with red vinyl-backed chairs.

Ron stood. "Hey, good morning. I hope we didn't wake you. Maggie and I.... You know, we go way back, so I thought I would barge in and get you started."

Adam pushed his hair across his forehead and offered his hand, but Ron approached with a quick, strong hug.

"Good to see you. You haven't changed––much. That's a good thing, I guess," Ron joked.

"Nope," Adam replied with a grin. "You haven't changed either––much."

It actually seemed that Ron had not aged much and looked the same except for more hair and a little more beard with a few gray strands. Straight and slender, he stood wearing a heavy ribbed sweater over a shirt with a crisp collar at his neck. A long wool coat hung over the back of the kitchen chair. Ron sat again and motioned toward the chair at the side of the table across from Maggie. As Adam sat, he noticed how the sunlight caught Ron's red hair and beard, and it made Adam think of old paintings of Catholic saints he'd seen somewhere, with halos that glowed around their heads. He smiled to himself because it was not a great leap for him to regard Ron that way. Ron had been a Jesuit. Few people knew that the director of Eastern U.P. Behavioral Health had gone to a seminary. Ron had never been preachy or self-righteous, for which Adam was grateful. Though Ron struggled silently with his former sanctified life, no one was more knowledgeable about faith and theology—or just about anything else. His hungry intellect extended well beyond an interest in faith and religion and included vast areas of science and history. But all these interests from science to the spiritual merged when Ron was able to share insight into his true passion: anything that had to do with Lake Superior. His knowledge regarding the biology, hydrology, and history of Lake Superior was boundless, and his local presentations and university seminars were well attended.

While working with Ron, Adam had never had a chance to fully appreciate this man's breadth of intellect because he was swept up in the early years of his career and his relationship with Julie. Ron was always just--*Ron*. A trusted friend, ready to listen, but often difficult to fathom and sometimes distracted by another avenue of interest. Being in his presence again, after several years away, Adam saw him from a different perspective. He could appreciate him more. Ron looked up and engaged his stare a few seconds.

"We have some catching up to do and a lot to talk about," Ron said.

Adam answered with a single nod.

Maggie left the table and bustled about the kitchen with her rocking gate and deliberate movements while the two men discussed Adam's harrowing trip.

"Very grueling, but what a relief when I got here. This place is exactly what I needed."

"Coffee?" Maggie asked as she slid a platter of eggs, bacon, pancakes, and a biscuit in front of Adam.

"Damn! God, that's perfect. Yes, black, no sugar," Adam said.

Maggie cleared her throat with a tiny note of dissatisfaction that caught Adam off guard, but she said, "I can make toast, and I have orange juice. Or I have some cranberry juice, too, if you like."

Ron looked up at her, catching her slightly affected tone.

"No, this is great," Adam said.

"Ron, you need a warmup? Would you like anything else?" she asked.

"A splash would be fine." Ron slid his cup over.

They were silent for a while as Adam started his breakfast.

"Go ahead; we ate," Ron urged.

Maggie glanced at Ron and he began.

"I actually wanted to catch you while Maggie was here because I think we have some things to talk about that may go well beyond the regular job description." He continued slowly. "Some strange things are happening in the area. I know it's all kind of sudden, but I thought you'd want to know."

Adam looked at Maggie, then to Ron. "Go ahead; you've got my attention. Sounds like weird shit, but I'm listening." Maggie cleared her throat again and Ron glanced at her.

Ron took a breath, then began, "When I told you we were busy, I wasn't kidding. The agency's been swamped. I don't think we've ever had volume like this. We have four therapists, and they're all booked out two weeks or more. We've even had to contract with another locum psychiatrist from Petoskey twenty hours a week for prescribing."

"What's going on?" Adam shrugged while he halved the biscuit.

"Well, that's why I came over here to the inn before you got to the agency. It's...how do I say this? Controversial."

Adam raised an eyebrow.

"My goodness, you beat around the bush, Ron. Tell him, already!" Maggie insisted.

Ron still hesitated.

"Go ahead; I think I can handle it." Adam smiled and sipped his coffee.

"Mmm. There's debate at the agency, you know. Some of the staff are sort of sensitive about all this."

"Heck, they're in denial," Maggie interjected. "They don't get it."

Adam laughed. "Come on, Ron. Mass hysteria? LSD in the water supply? Zombies?"

"Mass hysteria would be close, for sure," Ron said.

"Ghosts—Ron, tell him. Everybody's seeing ghosts!" Maggie blurted out.

"No shit?" Adam said. Ron glanced quickly at Maggie, and there was silence again before both Ron and Maggie laughed quietly.

"It's the language," Ron said. "Maggie could probably stand for smoking in her inn before she could tolerate cursing."

"Cursing? I'm so sorry. Now I'm embarrassed," Adam apologized. He set down his fork and wiped his hand across his forehead nervously. "I'll have to clean up my act."

"Oh, Ron, you didn't need to say anything. Don't apologize, Adam. I'm a *believer*, and I would only get offended if it were to get out of hand. I'm a little sensitive about that." She waved her hand. "I've only kicked out a few couples because of their swearing." She smiled sheepishly.

"Really? Crap! I mean...."

"Stop. No. It's okay. Just kidding. I only ever had to ask *one* couple to leave. And they were doing a lot more than cursing." She rolled her eyes.

"I'll try. Old habits die hard, but I'll stay professional." Adam smiled, picked up a piece of bacon, and crunched. "I'm truly sorry, Maggie. I should have been more thoughtful or at least shown some basic courtesy."

Maggie flipped her hand and shook her head. "Forget it."

Adam turned back to Ron. "This is really weird, Ron. What are you trying to say? Hysteria? Ghosts? What the h--heck is it?"

"Go ahead, Ron; tell him everything." Maggie stared intently at Ron.

"Okay, Maggie, but I have to explain it *my* way first." He turned to Adam. "So, Maggie's here for a reason, as you probably guessed, and we'll get into that shortly, but I'll tell you what *I* know, first." Ron cleared his throat. "Anyway, remember years ago when we talked about that book *Wisconsin Death Trip*? Where it seemed things were happening within small communities in Wisconsin, back in the nineteenth century, that created a sort of mass hysteria, as though one bad event led to another, then another, and so on?"

"Here in the Soo, you mean?" asked Adam. "That sort of thing is happening here? Like in the book where there's a domino effect; Aunt Mary commits suicide, then Uncle John has a fatal accident, which makes cousin Jimmy go nuts, and he shoots his sister, which causes her boyfriend to kill himself and stuff?" He looked at Maggie. "Sorry. Head shrinker stuff."

Maggie laughed. "You're not going to bother me with that."

"I know," Adam said to Ron, "that it happens in more isolated cultures or even in those intertwined social situations like Indian Reservations and urban settings, but are you saying that something like that is happening here?"

"Not really, not *yet* anyway. Thank heavens murder and suicide are not on the rise—yet—but anxiety and domestic issues are more and more common. Something is definitely happening, and I have to say, talking with some of the clients I've seen, it has to be more than just a few Yoopers with vivid imaginations. Something strange has begun. I'm afraid it will get worse, and that's the main reason I had to make a desperate move and get you involved. I know you're a good therapist; you don't stand for a lot of nonsense. You're sensitive." He leaned forward and tapped his finger once on the table. "Sensitive is the key, here. You see things in people that other people may not see." He paused. "I can't forget the Reilly case...."

"Oh, Ron, don't go there," Adam interrupted.

"No, really, it was amazing how you worked that out. You knew darn well what was going on, and you worked through it with them. And I guess that's where Maggie comes in." Ron looked at her.

Adam shook his fork. "No, wait. I don't want that damn--sorry, Maggie—reputation as some ghostbuster, just because I helped someone come to grips with the fact that they saw what they thought was...a ghost."

"It wasn't just the Reillys, Adam," said Ron.

"I started to get referrals from every provider who had a client who was seeing things," Adam said. "I don't want to get into it."

"You *know* it was more," said Ron. "You helped them, Adam. You had a technique; you helped them all."

"I'm not sure what I did," Adam replied. "I focused on their anxiety, which was caused by what they thought they saw, and I didn't try to explain it one way or the other. I always wondered what I was dealing with, but I was never sure. I realized that when people could accept their *reaction* to what they thought they were seeing, and not focus on what they were actually seeing, they coped much better. I focused on their reactions and emotions."

"Exactly. You did all of that. But you did more. You went further."

Adam seemed intent on attacking his pancakes while he thought of a way to respond.

Ron spread his fingers on the table and looked at his hands. "You had a dream. And you had other dreams that not only helped with the Reilly case. To me, they were quite amazing." He let that hang in the air while Adam chewed.

Adam set his fork beside his plate and touched a napkin to his lips. He looked quickly at Maggie, then at Ron. "Ron, you know I've been more than a little uncomfortable about this, but...." He hesitated as the dream about Julie's Dad trickled through his mind. "I get wary because I never knew where it was going to take me. I understand I might have to try to understand these things a little differently. I don't know. I'm working through it, but I'm willing to listen, and I'm willing to help, if I can. But it makes me very--uneasy."

"Adam, I don't understand it, either, but I think you have some sort of talent or even a gift. I think I've told you this before," Ron said as Adam met his gaze.

Ron continued. "You can't deny how uncanny it was. Honestly, Adam, it was not only the Reilly case. I can remember at least two other times that amazed me. One of those was after my father died." Ron paused. "You know what I mean. I don't have to tell you." Ron looked at Adam as the silence stretched on. Adam looked down at his plate.

Ron's father.

The week Adam had attended the funeral had been odd. Everyone was a stranger to him, including the deceased. He felt he was moving through the gathering like a ghost, unseen and unknown.

Only a couple of months into his job at the agency, Adam had been invited to travel three hours to Marquette to attend the funeral of Ron's father. Alone with Ron in the car.

Ron had offered it to Adam as a chance to see Marquette and to ride through some of the most desolate landscape and most beautiful shoreline in the U.P. Not to mention the chance to experience the Seney Stretch, a twenty-five-mile slab of soporific highway built on an old railway bed that had been surveyed, arrow straight and flat, carved through savannah-like openings and cedar swamps. It was along there that Ron disclosed his seminary years and his counseling career after ordination.

Ron told Adam he had been seeking a spiritual quest after ordination. But in Detroit, he was assigned to an urban outreach program for Native people who had migrated to the city from all over the region. In only a couple of weeks, he was being pressured to knock on doors, hand out literature for political candidates, drive people to the polls, and parade around with signs. He would not. The outreach program was fine, and the issues were not reprehensible to him, but this was not what he had been seeking. He wanted to work for a different Kingdom that was beyond this political charade. His superiors were obstinate. So he left. In only five months, he'd gone from priest to disillusioned lay person. His life as a Jesuit was over. Adam had been fascinated with the story. He had many religious clients, but he had never met someone with a depth of character and resolve like this.

To Adam, Marquette was a college town with a frontier atmosphere—a pleasant escape despite the difficult circumstance of his arrival. Ron settled Adam at a quaint old hotel downtown. Thankfully, Ron did not arrange to have Adam stay with the grieving family. In addition to the pain of losing Ron's father, his family was dealing with another recent loss. Only a year earlier, Ron's brother, Jan, had lost his wife. Jan and his children were at the funeral, and Adam recalled Ron's deep concern for his niece, Samantha. She was the youngest. Ron had mentioned his concerns to Adam on the drive over; he wondered how she and the other children would deal with the loss of their dear grandfather so soon after their mother had died. Ron, true to his character, never mentioned his own private grief over the loss of his father and sister-in-law, but instead focused on the others who were affected. In one vivid memory, Adam recalled young Samantha at the funeral home, maybe thirteen, looking aside, her cheeks shiny with tears, stroking her braid with one hand and holding a tissue in the other while she leaned into Ron, his hand clutching her shoulder.

After the funeral, asleep at the hotel, Adam had a dream. It was brief, but lucid. He was walking the cliffs at Presque Isle, north of Marquette, overlooking the lake. In the early morning light, a fresh breeze rustled the pine boughs and the air smelled of sweet spring. Adam approached a man who stood looking away from him over tranquil waters. Warm light reflected on the face of the handsome older man, who was tall and straight, with neat gray hair, and wearing jeans and a flannel shirt. It would have been a casual encounter along a common path until the man turned toward Adam and smiled. It was Ron's father.

He met Adam's gaze, then looked back over the water, spread his arms in a grand gesture, and said in a strong, steady voice, "This is my legacy; Keeper and Counselor."

It seemed like a weird heraldic phrase, completely out of place.

On the ride home from Marquette, Ron was telling Adam a small anecdote about his father when Adam casually replied that he'd had a dream about him. He described the dream, including the odd phrase Ron's father had used. Ron didn't respond immediately, but it seemed to affect him deeply. Soon he pulled the car into a muddy parking area next to a creek that ran under the highway. The water carved a deep, black channel through a peat bog. They talked a long while. Ron was intrigued that Adam had uncovered this truth about his father in a dream. He didn't explain the meaning of the strange phrase; he only offered that his family had a special affinity to Lake Superior that stretched through generations. And he also confided that he was not the only lapsed Jesuit in the family. His grandfather had also foundered in his religious vocation. But Ron said little more about his family after that.

§ § §

"So, are you still having those dreams?" Ron asked across the kitchen table.

"Yeah, I suppose I am." Adam snapped out of it. "We've talked about all this before." He folded and refolded his napkin and did not answer Ron's question. "But I just have to think about it again. I'm working it through; honestly, I am."

"Sure, of course. You know I won't force this on you." Ron inhaled and nodded to Maggie. "And Maggie knows I want her input, too. She obviously has some urgency." He smiled.

Maggie turned to Adam. "Oh, I go back and forth. Mostly, I just want clarity. But if Ron wants me to be part of it, I know it won't do any good to come in here kickin' and screamin' about it. I told you that I try to tell it like it is, so––I'll tell it like it is." She folded her hands on the table. "I can see things. I mean, things that others probably don't see and not just about somebody's mental needs like you do. I can see things. Ron used to think I was nuts, and he even tried to get me to see one of his shrinks, until I convinced him. Thankfully, Ron has an open mind."

Adam moved his fork to his plate, slid the plate back, sipped his coffee, and smiled at Maggie. "A week ago, I would've probably thought you needed to see someone too, but getting back here, and some of the things I've.... Well, I'm willing to listen, anyway."

Maggie went on. "I'll lay it out simple; it's about ghosts. People are seeing ghosts. Everywhere. I've seen 'em. Something's disturbing the fabric of life here, and we have to figure out what it is."

"You see ghosts," Adam said flatly.

"Ghosts," she replied.

"Could you be thinking, or I should say, are you influenced by all that's going on?" he asked clinically.

Maggie turned to Ron. Ron said, "No, Adam, she's not. She's more sound than you or me. I can't explain it either, but I'm not ready to disregard what she says." He looked at her and smiled. "Yet!"

"That's right. It's good for you to listen to someone else once in a while." Maggie nodded to Ron, then turned to Adam. "You will need to stay open-minded here in the days ahead, I guess."

Adam raised his eyebrows. "Maggie, you're going to have to tell me more. I have so many questions. But, Ron, what do *you* really think? I mean, how are you counseling people who are seeing...ghosts?"

"Right now, I'm focusing on their emotional response, sort of like you said. I try to find out how it's affecting their lives, and I'm letting them sift through their own ideas of what they think may be happening. And, I'm keeping Maggie close for my own sanity. That's really the main reason I set this up and thought you should stay here. You will need her as a resource, and I agree with Maggie; keep an open mind."

"And don't listen to the Indians!" Maggie blurted out. Ron rolled his eyes.

"I mean it. It's trouble," she said.

Ron turned to Maggie. "Maggie, you'd better explain yourself. I'm sure Adam will be interested."

Maggie leaned forward. "Oh, I don't mean all the Native people. I'm sorry. But some medicine man came here from Minnesota, or was it Wisconsin? No, he's from out west, I think, and he's got a bunch of the Native people and others following him and thinking that Git-chi-Gami is going to rise up and swallow everyone. He says people have to get behind him or some beast or creature or something will come out of the depths of Lake Superior and get them.

"I, at least, hope that I'm able to stay on the side of goodness and light, or at least on the neutral side. I try not to read too much into anything, and I think that a ghost or apparition is just whatever it happens to be. Nothing more. I can't claim to really understand it." She tapped her finger firmly on the table. "This shaman is *not* neutral; he's not looking for goodness and light, and he is trying to get everybody stirred up."

"James Graves," Ron added. "He's from Denver, we think. His parents were probably Potawatomi from Oklahoma or someplace."

"What do you mean, Maggie?" Adam asked. "First we're talking about ghosts and now it's shamans and the Creature from the Black Lagoon? Really?"

"Like I said, I'm a believer. I know the evil side is real, and I know it can masquerade as lots of things. Whatever is happening with the ghosts and all is one thing. It's something that just––is. We can't understand it, but maybe it's something just sort of natural. Maybe it is mixed up with Native lore and everything, but it's something that needs to be left alone to take its course." She looked from Ron to Adam. "But I'm worried about people getting the evil stuff mixed up with it. Like I said, I don't know if I've ever really been able to decipher what a ghost is. But I sure as heck know evil when I see it."

Adam thought for a while and looked at Maggie. "Have you talked to your priest? What does someone like that say?"

"I'm not a Catholic, or a former Catholic like some people." She smiled at Ron. "I don't think this medicine man needs an exorcism. You've seen too many movies 'cause most of us believers aren't necessarily Catholics doing the Sign of the Cross and carryin' a rosary, you know. I don't even consider myself religious. I mean I don't go for all those rituals and such." Her hand made circles as she talked. "I don't always know what I'm seeing, but I know the dark side is real, and I know where it comes from and what it intends. It can lead people astray and cause real misery. I think we may be able to figure out what's up with all the people seeing ghosts, but that shaman is just going to lead people the wrong way."

Adam looked intently at Maggie a while. "Okay...that gives me so much to think about. I can't thank you enough for your honesty. Really. A lot to think about."

There was a long pause.

Adam spoke to Ron. "When do you want me to come down to the agency? I suppose you need some paperwork done and stuff."

"Come down today some time if you want to take a look around and do all the bureaucratic stuff; then you can start seeing clients when everything is in place and you feel like starting."

"The sooner the better. You both have me really interested."

Ron looked at Adam for a long time until Adam had to raise his eyebrows. *Well?* Ron leaned toward Adam, began to speak, hesitated, then started again. "I've known you quite a while, and I have a hunch there may be something else on your mind." Ron paused briefly. "I'm not sure you actually came all the way back up here just to help an old friend out during a weird time like this. I have to guess there may be something else that...."

Adam pursed his lips and looked at the table.

"Is it something you'd rather talk about privately?" Ron asked.

"No, it's fine. You're good at what you do, Ron." Adam looked down with a wan smile. "I think you got me."

They waited.

"I could step out," Maggie offered.

"Oh no, no, it's nothing that I...." Adam's eyes became moist. For an eye blink, Ron looked surprised; then he reached over and squeezed Adam's hand. Adam continued, his voice cracking. "I knew it wouldn't be easy coming back here. There's something I feel is just... unfinished. A lot to think about and work through." He sniffled and quickly pulled himself together.

"I'd like to talk about it whenever you think the time is right. No hurry. Is there more? Is there anything else?" Ron asked.

Adam looked up at him, then back at his hands. Ron let go of Adam's hand and leaned back in his chair.

"Yup," Adam replied, still looking at his hands.

"Are there more? Are there dreams we need to know about?" Ron asked.

"Yup."

"Would you like to tell us?" Ron asked.

Adam took a deep breath. "Did you ever hear of Julie's dad, Skipper LaFave?"

CHAPTER 7

THE SITTING ROOM

THE FIRST FEW DAYS AT the clinic passed slowly with each day a little longer and more difficult than Adam had anticipated. It was mostly routine, but the undercurrent of anxiety and confusion made each session more complex--and strange.

Adam was curious as he tried to tease out the underlying mystery behind the events people were reacting to. It was uncanny. Not all, but many of the forty or fifty encounters he'd had with clients during the week seemed strangely connected, like tortuous arteries tapping into one hidden, beating heart. Distractions and awkward pauses were common during these sessions as people, who were otherwise sane and sincere, tried to grapple with the bizarre anomalies they had encountered. He would often run beyond the scheduled time during these complex meetings, which only compounded the next client's distress. Each day felt unsettled and chaotic. Although Adam was experienced and competent, he was trying to navigate a bewildering sea.

It was evening, and he was weary. Up in his room, he ate takeout food from an Italian place, grabbed a book, shuffled down to the sitting room near the front entry, and fell onto the couch. He felt wrapped in the room with its large fireplace, dark furniture, and nautical arrangements. Two nights ago, a couple had arrived at the inn. They were staying in one of the second-floor rooms near the front, and they were quiet and kept to themselves, so they were not likely to intrude on his refuge. He needed solitude, and he was looking for a change of scenery from his room.

Adam left his book and stoked the fire, adding a rough log and turning it with the poker. Back on the couch, he sat with his feet outstretched on the footstool. Resting his head on the back of the couch, he closed his eyes. He noticed a vague metallic taste and the smell of rain, but these sensations drifted by without arousing his fading consciousness. Dozing, his head nodded forward until his chin rested on his chest. He awoke, jerked his head back, but kept his eyes closed, trying to sleep again.

Dread—a horror swept over him. He squeezed his eyes tighter, shook his head, but the emotion was powerful and tenacious. Agitated, palpable fear surrounded him and stirred the room. He pressed his temples, feeling lost and sinking into cold depths.

An appalling smell of stagnant lake water and sewage made him gag. He found himself face down on coarse wood, soaking wet and staring into near darkness, feeling the violent rolling of the deck. Below him, he saw rough walls and thick rafters of hewn beams hung with swaying bags, nets, and a dying lamp that swung wildly. The moan and thunder of wind and great waters was deafening. In the dim cavern below, a thin plank floor had splintered and bilge splashed thick and rancid against cargo. The roar of waves crashed around him, while far above, sails whipped and snapped like rifle fire. Suddenly, he was raked by a rending, whining eruption, like great oak trees torn and twisted from crown to roots. He felt his body lifted, cast into terrible cold, then sinking and spinning like a tiny leaf into freezing depths of blackness as vast and endless as a night sky. Deeper and farther down. He awoke drowning, gasping for air.

Adam sat straight up, rubbing his face with both hands and breathing heavily. Looking at the fireplace, he recognized his surroundings and lay back.

A man emerged through the window off the porch; he walked between Adam and the fireplace along the length of the room; water dripped from ragged bib overalls and a torn flannel shirt. A flat cap sat on dirty, yellow hair. The figure proceeded through the glass of the closed pocket doors. His bare feet were soundless on wooden floors as he moved across the darkened library and vanished into bookshelves. The man never paused, never looked around, and he seemed so purposeful and unaware of his surroundings that it hardly surprised Adam. The apparition had simply walked through the room and left.

Adam was staring numbly back and forth from the window to the library when he noticed a puddle to the right of the fireplace and a set of wet footprints across the carpet. The damp faded in rapidly contracting circles and disappeared.

He jumped at the sound of the antique doorbell, which sounded something like an old wall phone hooked to a fire alarm. He was reaching for reality. He knew Maggie was in her suite on the third floor, so he tried to pull himself together as he stood to answer the front door.

A dream. This had to be a dream.

Adam felt dazed as he left the room and opened the front door. No one was there. *Now what?* he thought. He leaned out, but saw no one on the steps or the walkway to the street, no car in the driveway except his. He looked left along the porch, then right. There, standing under the light, was a short, stocky, Native man leaning against the wall, staring into the street. Adam hesitated. He had to wonder for a second whether or not the man was real. The man's long-sleeved calico shirt strained at a belly that slumped over a wide belt buckle.

He stood in dusty black jeans, tattered cowboy boots, and wore no hat or coat, though the evening was cold. Cigarette smoke curled up his right hand.

"Whoa," the man said. "I must've got a little dizzy, eh? Did you see that? I mean that guy just...."

"Can I help you?" Adam asked slowly, still testing reality but thinking maybe the man had wandered along the locks from one of the taverns. But the sweet, smoky smell coming from his clothes indicated a different form of intoxication. The man turned and looked up at Adam. He had exotropia, so his eyes diverged to the extent that Adam tried to focus on one of the man's eyes without seeming to be too obvious or impolite.

"I'm lookin' for Maggie. Is she here tonight?" He tried to duck into the entryway, and Adam was about to put his hand out to stop him.

"I'm here." Maggie came up behind Adam. Things were still moving a little fast for Adam after events in the sitting room, so he stepped aside.

"You'll be James Graves," Maggie said, with her arms folded and a thin smile at the corner of her mouth. "Why did I know that someday you'd come looking for me?"

"And you'd be Maggie Stewart. Guess we're psychic." He smiled an empty smile as his divergent, yellow-tinged eyes looked toward her. Countless wrinkles mapped his face, and his hair was thick, gray, and ruffled. He slid over the threshold.

"The smokes have to stay outside," she said.

The glowing butt was flicked end over end off the porch into darkness.

"What can I do for you, Mr. Graves? You'd have to know that it seems odd meeting like this. What do you need? Because, if I had a choice...I'd rather not say." She never left his gaze.

"I don't know that I deserve such a won'erful greeting. I expected you to be a better host." He sniffed. "I just want to talk. To pick your brain as they say." He looked with one eye toward Adam. "But what we need to discuss will have to be between you and me, Mrs. Stewart. Can we talk in private?" His head swiveled slowly, and both eyes scanned Adam more completely. His creepy gaze caused a chill: physical, cold. Adam was certain that Graves blinked and furrowed his brow in brief recognition. Graves stared uncomfortably long, then looked toward Maggie.

She studied him for a moment; then with a little sigh, she offered, "Okay, let's go down here." She marched down the hall, steady and quick, instead of her usual rolling gait, until she was standing at the breakfast room's door. Graves sauntered, taking in the walls, rugs, and furnishings.

"Are you sure you don't, uh, need anything, Maggie?" Adam called down the hall.

"We're fine," she said. When Graves arrived at the small room, she led him in and closed the door.

Adam leaned against the doorframe to the sitting room, where he could hear Maggie; her intense voice interspersed with Graves' occasional deep, mumbling. This went on for some time. Suddenly, there was silence for an uncomfortably long stretch; Adam wasn't sure if he should walk down and knock on the door. He didn't know if Graves was dangerous. Or was there some strange ritual performed by ghost whisperers and medicine men? He walked a short way down the hall, then returned and leaned against the wall again.

Soon, the door opened and the stocky man ambled down the hall without looking to the right or left. Just as Graves reached the door, Adam leaned over to open it for him, but the man stopped him with a look, grinned, opened the door himself, and left. Maggie followed slowly down the hall with her rocking pace, again. When she reached the door, she latched it and hitched the chain lock, hesitated, then undid the chain lock. "I'm not sure if our guests are in for the night," she said, mostly to herself.

"Anything you need to talk about?" Adam asked, aware that he might be sounding too professional.

Maggie leaned with her back against the door a long time. "I just don't like this." She paused again. "He thinks I should...." She wiped her forehead with her handkerchief. "Oh, let's sit. We can talk about it, then."

Adam followed her into the sitting room. She sat in one of the stuffed chairs, and he sat on the couch.

She sighed and looked into the fire. "He thinks I should help him. Can you believe it? Of course, he didn't hesitate to add that he wasn't sure about working with a woman." She smiled. "Especially a *white* woman. He wants me to conjure for him, but like I said before, I don't do séances, and I have no idea how to make spirits appear. And I wouldn't if I could. Not for him." Reverting to her full accent, she added, "I'm neither crone nor carlin!" She looked back at Adam with a slight grin. "That's a sort of witch in Scotland––I think."

"So, what did you say?"

"What do ya think? As my da used to say, he's all bum and parsley. I told him I don't *call* spirits. When I used to see 'em, they would just show up when I was around. I also told him he doesn't know what he's messing with out there, and I don't do the dark side. In fact, I explained to him that now I'm only a spectator. I don't want to be involved. I would never have been interested in promoting his brand of nonsense. When I had the chance, I only wanted to help the people who were visited, and maybe help those on the other side to move along, if that's even possible. I'm not always sure I know what my role is now, but I know it's not messing with his mumbo jumbo."

"I guess you made it as clear to him as possible. You don't do the ghost circuit anymore." Adam had set aside his dream, or whatever it was, that he had while sitting on the couch, before James Graves showed up. He leaned toward her. "Maggie, can I ask you something? I sure don't mean to, uh, aggravate you right now by asking a question about this, but I…. Maybe it's sort of related to Mr. Graves showing up. I hate to bring it up."

"No, of course. You can ask me anything as long as you don't ask me to conjure up anybody who was lost…." She had momentarily forgotten about Adam's tragedy. "I'm so sorry. Really, I am. Now I feel embarrassed."

He laughed. "Oh, gosh, don't apologize. I try to be thick-skinned. Sometimes too thick-skinned, some might say."

Maggie looked down at the floor, shaking her head, still embarrassed. "He's got me rattled. And I have to believe this was only a brief skirmish. It was his way of scouting out our territory. But I shouldn't've made a joke about conjuring. I'm sorry."

"No, really. Don't be embarrassed. I know we've both been through it––losing a spouse. I probably deal with it just like you have, and a little humor is one of the best ways of handling it, sometimes."

She looked up and nodded quickly. "Adam, I did say *our* territory, you know."

Adam shrugged. "What do you mean?"

"I saw the way he looked at you. And I have to tell you that he asked about you in there." She nodded in the breakfast room's direction.

Adam raised his eyebrows. "That's strange."

"He called you *that Dreamer*. He was real interested in you, but I didn't tell him anything."

"I don't know what to say."

"There is nothing to say. But you're already here, and I'm afraid you're already involved. I'm sorry." She leaned forward and tapped him on the knee. "Now that I laid all that on ya, what was it you wanted to ask me?"

"Well, it just gets stranger and stranger. But there are some things you could probably help me with. I mean, it's not only all this stuff that's going on with my clients. I think there are some things—How should I say this?—some things I need to understand, to get my head around."

"This is as good a time as any. I have a lot on my mind, now, and I wouldn't mind a chat." She sat back in her chair. "Now, you're not going to diagnose me, are ya?"

"I'm not sure there is a diagnosis for *ghost whisperer*," Adam smiled. "Besides, I think I may need you to diagnose *me!*"

She smiled and waited for him to continue.

He looked at the carpet a while. "Actually, this is weird, but I'll start at the top." He inhaled. "I was right here on the couch, and I think I fell asleep for a while. I had this vivid nightmare, like I was on a sinking ship. I thought I had awakened, but suddenly, when I looked up…. Don't think I'm nuts; I'm supposed to be the therapist here, but I saw someone walk through here, in old, wet clothes, as though they hadn't a care in the world. He walked in front of the fireplace, through the library, and went right through the bookshelves. I *must* have been asleep, but it seemed so real." He scratched his head. "You know I wouldn't tell anyone but you about this. I think I'd be afraid to tell Ron; he'd probably have me committed."

Maggie stared at him earnestly; it took a long time for her to respond. She finally looked into the fire and said thoughtfully, "I don't know. Maybe it was just a dream. I haven't said anything about it or told anyone either, but I've seen a couple of things here lately, too. *Heard* a couple of things I should say, back in that dang old infirmary. I was thinking maybe that's what you wanted to talk to me about."

Adam shook his head slowly. "No, I haven't heard anything back there. Nothing."

"Good, because this has always been what I would call a quiet house—no hauntings, no bump in the night. I have never even had one of my guests say they saw anything in this big old place—until *now*."

"Oh, I'm sorry," Adam said.

"No, I don't mean you," Maggie said. "Those other guests checked out today. They gave me some excuse about an aunt in Maryland, or something, but they were looking around like they expected Dracula to pop out of a linen closet."

They laughed.

"I've always let people check out early without a penalty. It can be a pain, but it keeps good relations here." She smiled. "But like I said, I've never seen anything here—in the house, I mean. The infirmary is another matter, and I sincerely do not want to get into that right now. It's different. But now it seems it's not only that infirmary, but everything is strange--everywhere."

"You've never seen or heard anything here before?"

"Yeah, I know; it's hard to believe that could be true in a big old place like this with that weird old infirmary back there. We've never seen anything here in the house, before. But I never go into the infirmary, so ghosts could be having the Admiral's Ball back there every night and I'd never know it." She laughed.

He smiled. "I'll have to check it out and maybe take a turn on the floor."

"No, no; don't go in there. I stay out of the infirmary for a reason." She scratched her arm nervously before continuing. "When Mr. Stewart was alive, we went in there a couple of times to figure out what we might want to do with it, but I never liked it and wouldn't go in there with him anymore. It gave me the creeps. I think it's just...." She trailed off as she shook her head. "It's a discussion for another time."

Her response puzzled Adam since she had been open with him about everything else. He was not going to press her on it. "Yeah, I can understand how a place like that could be disturbing. Don't worry. I'll stay away from there."

Maggie seemed nervous as she walked over to the fire, laid another log on the flames, and returned to her seat. She sat with a sigh. "Can I get you anything? Tea? A cola?"

"No, I'm fine, thanks," he said. "Are you okay talking about this?"

She studied him, tilting her head, elbow on the arm of the chair, resting her finger on her cheek, her thumb under her jaw. "You understand people. It's your profession, so I'm not going to lie to ya. Yeah, it's a little upsetting, but I very much want to talk about what you may have seen out here in the sitting room."

Adam sat back, folded his hands, and smiled. "Thank you. I honestly value your opinion. Anyway, some of the clients I've been talking to--well, I don't know what to say. I can address their anxiety, but some of their stories seem so real, and they come from people who don't normally come up with this kind of stuff. Just what *do* you see? What do you mean when you imply that you've seen ghosts?" He stopped. "Sorry; I didn't mean *imply*."

"*Imply* is aw'right. I feel the same way. I never tried to explain what I saw. But I can tell you what I think."

"That's good enough. At least I can get some handle on it. But there is one thing I have to ask--as a shrink, I mean." He smiled.

She nodded.

"You seem to refer to your sightings as occurring in the past. Do you still see apparitions, or am I reading too much into it? Am I asking too many questions?"

"No! I mean, no, you're not asking too many questions." She rubbed a finger on the arm of the chair, gathering her thoughts. She looked up. "That's the problem with Graves showing up here."

He smiled flatly and nodded for her to continue.

"It bothered me because I don't do the ghostbusters anymore," she said.

He blinked. "You mean you don't see things anymore, or...?"

"No, not that. Mmm, I guess I would say I don't *look* so much anymore," she said, looking at the ceiling for a while and then back to Adam. "Let me explain. I came to a point where I had to quit. After Mr. Stew...Leslie, passed away, it was not the same anymore. I couldn't do it. For one thing, it took too much of my time when he was sick, but then after he passed, it was just too strange." She paused. "How do I say this? After he died, it was as though I was always searching, always waiting for Leslie to show up in one of my encounters. It was torture. I had to quit."

"Do you still, uh, see things or feel things?" Adam asked.

"To be honest, I do," she said, nodding. "And I've helped some of my friends lately with some of the things they're experiencing, but I won't do the routine."

"The routine?" he asked.

"There were three of us. Jo Sparks from Sault, Ontario, and Leland Howard, who was a young professor at Lake Superior State, and me. We would go to homes in this part of the state and in Ontario to help people with sightings. We didn't advertise, of course, but we didn't need to." She sighed. "But I don't have to get into all that. We all knew it was time to quit after my Leslie passed."

"No, of course." Adam shook his head. "I understand completely."

She leaned forward, grasping her fingers around her knee. "Back to what you asked me before. What was it? Oh, yeah. You wanted some insight into what you might be experiencing. Like I said, even with everything going on in the area, I haven't had sightings here at the inn. But that doesn't mean I haven't seen things—things around town, things at people's houses. I try not to see, but I'd have to be blind."

"That's what I mean," Adam said. "What is going on? You're not trying to see things, but you're telling me you *are* seeing things."

She waved her hand. "Okay, so let's cut to the chase. I'll give you Maggie's manual to meeting ghosts; maybe it'll help you. And mind you, ol' Ron thinks I'm an expert because I.... Never mind; I've probably told him too much." She smiled. "He's worse at picking my brain than you are!"

"I really don't mean to—"

"Oh, stop! I love talking with someone like this. Free therapy!" She laughed.

She put her hands on her lap. "This is what I think," she said as she slid back in the chair again. "I think most people see ghosts sometimes, but they just don't know it. Wait; let me back up. I think there are at least two types of ghosts, maybe three. Over the years, I've truly seen *something*. The something I've seen is probably of two types. Stay with me here."

He nodded and she continued.

"I have no idea why I see them—or saw them, and when I saw them, it was as natural to me as seeing a stray cat. It baffles me why others don't see them. I have no answer for that." She shrugged. "The types of apparitions you hear about on those TV ghost chaser shows and on the internet are mostly what I would call *loops*. Like a film loop that plays over and over again. But when I see those apparitions, the loops can often change." She motioned around the room. "Lady walks through door and sits down; lady walks through door and goes to the fire; lady walks through door and goes to the table. They're different actions, but the same loop, I think. That's where you hear about the old tavern that is haunted by the ghost of a sea captain. It's a loop. Some wisp of that person's life that comes from--who knows where—and lingers after they're gone. I'm sure it's not really an entity."

He nodded. "You've given it some thought. I need someone who actually has some rational explanation. Now, somehow, *rational* doesn't sound right. Are we dealing with something rational? You know what I mean. I just saw something no one can explain. Is that rational? But go ahead; what's the other type?"

She smiled, then continued. "I really don't know if it's rational or not. That's your field! But the other type I've seen is harder to describe. They're more—how would you say it—fleshed out. Actually, quite solid sometimes, and I'm pretty sure just about everybody has seen them. They're everywhere, it seems to me. How often, when you are driving through town, or even out in the country, do you see someone who just looks out of place as they're walking along? Or you're going by a house and someone is sitting there staring out the window. How do you know that's not, what you would call, a ghost? You don't know. You will never see them again."

"You think it's that common?"

"Maybe not *that* common, but that must be what we see, sometimes. Those sightings are more like actual entities, I think. Not just loops. I could be wrong, but I don't think they are actually souls, so to speak, but more like a stream of existence left behind. Continuing like a river. I don't mean to be all New Age-y. I'm not like that. But we humans are powerful and complex spiritual creations that happen to inhabit this clay vessel, as I've heard it said. Let me think of how to describe it." She looked at her hands, then back at Adam. "Sometimes, after someone dies and their spirit leaves, I think it's as though the person has passed through a door. But the door is slightly ajar for some reason, and their essence lingers on this side." She scratched her head with the tip of one finger and continued. "The more unsettled the circumstances of their death, the harder it is for them to pass through. Their souls are in tatters, and the trailing shreds get caught in the door."

She blinked. "As I grow older, I think I have one more theory. I hope I'm not going on too much."

"Lead on," Adam said, motioning with his hand.

"This may be all too much, but as I age, I often feel it's almost as if the other side is somehow—how do I say this?—so much larger and more substantial than this side. The spiritual is pushing its way into our lives, and the thin fabric in between yields toward us. We're not leaning into the other side; the other side is reaching over here. Does that make sense?" Her eyebrows raised.

"Not a lick," Adam said.

Maggie smiled. "Well, of course it doesn't. We're talking about ghosts, after all. I mean, it's not so much that a wisp of a soul is left behind. It's more like something of them is pushing back in."

"Wow," said Adam. "That's somehow even creepier. But I wanted to hear what you had to say. I don't know that I'm all in, yet, or that I'm actually ready to accept it. What do you think is going on? Why is all this happening around here, now?" He stopped. "Wait; before you answer that, let me tell you this first. Here is what I've pieced together while listening to my clients. All of the ghosts that people are seeing, including this dream, or whatever it was that I just had, seem to be things coming from the lake." He looked toward the window where the apparition had walked through, and then he turned and looked at Maggie again. "All the cases my clients are telling me about seem like they are all people who have drowned or something. You remember the dream I mentioned the morning after I got here? About Julie's dad?"

"Yup. I think you may be on to something with the spirits leaving the lake." Maggie pushed her hair behind her ear. "Now that I think about it, it's been this way from the start. I'd have to say it was probably in August when people started to get sort of loopy. Ron has probably filled you in on some of the history of what's been going on."

"He filled me in a little when it started," Adam said. "He said he talked with you about the guy who got struck by lightning."

"Right, Matt Tolles. He was out there at The Shallows with his sister's kids, and he got struck by lightning and killed. The kids swear there was a woman sitting on a rock and that their uncle went out there to get her. The older one, Todd, said she looked like she was wearing an old swimming suit, but they never found any sign of anyone else, and the kids said she was gone after the lightning struck. It was a direct hit on the rock. The mark is still there. Why would he have gone out there in a storm if there was nothing there?" Maggie looked down and shook her head slowly. "What a sad, sad thing for those kids to see and go through."

"Yeah, I know; one of the clients I saw was connected to that tragedy."

"There's not only the sightings. People are talking about all sorts of strange things. My neighbor, Ben, was visiting his sister near Grand Marais when they saw these strange lights and rumbles far out on the lake. He said lots of people along the shore are seeing these things, and they are not Northern Lights. It's on the lake! They describe it as everything from gas bubbles to aliens, but no one has a clue. Everyone is stumped. It's been going on all through the fall, and the authorities are saying nothing, even though the police scanners are chattering away all night."

"Some of my clients mentioned stuff like that," said Adam, "but I didn't know it was so widespread."

Maggie looked at him intently, then sighed. "I can tell you this much, I suppose." She rested her arms on the chair, then inhaled deeply. "I try to be strong and ignore it, but now I have to confess that all these sightings are getting to me. I can't deny it. I hardly go out anymore."

"What do you mean?"

"Maybe I'm not being honest with myself. I'm seeing and sensing more than I want to admit, I guess." She looked into the fire. "I know I'm supposed to be the one who doesn't hold back, but I haven't said everything." She took a deep breath. "I go out to the store and all, but I can't hardly walk down to the locks or along the strip, or drive out to the department stores without seeing what looks like some drowned soul shuffling along." She was shaking her head slowly." I can hardly stand it anymore. So, I don't go out much. They walk right past other people on the sidewalk, but no one sees 'em. I even let the phone go to voice if I don't recognize the number 'cause I still have so many people calling me about ghosts. I don't exorcise ghosts, like I said; I don't do séances to bring back their loved ones who drowned." She looked quickly at Adam. "Oh. I'm so sorry, again. I didn't mean to...." She wiped the corner of her eye and sniffled. "Here I am just bletherin' on and on. You got me. You're doin' that dang psychotherapy on me, aren't ya?"

He smiled. "Nope. You're doing a pretty good job on your own. No, that's okay. This rattled me when I started to realize what seemed to be going on, but I'm really sorry to hear what all of this is doing to *you*." He patted her hand once. "I didn't know."

"I think," Maggie said, "that I understand more now after I lost my husband. He died peacefully here with the wonderful help of hospice, and I never heard anything after that from him, and I should've known I wouldn't. I told you how it bothered me when I was working with the others. I thought of him all the time, but I know that was my own fear and my own imagination. Even hearing that rattle in the infirmary now...." She looked away. "But when you lose a loved one, there is never any real comfort, is there? We only get used to it. You learn how to live with it."

He sat back, nodding.

She folded her hands and looked at them, then looked up at Adam. "I want to tell you something more about spirits and such. I think this is important." She looked back at the fire. "I left my home in Scotland with my husband, Mr. Stewart--with Leslie—to come here thirty years ago, leaving my whole family behind except for a sister who now lives in Milwaukee. My family wasn't really bosom-close, and my da especially was a quiet man who rarely smiled until his Saturday pints. I don't think he even saw us off at the airport when we left for the States, and then I got back there only twice in the first ten years after we came here. But about fifteen years ago, my da got really sick. We hadn't been back in a long time."

Her accent sounded more like home. "Leslie and I were sort of getting this place started. Money was tight. Da had a lung disorder like lots of them old miners, of course, and we knew it was terminal. We'd just about scraped together enough to make the trip back to the farm north of Edinburgh, and I had talked to Mama day or two before. She said he was still hangin' on, and she thought he'd be fine 'til we could get there." She touched the corner of each eye. "About two nights before we were set to leave, I had a dream. No, it would nae be a dream, but I have to *say* that it was, I suppose." She hesitated, wiped her nose delicately, and continued. "All I saw in this dream or vision, was my da. Close, like he could be in this room, but mostly just his face, and he seemed to be surrounded by others, but I didn't see their faces. For a second, I didn't even recognize him. He was young and his cheeks were red and washed with tears. At first, I thought he was crying, but he had a smile like I'd never seen. Complete joy. Weeping for joy, I tell ya!" She smiled as a tear escaped the corner of her eye. "I knew he was gone, but maybe it was his way of showing us it was okay—that we didn't have to make the trip back and see all that old gray death and toothless gasping."

Adam reached out and held her hand again.

She looked at Adam and continued. "We did go back for the funeral and all, but I know the way he looked in that vision is what we look like in the afterlife. I know it. We do not look like these shriveled, lost things I've seen." She smiled. "And now, I guess, that you are seeing, too."

Adam's eyes followed across the sitting room again where he'd seen the sailor walk through the room and disappear. He stared into the fire, nodding slowly.

CHAPTER 8

THE CLINIC

"THAT WAS THE WEIRD THING about it. I wasn't scared," she said.

Friday afternoon of Adam's first week and Mandy was the fourth client. She sat in a large chair in the corner of the small therapy room, her posture relaxed. She kneaded the purse on her lap, thinking about the Ativan bottle inside. The room was almost too close, set around with stuffed furniture and a bookshelf. Adam had pulled his chair to the front of the mahogany desk and faced her, his arm resting on the blotter near a laptop. Afternoon sun through the tall window made the room warm and bright in this big old house that decades ago had been converted to offices. It still contained some of its domesticity along with a dusty, dank odor that was barely covered by a few scented candles.

"You saw a ghost, but you weren't scared?" Adam seemed to be asking himself, recalling the night before in the sitting room.

"I *thought* I saw a ghost. That's why I'm here!" She paused, then smiled shyly and looked down. "I'm sorry." Confidently, she looked up again. Her strong features were attractive. She'd taken off her jacket and wore a white blouse and gray skirt; her legs were crossed, a black shoe bobbing.

"Oh, no, that's okay." He scanned her intake sheet again: a history of panic disorder well controlled by previous therapy and an occasional Ativan. But now she seemed to be struggling to find a reason she was here. She was unsure.

Adam smiled. He was comfortable with the way the session was starting, and it was certainly not the first time this week when ghost-spotting had been the topic.

"Did you have a panic attack?"

"I had one the following morning when I was getting ready for work, and I just talked myself down as usual, but I did not have one that night when it was happening. Like I said, that was the weird thing. It wasn't scary. Here's exactly what happened." She set her purse beside her chair and folded her hands, leaning forward. Adam changed position in his chair and set the intake sheet on the desk to give her his full attention.

"We live west of town on what they call Mosquito Bay; it's right on the sandy bluff of an old dune. There are some big trees in the yard. It's not totally isolated because there are other houses around, but I get a little nervous some nights. Not really scared, just a little jumpy." She glanced at her purse on the floor. "But anyway, I thought I heard the wind come up off the bay, and the cover on our grill sometimes flaps around when it gets windy. We also have a couple of lawn chairs that might blow around out there, so I got up to look outside."

She stroked her hair. "Our daughter, Katie, is away at Michigan Tech, and the house seems weird anyway with just John and me. It was about two-thirty in the morning." She stopped, staring at the ceiling, organizing her thoughts. Then she looked at Adam. He remained silent. "I'll tell you exactly what I saw; you'll have to tell me what you think. And yes, I know I was awake and I hadn't taken anything to help me sleep." She took a deep breath and continued. "So, we have a patio door and two large windows that face the bay. And...I saw a girl—maybe twelve years old in a long dress that sort of clung to her like it was wet. She came straight from the edge of the bluff toward the house."

Mandy smiled, and nervously looked away for a second. "God, this is weird. Anyway, the girl was like, determined, I thought, just heading straight toward the house. So, I hurried up, unlocked the door, and slid the patio door open. I figured she was in real trouble and needed help." She set her finger on her lips for a moment. "But she didn't come through the open door. She walked right through the window, went across the living room, out the kitchen, and through the south wall. Just like that. I couldn't move at first. I actually laughed out loud because it was so weird. I knew right away that I'd either seen a ghost or something was seriously wrong with my head." She picked up her purse from the floor and clutched it on her lap. "She walked right past me. I saw her perfectly clear. She had dirty blond hair, a pretty nose, and I could see that her chin was up, like she knew where she had to go. She just passed right through the house." Mandy sat back and rested her hands on the chair's arms. She stared straight ahead with a crooked smile. The smile faded and there was a long pause.

She sighed. "Suddenly, it was like a mother-thing, I guess. I ran to the other side of the kitchen and looked out the window. She would not have made it to the driveway, yet. But I couldn't see her anywhere. We have a yard light above the garage, and I turned on the front porchlight and went outside. I ran back and called John--that's my husband—until he finally came out to see what the hell I was doing. We saw nothing." She put both hands over her face as Adam waited. She brought her hands down. "She was lost. She was somebody's little girl and she needed help, and I couldn't help her."

Mandy picked at the chair's cover and brushed it smooth. Her lip quivered. Adam offered her the box of tissue; she took one and wiped her nose. "What the hell happened?" she asked. "I don't believe in ghosts. I don't think I even believe in an afterlife, and John thought I was totally bananas; that's why I agreed to talk to someone."

"And you said you hadn't taken anything for sleep, and you haven't been under an unusual amount of stress? Did you call the cops?"

"No, we talked about calling 911, but what the hell would I tell them? I know she walked through the wall, and I know she simply vanished. John asked me about my pills and stress, too, but I've been feeling good and hadn't been taking anything. Everything is good. This is our daughter Katie's second year at Tech, so I'm pretty good with the empty nest thing, and I like my job. I just saw a ghost--or something, and we can't figure it out."

"Have you talked to anyone else: friends, family?"

"That's part of the problem."

"Go ahead."

"Our neighbor, June, she's my friend, but John calls her *June the Loon*." She covered her mouth and laughed quietly. "She's into those ghost hunter shows and knows all the haunted houses in the U.P. and even attends a ghost club in Sault, Ontario. John thinks June has planted ideas in my head. She says she's seen two ghosts fleeing the bluff, and she's even heard of other people along the bay who have seen ghosts leaving the lake. I guess the ghost club in Ontario is all atwitter about it." She fluttered her fingers.

"I'd have to make my own assessment whether June is, in fact, a loon. It's not really a clinical diagnosis. At least not yet." They laughed. Then Adam paused, brushed the hair off his forehead, and looked out the window as he again remembered the apparition from the night before. "Are June and the ghost club talking about ghosts that are—?" He continued to stare out the window an awkwardly long time.

"Dr. Knowles?" she finally said.

"Oh, I'm sorry; I was just remembering someone who--or, I mean, something that someone else was telling me." Adam shook his head. "Go ahead. You're friend, June...."

"Yes. Just like the girl I saw, June tells me ghosts are leaving the lake. It sounds so weird when I say it."

"I don't know what to tell you, Mandy. Maybe you could talk to the psychiatrist about meds." He hesitated again. "But I understand what you're saying. Maybe you just saw something we can't explain right now. I mean, you've heard some of the talk about all the people seeing ghosts and stuff." He scratched his head. "From a professional standpoint, we're looking at it as sort of a mass sighting or mass hysteria thing, but I'm not convinced that's all it is, and listening to people like you--I don't know. I think you can just wait and see. If it's not a problem with your daily life, I think you can just file it away as *unexplained phenomenon.* You seem like someone who's learned how to manage your anxiety pretty well."

Adam leaned forward and folded his hands. "I don't know what to tell you about your husband. You'll have to talk to him about it, and I'd certainly be happy to help. Other therapists and the authorities are advising people to keep it to themselves to avoid creating a sensation, but I don't think it makes a difference. We'll have to see how it plays out—as long as no one is getting hurt."

"As long as no one is getting hurt? What do you mean? Is it *really* that widespread?" She blinked. "That's amazing. What else are you hearing? Do you think it's related to the other stuff going on over the lake?"

"Like what? What do you mean?"

"Well, you know, the lights and rumbling and shifting water levels. People are talking about that, too. It's eerie to see it across the bay at night," she said.

"Yeah, I've heard about some of that, but I think you're the first client who's mentioned it. I honestly don't know, Mandy, what's happening or how this will all play out, but we hope it just blows over."

She clutched her purse with both hands; her expression was troubled.

"I'm sorry," said Adam, "if I gave you too much *inside sports* about what some of the clients are saying. And I hope I didn't make it worse for you. But I think you're okay, and for you, as an individual, your mental state is fine. Again, I'd be happy to talk with John, or both of you, if you think it would help, but I think it may be better just to work it out with him––and maybe avoid June for a while."

She smiled. "I'm good. I have a lot to think about. This weird supernatural stuff makes me think of some spiritual things, too. I won't go there, now, but I appreciate the help. I feel much better."

"Thinking about spiritual things is good. I won't deny it. How about I see you again in two weeks just to get your insights? If you feel okay, you can cancel the appointment, but I'd really like to know how you're doing."

They shook hands. After Mandy left, Adam pushed the desk chair back and sat at his desk to make a few notes. The lowering sun through the window cast the room in warm yellow. He reached for the hand sanitizer and turned over a folder on his desk. He leaned back in the chair, set his elbow on the desk, and put his finger across his lips while staring out the tall window. "What the hell is going on?" he muttered.

§ § §

"Daniel Sayles!" Adam called as he stepped into the waiting room.

A short, nervous man was standing, looking out the window. He turned and smirked.

"You can call me Danny."

Danny dropped into the seat in the exam room and slapped the arms of the chair, causing motes to rise in the late afternoon sun. His hair was medium long, receding, and he had a thin mustache under a blocky nose that might have been broken a time or two. While he gawked at walls and furniture, he zipped and unzipped his worn, tan jacket, which opened and closed over a white Star Wars T-shirt. The quiet room was possessed by his restlessness.

Adam leaned casually on his desk to read the man's intake information and medication list; no psychotropics and only an ACE inhibitor for high blood pressure. He was thirty-four and had no prior psychiatric history, but he had a court order to avoid drugs and alcohol while he was on probation for an unspecified offense.

"So," Danny interrupted, "how does this work? Do ya want me to spill my guts and tell you that a priest fiddled me when I was an altar boy, and then I can be on my way?"

Adam placed his finger across his lips to hide a smile. "Tell me why you're here, and maybe I can help you."

"I'm here 'cause my ma called the cops after I shot a hole through her sofa trying to get some bastard out of the house. The judge said I could get off easy if I got some counseling, so here I am. I was waitin' out there for half an hour."

"I'm sorry if you were out there too long, but I think your appointment was at four, and it's only ten minutes after now. But let me get to know you a bit. I want to hear your side of it."

Danny was drumming his fingers, and he looked incredulous. "Oh, I'll tell ya my side of it, but nobody seems to want to believe me. Some bastard looked like he came through the wall while I was at my ma's. I have—I should say I *had*—a CPL or concealed pistol license until that fu...f'in judge took it away."

Adam decided to go with it for now. Let him vent. Maybe he would settle down.

"Who came through the wall?"

"President Donald F'in Trump! I don't know who the hell came through the wall. Jeez!" He grabbed the chair's arms with both hands. "Besides, he didn't *really* come through the wall. I said it looked like he came through the wall. I don't know who the hell he was. My ma didn't even see him. He looked like shit warmed over. Some bum or homeless guy or something in old coveralls that looked like he was drowned for God's sake, so I whipped out the pistol, but the damn thing went off before I got it up and the guy was gone."

"Did he go out the door or vanish back through the wall?" Adam immediately knew it was the wrong thing to say.

Danny swept the air with both hands. "Go to hell. You already think I'm nuts. I don't know where the hell the guy went. He was gone! The asshole didn't even look at us when the gun went off. He just walked straight through like he knew where he was going, and then he was gone. Gone! Flew the coop! I don't know what I saw." Danny looked at the floor worried, intense. "I don't know what I saw."

"I'm sorry; let's start over. We didn't get off to a good start, here."

"No. Nope. This is bullshit. I really don't want to be here. I'm gone."

"Wait; I think we can make this work."

"No, I'll take care of it. This is crazy. I'm not the problem here!"

Danny tore out of the room and through the empty waiting room. Adam stood to listen to Danny tramp down the creaking steps. He sighed, turned back to the desk, sat, and paged through the intake folder.

"As long as no one is getting hurt." *This guy could've killed some-one*, he thought.

"Hey," said Ron, leaning into the room, "if you have a few minutes after you see your last client, why don't you come down to my office?"

"Actually, I'm done; I'll be right there."

Ron looked back at the waiting room. "Was that *your* guy?"

"Yeah; all in a day's work, so they say." Adam grinned.

Ron's office had two tall windows that provided a wide view of the Sault Locks and the International Bridge as it made its winding course over locks and channels all the way to Sault Sainte Marie, Ontario.

"How was your day? Do you want a coffee or anything?" Ron asked as he sat at his desk with his hands spread, palms down on each side of his cup and looking up at Adam.

"I'm fine, thanks. No, it was only a three-ghost day, so maybe things are getting better. It's just very strange; I hope you can help me figure this out some time."

"Good luck with that. I have some ideas, beyond what we talked about before, but I'm not sure if I have it all put together enough to share, yet. I have a few things to show you, or discuss, actually." Ron pushed his cup aside with the back of his hand and folded his fingers loosely. "Maggie called me this morning; she was a little upset about James Graves showing up at the house last night. I don't blame her. She really doesn't want to be involved in this kind of stuff, and some-times, I worry about her. But she said your talk really helped. I'm glad you're there for her."

"Yeah, we talked for quite a while after he left."

"Adam, I guess I don't have to tell you that Graves is trouble. If a little knowledge is dangerous, then he's very dangerous, because I think he has very little knowledge about what he's doing. And I hate to say that because I know he's an important guy to many of the Na-tive people around here. But do you remember that time when Cam had trouble with him? Graves made one of his visits to the area while Cam was doing some part-time work with the tribe."

"I didn't know about that."

"Yeah, I suppose it would've been after you lost Julie, so you wouldn't have known. You didn't see Cam again after that, right?"

Adam shook his head.

Ron nodded sympathetically. "Well, Cam thought Graves had been inappropriate with some female followers or clients or what-ever, so he brought it before the tribe. There are legitimate tradi-tional healers within the health division, and they supported Cam. They were incensed about what Graves was doing. But the tribal administration and the healers felt their hands were tied because

Graves was seen as a powerful medicine man by some. I have to think it was kind of political. There was a lot of support for Graves, and someone would've taken heat if he got canned. It was a mess, and it probably had something to do with Cam quitting his job. I can't help but think it was one of the things that pushed him over the edge. He was sort of drifting after that. I tried to reel him in again, to find out what was going on, but he didn't want to talk to me."

"Really? I didn't know about all that. I can certainly see that Graves could be trouble, and Maggie is even more concerned. He was pretty weird when he showed up at the Inn last night. And you're right, I never talked to Cam after Julie died. And we had been best friends. You know he was friends with Julie and her family since they were in high school. I'm sure it was really hard for him, too. But, to be honest, I always wondered if, somehow, he sort of blamed me for not taking better care of her. Like it was *my* fault that she drowned. I don't know what made him drift away." Adam tapped his chest. "Back then, I sure as hell had more to deal with than mending fences with Cam." Adam rested his forearm on the desk's edge and rapped his knuckles lightly.

"You guys were pretty close. Then you took off to Indiana, and he went into the woods. Sounds like you both need a good therapist," Ron said.

Adam smiled.

"Anyway, Cam is really the reason I called you in here." He stared at Adam. "I'm really debating with myself whether I should share this with you, but...."

Adam looked up at Ron. "No! He came back?"

Ron smiled. "No. No, he's not back--yet. It floored me when I got here this morning and there was a message on.... Here, listen." He punched the audio button on his desk phone and entered a four-digit pass. There was a beep and a voice that said, "Press one to play messages and...." Ron hit the key.

"Hey, Ron, it's me, Cam." There was a sigh over the phone, silence, and then the message continued haltingly. "I'm going to be in the Soo in a couple of days and I need to talk. Just wanted to give ya a heads up. A warning, I should say." He sniffed. "I'll call you when I get there. Thanks, Ron. Bye." Then a tone. Ron pushed a button and the phone was silent.

Adam stared at the desktop. "Really, it's amazing to hear his voice; I don't know what to say."

"I know," said Ron. "That's how I felt."

"What are you going to do?"

"Nothing. I just have to wait for him to reach out. He has my cell phone number, so I'm not sure why he left a voice message here at the office. I think he wants to hold me at arm's length. He wants to call the shots for now. I'll let you know what happens."

They sat in silence. Adam ran his fingers along the desk's edge and Ron looked into his cup.

"I'm sure you have some stuff to finish up," said Ron. "Hope I didn't ruin your day."

"No. I knew I'd have to deal with things like this as they came up. Lots of loose ends."

The receptionist peeked into the office. "Oh, good, Adam; you're still here. There's a message for you." She handed him a note. Adam read it. His lips parted, and he raised his eyebrows in surprise while he looked up at Ron. He turned the note for him to read.

Casino Back Desk at 7:00. OK? Call and ask for Harley if any questions. James Graves.

CHAPTER 9

CASINO

ORANGE, PAISLEY, SQUARISH COUCHES SAT on green and purple, block-print carpet: visual overload. Beneath pink and gold sunrises and tangerine sunsets, wolves and coyotes were depicted in birch-framed amateur paintings that lined the small back lobby at the casino. Contrasting the décor was a modern, curving maple hotel desk. *Meetings/Special Events* and *VIP Suites* were printed on gold plaques across the front of the desk.

Behind the desk, a petite, young Native woman stared intently at a screen, typing while biting her lower lip and squinting in concentration. Adam waited for a moment until she looked up.

"Can I help you?" Red lipstick smiled broadly. Too much makeup was mandatory for her job and suited her uniform of black slacks, a white shirt, and black bow tie. Her hair was tied in a neat bun. Her nametag said *Gracie*.

"I'm Adam Knowles, and I'm here to see James Graves. I was told I should check in here."

"Oh, sure," she said, still smiling, staring at his face a fraction of a second longer. "I can help you. One second." There was a momentary hesitation. She half-frowned as she turned from the desk and seemed reluctant to walk into the office behind her. He heard her conversing in hushed tones with a couple of men. The men's conversation was interspersed with low laughter, but hers was not.

Adam was still trying to decide why he was agreeing to meet Graves. He had talked briefly with Harley, whose name had been on the note. Even though he didn't get much information, the guy sounded pleasant and Adam was curious. He wanted to dig deeper into all that was going on. He would rather face it head on than wait for something unexpected to come at him. But his real motivation was to help Maggie. She didn't need James Graves bothering her, and Adam felt confident that he could tell him to back off.

Ron had become enormously curious about what Graves was up to and why he had summoned Adam. From what Adam had told him about the meeting with Maggie, he was aware that Graves knew about Adam's dreams. Ron cautioned him, though, and offered to accompany him to the meeting, but they decided against it. Both of them were interested in what Graves had to say, and he might refuse to see them or talk to them if both showed up. It was even possible that Graves just wanted to talk about clients, even though confidentiality would prevent anything like that. So, Adam accepted the invitation with trepidation.

After a minute or two, Gracie returned to the desk with a young man, who stepped behind the desk and stared at Adam with a smirk. He held a small, black tray in his hand with several wrapped candies that he held out for Adam. He was tall and slender, his black hair was slicked back, and he wore a neat white shirt and jeans.

"Complimentary maple sugar candy produced by our own hands in the deep forest by real Indians." His smirk became a smile, but not any more genuine. "I'm Harley Graves; like I told you on the phone, James is my uncle." He held out his hand, shook, then plucked a piece of the candy from the tray and handed it to Adam. He held another piece to the receptionist. "Gracie? Sweet for the Sweet?" She rolled her eyes and walked away. Harley followed her with his eyes, then turned back to Adam.

"The maple candy is left in all the rooms. It's a little side job of ours in the spring. Anyways, I can take you to Uncle. By eight or nine, he usually likes to hit the floor and do the tables and slots."

Harley came around the desk and led Adam down the dim hall past small, dark conference rooms and closed doors. "It's a little hard for him to get around sometimes, so I'm glad to help out when I can. I usher people around for him."

Adam took a few steps down the hall, then stopped. "Harley, can I ask you something first?"

"Sure."

"So, as you know, I'm not really here for a consultation, or healing, or whatever. James asked to see me, but I'm not sure what it's about. I'm a therapist, so maybe it's about some of the people we have in common or whatever. But I was wondering if there is anything I should offer him, or any custom or etiquette I should follow? You know what I mean?"

Harley smiled again. "You just give his nephew fifty bucks and he'll be all set." They laughed. "No, bro; do you smoke?" Adam shook his head, puzzled. Harley reached into his shirt pocket and pulled out a pack, took out a cigarette, and offered it to Adam. "No, just give him this. It's good to offer tobacco as a sign of trust and respect." Adam took the cigarette. "Some people give him twenty bucks or even a hundred, or they give him casino coins. Jeez, one guy even gave him a haunch of smoked venison. You don't have one of them on you, do ya?" Harley laughed too loud and slapped Adam on the back.

"Don't worry about it," Harley said, waving his hand. "He wouldn't expect you to pay him just for a chat. It's just a chat, right?"

"Yeah, just a chat. I'll offer him the cigarette and save the haunch of smoked venison for next time." The small joke went past Harley without response. They turned and continued down the hall.

After passing the dark meeting rooms, they walked through an alcove with vending machines and restrooms on each side, and came to the end of the hall where a single can light in the ceiling shone on a setting of two chairs with a side table set between. A garish arrangement of dried flowers and weeds was on the table next to a lampshade with a painting of a scantily dressed Native man and woman embracing. For some reason, a deer, wolf, and rabbit were looking on. *What happens next?* Adam smiled to himself. His silly thought told him he was trying to distract himself and was more nervous than he realized.

Harley stepped up to a door overhung with a small cedar branch. He put his ear to the door, said, "They're just talking, I think," and knocked very lightly with the knuckle of his index finger.

"It's Harley," he said softly. "I have someone here." There were steps and rustling inside for a few moments; then the door opened narrowly as the side of James Graves' wrinkled face appeared in shadow. "Be right out," he said hoarsely.

It was a long time before the door opened wider and a stocky, middle-aged woman with poorly dyed reddish-brown hair and heavy makeup, squinting at the light, came out clutching a purse and pulling on her coat; she looked confused and disheveled. She turned, said haltingly, "Thank you, Mr. Graves," and cleared her throat. She met Harley and Adam's gaze, looked down, and walked slowly away. Adam turned from her to the door to meet the unsettling, diverging glare of James Graves.

"*Mister* Knowles knows all. I'm sure you don't mind if I call you Mister. Or how about Adam? We're all friends here." He continued to stare with a slight grin. He looked quickly at Harley and nodded once toward the departing woman.

Harley nodded back and headed quickly down the hall. "Catch ya later."

Adam tried to decide which of the medicine man's red-rimmed, yellow eyeballs he should follow.

Graves stepped back to open the door wider. "Adam; 'at's a Jewish name. You a Jew?"

Adam smiled. "Nope, 'fraid not. I was told once I was French and Italian. But...." He decided not to give Graves any more than he needed.

"Oh, a big wop, then," James replied, "Well, come on in, ya mutt."

James knew Adam was a psychologist, so Adam figured he was using this weird ethnic stuff to throw him off and level the playing field. The cigarette would stay in his pocket. There seemed no point in giving Graves the satisfaction of a tobacco offering.

Adam entered a dark room—a suite probably used for entertainers or high rollers—that smelled heavily of spicy smoke. On the counter, a CD player warbled Native vocals and drums. A rumpled king bed was in a dim alcove with a desk and table, and in the main room was a sofa, chair, and kitchenette. A light and fan were on in the bathroom, the door to which was slightly open. Adam's vision adjusted to several candles around the suite and to a dim light over the stove where a foil pie pan held a smudge, drifting a wisp of smoke into the quietly whirring range hood. A half-eaten meal of fry bread and some kind of shredded meat sat on a greasy paper plate.

"Home away from home. Actually, hell of a lot better than home away from home." The lower half of James' creased face smiled, but his eyes hadn't changed. "Glad you came. You got past our little pest at the front desk?"

"You mean Harley? No, he was fine."

"No. That little Gracie Bird that flits around like a wren but has the eyes of a hawk--and the talons, too."

"The desk clerk?" Adam replied, incredulous.

"My keeper...." James trailed off and looked at the floor a long while, then looked back at Adam. "She's a pretty little thing, though." He grinned. "And you like our Anishinaabe girls, don't ya?"

Adam responded with a thin, tense smile.

"And how's our Maggie doing?" Graves asked. "You seen any ghosts, or does she just keep those for herself?"

Adam paused, realizing this could be more of a fencing match than he'd anticipated.

"Isn't everybody seeing ghosts or something? Isn't that the reason you're here in the Soo now?" Adam parried.

"Is that why *you're* here? That's why you came back around again, isn't it?" James continued to grin and turned to glance at the smudge. "Have a seat." James pointed with his lips toward the couch. Adam sat down and thought immediately that this must be the most comfortable hotel couch he'd ever sat on. It must be nice to be in the VIP class on the medicine man circuit.

Adam maintained professional composure as he prepared to hear what James had to say, but he was enormously distracted, enveloped by the warm, dark room and the deep, soft couch.

"You help people, Mr. Knowles, and I'm here to help my people. Miss Maggie and Mr. Ron Jarvin called you here 'cause people need help, and sometimes they even need *your* kinda help." He pulled up a chair near the couch and wiped his mouth with a finger.

"I'm here to listen," Adam replied. "I suppose that's what I do. I see a lot of people who need help, but I'm not sure what the problem is here in the Soo, and that's why I was curious to see how you fit in; I mean, what you have to say."

Graves continued to stare at him in a way that made him feel uncomfortable. It was part of the game, Adam thought.

After a time, the medicine man spoke. "Maggie Stewart won't work with me, and when I saw that you was her doorman, I got curious. I got my people on it, and I learned that Maggie and Ron Jarvin snagged you up here. I got my ways, just like you."

Adam smiled and furrowed his brow. "My ways? I don't know what you're talking about. I never knew Maggie before I came to the inn. Ron was my boss for years." He felt off guard, but blurted out, "Maggie was a little, I have to say, surprised by your visit. It upset her. That's one of the things I wanted to talk about."

"Aw. I upset her? L'il ol' James?" Graves said, still grinning.

He's pleased that his visit bothered Maggie, Adam thought.

"The Reillys," Graves continued, "you were involved with them a few years ago. I was coming here even then, and they were tribal members who just didn't seem to have a use for *my* medicine, for the traditional ways."

"I'm confused," said Adam. "I don't know why you're bringing that up. I didn't know they were tribal members, and I really don't want to get into that case again. I only helped them with their emotional state at that time, and I don't think it's really appropriate for me to share more about their case."

James stared again for a time with his finger across his lips. "No, of course not; I'm sure you don't think it *appropriate*."

"Is that why you wanted me here? Because of the Reillys? I really can't get into that. Besides," Adam said, shifting on the sofa, "I may have a couple of questions of my own."

"No," James said slowly. "No, it's not the Reillys. That's not why I wanted to talk man to man with you. Like I said, I just put two and two together when I found out who you were and about your relationships with Maggie and Mr. Jarvin." He inhaled through his nose. "You know the reason Mr. Jarvin keeps you close, I suppose."

Adam felt exasperated. "Look, Mr. Graves; it really seems that we're on two separate, um, rails, or roads...tracks, I mean." He wondered why the word was hard to find.

Graves smiled at Adam's fumbling speech. "Maybe you have some dreams you want to share? I am very interested in your dreams, you know. Anything you need to tell me? And while we're at it, are you saying you don't know Mr. Jarvin's whole story, either?"

"No, I sure don't. Well, I do, but...no dreams. *No.* I don't want to talk about any of that." Adam was feeling more confused. The room was getting closer, and it seemed as though James was pelting him with confusing questions. Had Graves' chair moved a couple of feet nearer? "I won't get into any of that, and I don't want to. What do you mean about Ron Jarvin?"

"You sure as hell know that *Father* Jarvin was a Jesuit, as was his grandfather, and even his great-grandfather before that. It's all connected." Graves' eyes were animated as he bore into Adam.

His eyes! They're not diverging, now. Adam shook his head and giggled. He was immediately embarrassed and didn't know why he did that. *This is crazy.*

Graves' voice was rising. "Your Mrs. Stewart came here from the Old World after she and her husband inherited that inn, which long ago belonged to a Captain Stewart, whose grandfather was none other than General Brady. My people certainly had a history with that old soldier. Specially one of my great-grandfathers. You know who that was?"

"No idea." *What the hell is going on?* Adam felt very much like he wanted to leave as Graves drilled in, but he also wanted to stay and listen. And the couch was getting more and more comfortable.

"Shingwauk, the Great Shaman and storyteller, and before that, Myeengun: Great Chief. They were the last ones who could call forth Mishipezhu," Graves said, then whispered with veneration, "the Great Lynx."

Adam's head was spinning. "I—I don't know what...."

"Mrs. Stewart and Ronald Jarvin will want to stop me from calling Mishipezhu, but it is time. I thought I needed someone who could bring Shingwauk or Myeengun back from the other world to conjure the Lynx. That's why I figured I needed Mrs. Stewart to bring back his spirit. But now I believe that dreams are the only path to find the Great Lynx. I have tried, but I get nothing." Graves leaned forward, his face near, his breath rancid. "And, Mr. Knowles,

I just have a gut-feeling that you are the one who can see into the dream world."

This is bullshit--insane, nuts! What am I doing here? I'm so tired, so tired of this, so....

"Do you know who your real parents are, Mr. Knowles? Where did you come from? Maybe you're not the big wop you *think* you are. Hee, hee." Graves' laughter rasped.

A phone rang and Adam fumbled in his pocket, but his hands were slow and hard to control.

Graves' phone was in his shirt pocket. He slowly lifted it out. "This is James." It sounded as though Graves was on the other side of an auditorium, which finally made Adam realize something was seriously wrong with him, and he had to get the hell out of there. He was too tired and muddled. The couch seemed to be getting softer and deeper as he heard the phone conversation drone on, in Ojibwe now, sing-song, as though Graves were chanting. Adam could understand none of it. Maybe he could lie down for just a minute. It couldn't hurt.

The room was changing, and he noticed cedar boughs had spread from a dark corner above gray tree trunks in shadow. The whir of forest sounds grew and wavered amid mossy dampness. Rustling and whispers fluttered around the room. He flinched when he saw the glare of large, yellow cat's eyes through branches above Graves' head.

"What...the...hell...is...going...on?" He managed to say, but he was not sure it was audible.

James locked Adam's gaze with watery, dead eyes, and his lips continued to move. Was he talking? Chewing something? And on his shoulder, it was.... *What the hell was that?* A small character. A doll? No, it was moving while it stared at Adam. It looked somehow like Graves, except with a long nose, tiny eyes, and a spray of feathers on its head. It was naked, and it was chewing something, too, its mouth ringed with--blood? Adam couldn't move.

Warbling Native songs were swelling, filling the room in a high-pitched trill. Night sounds whirred louder, tree frogs and insects, rising and shrill. Adam wanted to cover his ears, but he could not move.

Adam opened his eyes to realize he was lying on his back. Tree frogs were covering the ceiling, creeping with small hands and tiny, suction-cup fingers. Chameleon-like, their colors changed from green to beige to brown and back again in waves across the ceiling like leaves in a breeze. And there were other sounds—scurrying. Something was knocked off the counter near the kitchen sink as another tiny person, with a spray of feathers on its head, walked on hands and feet, elbows and knees, thin and angular as it crawled into the sink and tried to suck out of the faucet.

Graves' mouth was chewing: grinding and chewing. And the ugly likeness on his shoulder was chewing and chewing. Both were staring, their eyes divergent again. Grinding and chewing.

§ § §

"Adam!"

"Ju-lie?"

"Adam!"

"Julie...Jules!" Her face was right there. Her breath smelled soft as wintergreen. He saw her hair, her smooth forehead, and her eyes with little green rings on the inside of dark brown irises. There was that little scar on her chin. And her lips....

"Dr. Knowles, it's time to wake up. You'd better go." Her face began to lift away.

"No, wait. Wait!" He reached for her.

"Adam, wake up. You have to go."

He gasped. It was the young woman from the front desk.

"Adam, it's Gracie from the back lobby; you'd better get outta here."

"What happened? I—I fell asleep. Where's, uh, Graves? What happened?"

"He's at the slots and maybe to the tables by now. I saw him walk past the desk, and then you didn't come out, so I waited for a while and had to come see what happened." She looked at the door. "That asshole Harley and his friend left, too, thank God. This is not the first time they left someone here unattended."

"I have to find him. What's going on?"

"Just go; you won't get anything from him."

Adam was awake. "Did he slip me something? I didn't drink anything, and I don't feel like I just fell asleep."

"Did you eat any of that maple candy?" she asked.

Adam blinked and looked at the ceiling. "No. No, I didn't. I don't like maple stuff." He shook his head. "I don't think I did."

As he began to sit up, a small dream catcher with feathers, beads, and netting fell off his chest.

Gracie snatched it. "Just take this dream catcher with you. Do not let Graves find it. Otherwise, he might try to use it or something. I don't really know what he does with these things. Just stay away from him. I thought you were just here to meet with him; I didn't know you had a *session*."

"I didn't either; I just fell asleep." He looked at her. "Dream catcher. I—I remember. When you woke me, I was having this weird dream; I was not in the room anymore; I was in a forest with music all around. There were some little people...and a monster coming out of the water! What the hell was *that* all about?"

"I have no idea. Come on. Let's get out of here. I really don't want to be in here if he or Harley come back, or I'll be in trouble."

Adam looked around the room to be sure he had everything; he felt his phone in his pocket, his wallet. He followed Gracie out of the room and down a branching hallway within view of the desk. A taller, middle-aged woman stood behind the desk, looking into a screen.

"Francie," said Gracie, "I'm just taking him to the front lobby and I'll be right back." Francie waved but kept looking at her screen.

They turned down another hall and Gracie stopped and turned to Adam. She was close enough that her subtle perfume reached him. "I'm really sorry," she said. "I should've warned you when you came to the desk. I try to keep track of his schedule. I didn't see your name on the list, but when you introduced yourself, I was pretty sure you were just there for a meeting about a client or something. But you can never tell with Graves."

Adam blinked. "Like I said, it was—it was supposed to be just a meeting."

Adam looked carefully at her. "I'm sorry; do I know you? You said you didn't see my name. How would you know who I am? I saw a lot of clients when I used to work here. And were you...?"

"No, I don't think we ever met," said Gracie, "but I actually think you knew my husband."

"Oh, so who's your husband?" he blurted out. Adam felt a little twinge of regret somewhere inside when he learned she was married. He looked down at her a moment longer, still trying to revive the image of Julie that he had imagined. "Duane Bird. He was in the Marines and was going through some wicked PTSD after serving in Afghanistan. He got his CJ degree, criminal justice, at LSSU."

"Yeah, of course! I do remember him--vaguely. Tall, friendly, nice guy. Where is he? I mean, what's he doing?"

"He works for the FBI in Wisconsin. And we came here—I mean, I'm here 'cause Graves is here, but that's a long story. I don't want to talk about it." She hesitated. "Actually, Duane's making some plans, and then I'm going home. Anyway, I'd better get you out of here."

"Wait, Gracie; what did he do to me back there?"

"I really don't know. People coming out of that room don't usually seem hungover or act drugged, so I don't know if he hypnotizes them or if he uses something else."

"I don't know if there's a drug that would wear off that fast. Jeez, how long was I in there?"

"You were only in there an hour when I came to get you."

"So, I wasn't drugged."

"I hope not. But I never eat the maple candy, either. It's crap. I'm going to send a sample to the lab." She stopped and looked down. "Never mind. Pretend you didn't hear me say that."

Adam paused. "I don't think I had any of the candy, but I'm just not sure."

"Hang on to that dream catcher that was lying on your chest while you were sleeping. I know a little about that stuff, and I'm pretty sure that's what he wanted. He was trying to...catch something from you."

"I'm afraid to think of what he wanted," Adam replied.

"Let's go," Gracie said.

They wound through a maze of hallways, trying to avoid the game rooms and slots so they wouldn't see Graves or Harley until they came to an alcove partially enclosed by tall, potted trees. They were hidden from the main lobby, where a bustle of people trudged past, looking down, not making eye contact with one another. A couple waddled past with matching oxygen tanks in tow. Several others inched by in wheelchairs, moving their arms in unison, like rowers crossing the River Styx in rhythm to the incessant musical twitter from slot machines.

"Adam," said Gracie, reaching for his wrist. She grasped it firmly, "I don't mean to be.... I'm not sure if I'm saying too much, but I think I need to talk to you some time. I think you're in this now, and I'm kinda worried. That's why I'm back there at that desk. To keep an eye out."

"So, that's what he meant," Adam said.

Gracie looked surprised. "Did he say something about me?"

"He called you his keeper, I think, or something like that." He didn't tell her the other things Graves had said about her.

"That's not good," she said mostly to herself.

"Are you in danger? Should I tell someone?" Adam asked.

"No. Don't tell anyone. That's why it may be time for me to go back with Duane." She nodded slowly, then looked up at him. "It would be helpful for us to talk some more. I know you work with Ron Jarvin. To be honest, that's the other way I heard about you."

Adam was surprised. "How do you know Ron? What's going on?"

"Mmm...that's a long story, too." She smiled. "Maybe we should *all* get together. There's so much going on and so much to do here. I'm afraid that now you're part of it."

"Well, yeah, dammit! I have to find out what's going on. What *are* we doing here? I'm sure as hell worried after what I just went through. I'll do whatever I have to."

"I know; I'm sorry, but be careful. We can handle it for now, and we will all get together and talk about this," she said, finally letting go of his wrist. Adam looked down at his arm as though something were missing, but it was only her touch that was gone.

"I'd better go." She looked around nervously.

He paused. "Really? You're that worried?"

She just looked at him with a tight smile, nodding her head, then gave a small wave and patted her side. "Do you have the dream catcher?"

Adam looked down, felt in his side pocket, and could feel the little coil of feathers and twigs. When he looked up, Gracie was gone.

The large main lobby was a contrast to the back lobby where he had met Gracie. Here there were plush leather chairs and beautiful Native art hanging all the way to an arched ceiling. Steel tree trunks rose skyward, symmetrically branched with laminated wooden beams. Each branch formed part of the glass dome.

Adam looked around for Graves or Harley, then slipped through the doors.

§ § §

As Gracie strode around the corner leading to the back lobby, she stopped. Harley was slouched against a counter that ran along the wall behind the desk and was laughing with his acne-ed sidekick. The sidekick stood with arms folded, leaning near the office door, a pancake of greasy, black hair nearly hiding the kid's eyes.

"Where the hell's Francie?" Gracie demanded.

"Took a break, I guess. I told her I'd cover." Harley grinned and looked Gracie up and down while his stupid partner did the same.

"You guys aren't supposed to be around here without a manager." She stepped quickly past Harley and up to the computer screen; with a few key strokes, she checked the screen to be sure it hadn't been tampered with. It hadn't. These two wouldn't be smart enough to hack it anyway, she guessed. As she checked the room file and opened the key drawer, Harley walked behind her toward the office, allowing his hand to slowly brush the back of her slacks. He snorted as he and his friend made eye contact. Before he took another step, she turned, grabbed his right arm with her left hand, and as she pulled it back and outward, she neatly clipped him in the back of the right knee with her left foot. He crashed to the floor as she stepped smoothly aside. Her moves were trained and efficient.

"What the f...?" he sputtered as he flailed on the floor.

"*Never,* touch me!" she said.

As she turned toward the office, the other kid was standing in the doorway, looking stunned.

"Get out of my way, you pimpled prick!" she said and elbowed him neatly in the side. He coughed and backed into the office.

"I'm getting the supervisor." She didn't look back.

CHAPTER 10

GRACIE BIRD

FRANCIE DROVE GRACIE TO THE Sugar Island ferry dock on the Saint Mary's River, east of town. She parked away from the line of cars that waited to load so Gracie could walk on to the Sugar Islander ferry. They arrived a few minutes early; since it was late in the day and getting cold, they sat in the car and talked. Francie had not noticed the car tailing them from the casino, but Gracie saw it the moment they pulled from the lot: Harley's piece-of-crap 2002 Chevy with his mop-top friend riding shotgun. His car sat near the back of the line of cars waiting to get on the ferry. Harley's head was down because he foolishly thought then she couldn't see him.

The gate dropped, and cars from the island started to leave the ferry. Gracie said a few words to Francie, left the car, and walked briskly toward the dock. Francie drove away. Two large, Native men in white shirts, jeans, and black sport coats came down the ferry ramp toward Gracie. One wore his hair long, the other braided. When she looked up and smiled, they nodded quickly and walked past her toward the old Chevy.

The man with the braids waved politely to the car behind the Chevy to move back, while the other man leaned into the window of the car parked ahead of Harley's and asked them to pull forward. Harley's head swiveled back and forth between the two men. One of the men stepped to Harley's window, smiled broadly, and motioned for him to lower his window.

"What the hell do you want?" Harley asked before he got his window all the way down. "I'm getting on the ferry!"

"Oh, no problem, sir," the man said cordially. "Routine inspection; you can be on your way in no time. Could you just pull your car out of line for a brief moment, and then, like I said, you can be on your way."

The second man stepped up and also spoke pleasantly. "It will not help if you resist because...." Smiling, he lifted the side of his jacket to reveal the butt of a gun.

"Oh, for God's sake. What the hell is this? Do you know who my uncle is?" Harley whined.

"Yes, as a matter of fact, we do," the man said while ushering him out of line with his outstretched hand. Harley revved his engine and spun his tires.

The cars started loading, and Gracie walked up the ramp. A quick, thin *meep* sounded from the horn above the cabin. Gracie looked up. The captain gave her a thumbs-up. Gracie grinned and returned the salute.

"Hey, dammit, I gotta get on that ferry, *now*! You son-of-a..." Harley sputtered.

One of the men held up his finger. "One minute, sir."

Harley smacked the steering wheel with his fist.

When the ferry was loaded, the conductor brought up the gate. Harley glared at Gracie, who stood at the rail looking back. Her big smile showed perfectly. She reached around with her right hand and undid her long hair, shook it out, and stepped up on the lower bar of the side rail. Then she leaned forward and waved at Harley and his sidekick. He rolled his eyes and looked away.

"Okay, sir, like we said, now you can be on your way." The man pointed toward the road as he lost his broad smile. "And don't come back. We'll be here on the return trip, too."

Both men turned and stepped quickly toward the ferry, grabbed the gate, and neatly pulled themselves over. They gave a quick wave to Gracie before going up the steps to the cabin.

Diesel fumes mixed with the smell of crisp air. Clear river current rolled under the ferry as it rumbled across the channel on its brief voyage.

When the ferry reached the other side, Duane was waiting for Gracie. He stood tall, smiling in a dark blue sport coat, blue shirt, and jeans. His black hair was meant to be neat and trimmed, but it was jostled and thick. Duane and Gracie hugged briefly as cars growled over grates behind them and sped away toward the island's interior.

"You okay?" he asked.

"Sure," Gracie said. "Leo and Donnie took care of things.

"Harley?"

"Of course," she smiled. "How about we go back to the house. I think I'd like to go for a short run, then take a long, hot shower: get rid of the casino. Then we can eat and head to Lake State. Is that okay?"

"Sure, we don't have to be there until eight," he said.

§ § §

When Duane and Gracie returned, they drove onto the ferry to catch the seven-thirty back to the main land. The two big Native men, Donnie and Leo, came down from the cabin and took the backseat in the car. Gracie licked her finger and reached into the backseat to wipe Donnie's cheek. "Does it still hurt?" she laughed.

"Not much," Donnie said, "but next time, would you mind practicing your kicks on Leo? He's a bigger target."

"Aw, poor baby," she replied. "Remember, jiu-jitsu is about center of gravity. Next time, keep your head up."

"Yeah, I think you already told me that––after you hit me." He smiled.

Lake State University sits on the site of Fort Brady and incorporates several of the buildings from the old fort, including the barracks, post headquarters, and quartermaster's building. Overlooking the Saint Mary's River, the university maintains the character and stately beauty of the fort.

The choice of this facility for the meeting, on the old fort site, was not entirely coincidental. It had power. Everything would need to be done with precision and planning when doing battle with forces that few understood.

Yellow lights lit the walkways through the manicured university as the group of four crossed the campus. Gracie walked ahead, her small frame and long hair contrasting with the three tall men.

The rambling quartermaster's building housed the university administration complex and contained offices and meeting rooms on the second floor. The lobby had lost none of its early twentieth century character with deep wood trim, tile floors, and tall windows. Down the hall, their steps echoed to the elevator. When arriving on the second floor, they had only to follow the scent of sage smoke to find their way to the meeting room.

Seven of the eight high-back wooden chairs that rimmed the long table were already taken. One chair at the head of the table, near the door, was empty. The faces that greeted them with straight smiles were serious but not unpleasant.

Leo and Donnie walked over to stand against the wall with their hands crossed in front of them. Duane stood next to them while a man sitting near the empty chair motioned for Gracie to sit. With raised eyebrows, smiling nervously, she took the seat reserved for her. At the opposite end of the table sat a very old, very small man, his eyes narrowed. Gracie could not tell if he was looking at her or sleeping, since he sat slumped, lost in his calico shirt with sleeves that came almost to his knuckles. Long gray hair was loose around his shoulders and swept nearly to the table.

A small smudge burned in the back of the room, but there was no pipe and no ceremony. These people were of a more ancient creed. The stocky man on her left spoke first; his short, thinning hair was streaked with gray, and his eyes were magnified large in black-framed glasses. Silver rings were on three fingers, and a red stone bolo was pulled around the collar of his denim shirt. "We are eight, now. Four and four. We like to believe that four and eight represent fullness and wholeness. This is according to custom. So, let's get started." He nodded sharply and smiled. "Then we can get downtown before the Big Boy closes." A couple of beats of low laughter sounded around the table.

His tone changed, became earnest. "Many of us are familiar with each other, but it is not often we get to meet together formally in this manner. As you know, membership in this Lake Council has passed down through many generations, so we forget who's who, sometimes. When something needs to be decided, we have usually talked informally among ourselves. But this is different." He paused briefly. "I don't have to tell you that we are the ones granted the responsibility to preserve the lake's traditions and protect the lake and the people who live and work around it. No one else is aware of the spiritual mysteries and dangers this lake possesses." He tapped the table with a finger, and as he scanned the faces of those who sat around it, his magnified eyes grew intense. "And no one else should be allowed to divert its power. That's why we're here."

Several in the group nodded.

He smiled again. "We're not exactly into name tags, I guess, so why don't we go 'round and introduce ourselves. Just so everyone knows everyone. I think we have the lake surrounded, here. Somebody from every corner." He raised his hand. "I'm Virgil Clement from Michigan Intertribal Council in the Soo." He nodded to the woman on his left.

"Sharon LaPere, Bay Mills," she said.

The next man said, "Melvin Smart, Bad River Tribal Council, Ashland."

The old man just nodded slowly when his turn came, and the woman to his left spoke up, "Sophie Kakegamic, Fort Williams and Thunder Bay. My brother, Miles Laronde, is an alternate, and I *hope* he's back at the casino if we need him."

Virgil Clement spoke up again, indicating with his open hand the three seated across from him. "Dr. Kakegamic, Wally, and Carl are our Canadian First Nations folks."

"Wally Anemki, Red Rock," said the man beside Sophie. His voice was high and quiet for such a huge, round man. He was looking down at the table with his long braids beside his big face, and his ribbon shirt straining over his chest. He looked up. "Oh yeah, and I'm also for Pays Plat, where my Uncle Chet Anemki is an alt—alternate. Uncle Chet couldn't make it," he said shyly. "Anyways...." He just twisted his hand in the air, and looked up with a crooked smile.

"I'm Carl Odjig, Batchewana Band," the man to Gracie's right spoke up. He looked around the table with a huge grin while he tapped the table nervously with a pen. He was middle aged and wore a polo shirt and khaki pants. Gracie thought he looked like a high school teacher.

The old man at the end of the table mumbled something and the room grew silent. Members looked furtively at him, then away.

"Excuse me," Virgil said, offering a hand toward Gracie. "This is...."

"Waabishki Oniijaaniw!" The ancient voice was loud and clear, and his eyes were staring at Gracie. "You are Waabishki Oniijaaniw! And daughter of Waabishki Oniijaaniw!" He smiled broadly, revealing two rows of straight white teeth. "The White Doe."

"Yes, I've been given that name. Albino Doe is a little more accurate translation, but it's always been White Doe." Gracie lifted her chin proudly. "But no one would know that better than you, Jacob Payment. I'm honored to be here. Humbled to be in the presence of all of you, but especially a great spirit man like Jacob. And you can all call me Gracie." She looked around the table. "My work with the council has been kept private up until now so I haven't had a chance to—"

"Gracie Bird," the old man said, still smiling and turning to Duane. "And you are Duane Bird." Duane nodded. "Welcome." It was as though the old man had awakened.

Virgil extended an open hand toward the two men standing against the wall. "I also asked Leo and Donnie, two of the Ogichi daa, the warriors, to stop in just so we could thank them for their help and for their behind-the-scenes planning and strategy. They found this room and set it up for us and everything. I also want to thank them for the protection when we need it. And to offer our sympathies to them for quite regularly getting their rear ends kicked by Gracie while they train with her." The group acknowledged them happily, and the two men grinned, nodded, and turned to leave the room. Gracie waved.

"We'll be around if you need anything," Leo said as they left.

Virgil looked around the table. "There is trouble all around the lake. More than we can guess. Gracie knows Mr. Ron Jarvin pretty well. We all know who he is, I think. She will be meeting with him so we can understand some of the deeper physical and historical aspects and see things from the perspective of one of the true counselors or teachers like him. We also know there's been a little more going on here in the east where the Saint Mary's River flows out of the lake.

It seems to draw everything this way. That may be why there's more activity here," Virgil said. "But even up in Thunder Bay, some strange things have been happening that hit pretty close to home. Right, Sophie? It's okay if we call you Sophie, Dr. Kakegamic?"

"Of course." Sophie smiled and waved her hand, her lovely, weathered face and firm jaw framed in straight, gray hair. She wore a white shirt buttoned at the neck under a suit coat and black pants. A fine silver and turquoise necklace hung over her shirt with matching earrings setting off her dark features. "You want me to tell it?" She hesitated.

Virgil and a couple of the others nodded.

She inhaled. "Well, this is just one example. I'm sure we all have our stories. But my sister Susie and her kids were wading at the beach near Thunder Bay. I think it was Wild Goose Beach; I'm not sure. It's real shallow, so it stays pretty warm, and you can go way out there. It was a nice day last September, so Susie decided it wouldn't hurt to let them splash around." She paused and pushed her hair behind her ear. "Nobody else was there, and she wasn't paying much attention. One of the kids yells, 'Mom, look!' Susie looked up and here's a guy walking toward them."

"Somebody else taking advantage of Indian Summer?" Carl Odjig from Batchewana looked along the table at Sophie.

"Not at all," Sophie said. "He had a full-on snowmobile suit and was carrying his helmet under his arm. The kids scattered to their mom, and she just sat there frozen."

"Boy, I know, we have all seen some strange stuff, right?" Carl chattered nervously.

"That's not the half of it," Virgil said. "Let's have her finish. Go ahead, Sophie."

"Right," Sophie continued. "You see, we lost our brother a few years ago. He went through the ice with his...."

"Oh, no," Gracie said. "It wasn't!"

"Yup; my sister saw him. It was awful. It's like he didn't know where he was as he came out of the water. He just wandered into the brush across the highway and disappeared. Like I said, Susie was frozen."

"Oh, my God," both Gracie and Sharon from Bay Mills whispered.

Virgil nodded. "Like Carl said, I think we've all probably seen some strange stuff and would all have our own stories, but I wanted Sophie to share hers so we see what it means for all of us around the lake, even up in Thunder Bay. But we're here for more than that. We have another problem, maybe a bigger problem."

"James Graves," Jacob interrupted with measured disgust. The council waited, and he continued slowly, confidently. "We can do nothing about the restless lake. We cannot change what is happening in the lake or with those spirits that are leaving. But we must hold council to understand and record these things and know why souls are leaving. That's why we are here." He held up one hand, pointing into the air. "There are great signs that have not been seen for many, many generations." He looked around the table. "But we cannot allow a man to attempt to call up or try to control Mishipezhu. The Great Lynx is uneasy and may soon appear. We don't know why, and we don't know what it could mean. If The Lynx comes to stay in this world, the waters could be spoiled, children could be lost, and the forests will turn brown when the lake refuses to give up rain. Mishipezhu can bring misery."

Wally Anemki spoke in his high quiet voice. "This Bear Walk—*Graves*—brings the misery! He does not understand. He does not know." Wally looked down at his big hands formed into fists. "My mother, my mother was so sick, and she went to one of these bastards last year––these false medicine men. They killed...." His voice cracked and he rubbed a big fist near his eye and sniffled.

"We know," Sophie said softly and patted his arm. She turned to Gracie, then Duane. "Gracie's mother met a different fate at their hands. You could say she was cut down, assassinated. If they can do that to a young mother, then...I'm sorry, Gracie."

Gracie was looking at her hands. "That's okay, Sophie. Wally, I'm sorry for your loss, too. We all need to understand and take this seriously. We need to be vigilant and fight back."

Virgil broke in. "He is not a Bear Walk. He does not even rise to that level; isn't that right, Jacob?"

Jacob nodded. "That's right. He has evil power similar to that, but not at the level of a real Bear Walk. The Bear is an evil Midiwinini, who can shape shift and cast spells. Graves is not even a Tcisaki, or male diviner. He's a fraud, a sham. He hasn't achieved the status of a first level Mide'o. He's nothing."

"We all know how good medicine can help," said Virgil, "but we also know what this bad medicine can do. But how can we stop him?" He looked at Duane. "That's why we invited Duane to accompany Gracie today. As you know, he's with the FBI, working with tribal operations, and knows as much about Graves as anyone. Can you fill us in, Duane?"

Duane cleared his throat nervously and stepped forward while looking at the floor. "May I address this Council of Eight, Mr. Clement?"

"Go ahead, Duane. We will lay aside any formality tonight. I think that's okay with everyone," Virgil said, and the group nodded.

"As you probably know," said Duane, "there are criminal investigations involved here so, of course, I can't go into anything about that, but I'll give you a sketch about what I know." He looked around the room and inhaled before beginning. Gracie smiled at him and he smiled back. "I think many of you know a few things about Graves, but I'll give you the rundown anyway."

"Yeah; then we will all be on the same page," Virgil said.

"What we know is that Graves grew up near Denver. His father was a Potawatomi from Oklahoma and his mother was Lakota Sioux from Pine Ridge in South Dakota. He came to Michigan when he was in his thirties, looking for some long-lost Potawatomi relatives of his, and we think he wound up living off them for quite a while." Duane scratched his forehead with two fingers. "And that's where we sort of lost track of him. The best we can tell is that he was a dealer at a casino for a while until he fell in with a visiting medicine man and learned *the trade*."

"And the rest is history, as they say," Carl Odjig interjected.

"Right, sure, but it's a bit more complicated," Duane said.

"He has some skills," Jacob said slowly. "He knows things. And that's the problem."

"I think that's right," Gracie said. "He knows things and he does things. I've seen it at the casino."

"So, he's not entirely a charlatan?" Sophie asked.

"No, he's not," Duane said. "That's what we used to think, too. But he has not just stirred up trouble around here. He's been around to other tribes; he has connections, and he has his hands into some things that should make the Native community very concerned." He put his hands in his pockets and paced. "This cannot leave the room. I know this council is sworn to secrecy." He glanced around the table. "It's enough for me to say that...it may involve those three kids that went missing at Pine Ridge and Rose Bud last year."

Several in the group responded with small gasps. Duane nodded at Gracie.

"No, Graves is dangerous for several reasons," Gracie said. "He knows much more than you think. He dipped a finger into the well of mystery and got a taste. Now he wants more. He wants power. Power will get him recognition so he can carry out more of his heinous deeds and sleazy sessions for more money. Power and money, it's as simple as that. He has no idea what he's actually messing with."

"He has no idea," Jacob affirmed. The others turned toward him. "He seeks Mishipezhu, but The Great Lynx is more than he knows. It is a force," he continued grave and authoritative. "It is also a sign, a symptom of trouble in the lake. It can be summoned, and may even be guided, but not by man or woman. It is not of this world, but of the dream world. The vision world." He looked at his hands.

Thinking of Adam, Gracie and Duane exchanged glances.

Jacob looked up from his hands. "We see the Great Lynx in the pictographs on Agawa Rock in Canada. We believe that Myeengun or Shingwauk, the ancient chiefs, saw Mishipezhu in a vision quest, then made the paintings on the rock. But the nature of The Great Lynx is not truly understood." He held up two long fingers on his right hand. "It has two natures. Wait." He extended his index fingers on each hand. "It has two separate natures." He moved his hands apart with his index fingers still extended as he talked. "One nature exists in the dream world," he said, lifting higher his right index finger, "and one nature exists in the real world," raising the left. "It surfaces from one to the other like a salmon jumping out of the river."

Resting his left hand on the table, Jacob wagged his right finger. "But Graves is not a dreamer. And he's too damn lazy to do a dream quest or even move through the levels of Midewiwin, so he cannot see or summon The Lynx. He can only piss him off. And that is very bad. Mishipezhu will dive back into the dream world and leave when the lake settles down. But not if Graves has intervened."

"So how do we stop the son-of-a-bitch?" Wally shrugged, turning his palms and looking at Jacob. "We're not Midewininiwag; we do not do their medicine."

Jacob, staring at Gracie, said, "He can only be stopped while he's working, when he's doing the ceremony. Then he and his forces are open and vulnerable. And we know there is only one person qualified. One person who carries the ancient authority of her mother."

The others turned toward Gracie, who sat with her elbows on the table, her hands folded under her chin as she stared at Jacob.

Sophie spoke up. "Gracie, you know Mr. Graves. I think we have a good idea where he will be doing the ceremony." She looked around the table. "We know Graves must be stopped--at any cost. If he attempts to conjure, it could be a disaster. If he does something wrong—if he tries to intervene and he doesn't know what he's doing—it will be tragic. I know this: Mishipezhu represents that ominous, capricious nature of Lake Superior. For all we know, the lake could be devastated for a generation if this entity emerges: the fish could leave, people will die on the beaches and on the water, the forests around the lake could die. No one knows."

She looked around the room and her gaze settled on Gracie. "Now we need a plan."

CHAPTER 11

JAN JARVIN

A BURGUNDY GLOW REFLECTED FROM POLISHED cherry walls, as a single light haloed a seated figure bent over a carving on a low table near the fireplace. Wind rattled the windows and the flue huffed with gusts. Through heavy walls, the lake drummed, and between gusts and waves, there was the gentle rustle of sandpaper on smooth wood. Wavering strains of the French torch singer, Edith Piaf, played low on the stereo.

Jan had moved here—west of Wawa, Ontario—six years ago after their dream home was completed—a rare private stake on Lake Superior's north shore. He deeply regretted that Susan was never able to join him. She would have appreciated, in her funny, flippant way, that her life insurance helped cover the thousands of dollars it cost to build the road and run electricity.

"Hey, Jake, what're you thinking?" He continued sanding while he spoke to a sleek Husky that lay near the fire with its chin resting on its paws and its pale blue eyes restlessly scanning the dim room. The dog whined.

"You seem nervous, pal. Visitors tonight?"

Jan set the sandpaper on the table as he listened to Piaf's distant recording of "Je m'imagine," and followed Jake's eyes around the room to see only dark wood walls framed in stone. Leaded windows reflected three candles, one for each window. Under the windows stood a leather couch with chairs on each side and a low table in front of the couch. No curtains obstructed the view across the big lake during the day. Tonight, the windows were black.

This side of the house took the full force of the lake, raging against square logs set above stone walls. A narrow deck ran the length of the house, eighty feet above the water. Gale-force winds traversed a hundred miles of ragged freshwater sea before crashing onto cliffs, thrusting halfway up the rock face, throwing gouts of spray as high as the windows. Tonight, the lake was as cold, deep, and ferocious as any coastline on the planet.

From the lakeside, the house sloped upward two-and-a-half stories. The main floor contained an open living area with a span of oak flooring. It did not seem so vast and empty whenever the kids were here, but tonight he was alone, and the chattering storm echoed through the broad rooms and shadowed halls.

His youngest, Samantha, was at Michigan Tech, but she had been staying here more often since her recent unsettling experience on a Lake Superior research vessel. While working as an intern on the ship, she had seen and heard some horrifying things Jan was only now beginning to understand. *That young woman has been through a lot*, he thought, *but she has strength.*

This house, this time, here and now, that's what he loved. It was a healing place. The Toronto lifestyle and the Canadian biotech company were far in the past. If only Susan had made it this far with him.

The house seemed strangely waiting, dynamic. The small figure he was carving was part of a set he had been working on for nearly a year. This was the final piece. It was a Native woman, naked to the waist with a headdress of long feathers. Around her neck and across her skirt were precise decorations. The other pieces stood on a side table and had similar features: three men and another woman. They had all been cut from a strange piece of driftwood found along the shore: a three-foot, battered, cigar-shaped log. It had been oak or hickory, he thought, but he couldn't clearly identify the ancient waterlogged wood grain. When he cut into the hardened wood, it was swirled with color. Carved and polished, the wood shimmered.

The intricate figures of the men were carved with large headdresses. Jan's skill depicted woven feathers and bits of fur that sprayed from their heads. Long, broad loin clothes, cut with fine patterns representing beading, reached below their knees.

The figures of the women were also arduously engraved with similar headdresses of long feathers set in a band that perched on hair inlaid with elaborately plaited beads and tiny copper discs. Their hair cascaded to low slung skirts, covered in minuscule cones of metallic ornamentation made of inlaid silver. Around their necks, the women wore wide chokers with more inlays of red stones and green-tarnished copper. From these collars hung intricate plates that spread nearly to their breasts, glimmering with mother-of-pearl. It was a magnificent presentation: savage, angelic, and utterly human. Jan felt it was by far his best and most ambitious work.

Jan had been a woodcarver since he was a kid. His hobby evolved, as he grew older, from carving animals to his fascination with the human form. Gradually, his interests advanced to dream-like figures of sprites, elves, goblins, or any other faerie-like figure that stoked his imagination––while awake or asleep.

He knew someone was watching him before he looked up, and now Jake lifted his head, his eyes wide, in wonder more than fear. Just out of range of the craft light, he saw a torso with arms at its sides. It startled him. It was transparent; he could still see the couch below the window through a diaphanous striped shirt. Jan moved his gaze slowly upward. He was more curious than afraid. He was becoming accustomed to things like this happening recently. And he knew for sure that no one could have walked nearly ten miles from the Trans-Canadian Highway to get back here on a night like this. Jake would've thrown a fit if a person actually got in here.

For several months, Jan would see an occasional shadow move out of the corner of his eye, or a shoulder disappear around a corner. He became intrigued when Jake started to react to these apparitions at the same time Jan was seeing them. Not a bark or growl, just a whine or wag of the tail, as though he were about to get a friendly pat. Being the curious, pragmatic scientist that he was, this stuff fascinated Jan. He was not averse to the supernatural, and he was too confident in his stability--and Jake's stability—to be worried about his mental status.

It almost seemed ordinary, if that's possible. In fact, that was the reason he had the candles in the window. *Bait*, he thought, *like moths to a flame.* He wasn't sure what he was dealing with, but he was enormously curious to find out, and he didn't mind adding a little enticement to get things started. It had never occurred to him before to try recordings of French torch singers.

Tonight, things were becoming far from ordinary. He was seeing a full-blown apparition. He knew the striped shirt immediately: a French navy Breton pattern. The stripes rippled and faded, then returned, but the face he beheld was incandescent, floating near and shedding light on the figure Jan had been carving. As the face hung inches away from the statue, Jan could see that this was a young man as serene and curious as a cat. His half-grin was not leering at the woman, but it shown with recognition, and appreciation. He seemed fascinated by the statue, and he looked at Jan with approval.

"*Bonsoir,*" Jan whispered, and he smiled. Behind the sailor, four other figures sharpened into view. Two appeared to be sitting on the couch. They also wore striped Breton shirts and flat caps. Two more were in the chairs and had dark shirts with broad sailors' collars and dark hats. All their faces shown with clear radiance.

"Bienvenue chez nous. J'espère que vous trouves la paix," Jan said, then looked sideways at Jake. "I hope I just said something like 'Welcome to our home. I hope you find peace.'" The sailor near the statue smiled at Jake, and the dog stood, wagged its tail, and gave a happy "Woof."

It was as though the ghosts were moving in another dimension, distant but near, looking in through thick glass. They were looking *in*, but Jan felt like they didn't really know he was looking *out*. It didn't seem like they could hear or actually respond to him in real time. Only that approving nod toward Jan and that smile of recognition for Jake weaved through the warp and connected.

In seconds, the man near the statue looked up, gazing toward the east wall while the other four, as though hearing a signal, stood and looked east. Their expressions never changed. All moved past Jan and Jake and slowly walked through the solid stone next to the fireplace and were gone. The dog continued to stare at the wall and wag his tail. While all this was happening, the room had grown silent, as inside a bubble. Jan flinched when the rumble and whistle of the gale roared in, again, and Piaf was singing the frenetic "Ouragan (Hurricane)" on the stereo.

Jake stepped back near Jan. He scratched the dog's head and stroked his back. Soon the dog lay back by the fire with his chin on his paws as though nothing had happened.

Jan turned off the craft light, and clicked off the stereo with a remote. He pushed his table away, sat back in his chair smiling, his hands folded, and put his feet up on the footstool for a long while listening to the storm, the music, and the crackling fire.

Suddenly, he said, "I have to tell my brother."

He picked up his phone, grateful that he could get one or two little bars this close to the Trans-Canadian on a stormy night. It rang twice.

"Hey, Ron. How ya doing? Yeah, storming like hell, here. No, I'm fine. Jake's here watching over me."

He laughed. He and Ron had small talk, then Jan said, "The reason I called was because I wanted to know if you remembered those lost French mine-sweepers—the *Inkerman*, I think one was called, and the other one was called something else.... Yeah, that's right: *Cerisoles*. Of course, you'd know. Wasn't it in November of 1918? Yeah, weird. We were talking about how they were going to try to find the ships again." He listened. "Well, yes, right. I know. All seventy-six sailors were lost and a couple of Canadians who were on board. Well, anyway...."

CHAPTER 12

DEAR UNCLE RON

Hi Uncle Ron,

Let me know if you have any problems downloading this, and I'll put it in a different format or I can send you a link.

How have you been? I'm doing great. Dad and Jake say, "Hi." Jake would probably say "Woof!" but that's silly, I guess.

You've been on my mind, of course, since I got that gig working with the USGS. You're the one who got me interested in limnology, with all that you know about Lake Superior and with some of our discussions. And now I'm working on a minor in biology, also, like you.

We only talked for a minute about that article that was in the paper when I got off the boat. Thanks again for calling me. I'm lucky to have you for my uncle, and I'm really grateful for all you've done over the years.

I'm sorry I missed you when we docked at the Soo, but I knew you were up in WaWa with Dad then. Now that I think about it, I probably would've been too shook up at that time and wouldn't have known what to say anyway. I should've come up there with you and Dad.

My time on the R/V *Kite* (that's Research Vessel, of course) was amazing. Being out on the water is just my thing, I guess. To drift out in the middle of that incredible expanse or gaze into the depths of that huge lake and see it teeming with life makes me feel small.

As you know, some very weird and scary stuff happened out there, and I figured maybe you could help me understand it. Or at least hear me out. I'm still pretty nervous and have some trouble sleeping. I told Dad, and he understands, a little, but I'm not sure he really gets it. I was afraid he thought I was smoking weed or something, which I wasn't! (And I don't.) Do you know any good therapists to talk to?--lol. I know our family has a dark sense of humor, but what happened out there goes beyond the pale, as they say.

I decided to just forward the whole account that I wrote when I got back. It turned out almost like a letter--to myself, I guess. Good therapy, right? I want to share with you what I wrote. Don't worry; it's not too long, and I left a lot of the technical stuff out. I'd love to go over our data with you sometime. You'd be interested in it, too, I think. Some of the anomalies that we recorded were incredible.

A separate folder has some of the pics, too.

Hope to hear from you soon.

Love, Sam

§ § §

Ron's apartment near the locks had a similar view to that from his office. He could see the International Bridge with toy-like cars and trucks winding above the locks and heading to Ontario. Saint Mary's Rapids winked and glimmered like tinsel in the distance. The apartment also overlooked *The Strip* as the locals called it, where the tourists hang out to buy Soo Locks caps and Mackinac Island fudge. Late in the day, this time of year, the street was empty except for a few hopeful *Fudgies* gawking as they meandered the street looking for fish dinners and souvenirs.

He opened the attachment to Sam's email and downloaded the file. A separate folder opened with thumbnails of photos and a couple of maps. He clicked on the first photo, which showed a smiling Samantha standing with the rest of the crew next to the research vessel. He hit print to his photo tray and looked to the Canadian side of the river thinking about Samantha: the tearful little girl in braids. Her mother and grandfather's deaths had been devastating, and it bothered him, now, that she would have to endure this terrible experience on the research vessel. He took the photo off the printer and leaned it against the desk lamp.

He already knew some of what she had encountered. Newspaper accounts a few weeks earlier detailed the recovery of a badly decomposed corpse by the R/V *Kite*. Remarkably, the body was thought to be associated with a sunken cargo vessel that was lost in cold waters--nearly a century ago.

§ § §

My sweatshirt said "USGS: Science for a changing world," and now I think I know what it means. I saw a changing world. All of the other trips on the R/V *Kite* from June through October were pretty routine, and my scientific data is filed separately among other reports. I decided to highlight this last voyage in a different way and get it all written down while it's still fresh in my head. I don't know if the other academic team members are going to write anything up; I wish they would. I think the ship's crew made some sort of pact not to say anything because they're more afraid for their jobs or credibility. I understand that, but I was just an intern, so I guess I'm free to write what I want. I hope.

We were working for the university, and most of our time was spent taking fish samples and recording data, so we became immune to smelling fish after a couple of days. But on this trip, about three days out, we started noticing this odor coming from somewhere. It smelled like something rotten. There were eight of us on board and the captain had us go through everything to see if some garbage was stowed somewhere or if a raccoon got in when we were on shore and died somewhere (seriously?), but we never found anything.

As we were heading toward the east side of the lake on day six, the really strange stuff started happening. And thinking about it now, I'm glad the captain was the first one to see it because if it had been me or Sven, the other intern, they would've thought we were crazy or playing a practical joke. It takes a while for an intern to earn the trust of the rest of the crew, even though we interns are along on just about every trip. Besides, Sven is not exactly the type to play practical jokes, although I guess I might have considered it myself just to liven up a long trip. But I didn't.

The captain and the mate were up on the bridge. It was late afternoon, toward evening, and we were still bearing east. We had originally planned to harbor in Munising that night, but the chief scientist wanted to take a turn farther out and catch some surface samples early in the morning. I really wish we'd gone straight to the Soo.

Suddenly, the "Man Overboard" alarm went off. At first, we didn't get too frantic because we thought it might be a drill. It was pretty calm, and no one was doing anything around the nets or rails. Most of us were below cleaning up the processing area. It takes forever because there are all these stainless-steel tables and lockers to clean, and there is equipment that has to be stowed after we're done with the samples.

On the Station Bill, which hangs by our personal lockers and describes our duties and bunking arrangements, each of us is assigned a job to do for "Fire in the Engine Room," "General Fire," or "Man Overboard," so we each went to our stations. I was designated "The Alternate Pointer," the one to keep an eye on the person, or persons in the water, and I would work with Sven to secure the rescue line and get the inflatable life ring. I was afraid it was Sven who had gone overboard because he'd gone above to find the cover for one of the cans we use. But by the time I got on deck, Sven was already there. He had the ring and was going for the rope. I ran up to the rail and looked back at Sven, who was coming with the equipment. I saw the rest of the crew pretty much all at their stations.

About that time came the "All Clear," and the mate stuck his head out the window of the bridge and said, "Sorry, guys; false alarm. We're really sorry." He looked more worried than embarrassed, though, and I heard him say to the captain, "What the hell was that! What was it?" I couldn't hear what the captain said, but he sounded just as worried. Lots of quick conversation.

The engineer came along the rail behind Sven and me and went up the steps to the bridge, followed by the chief scientist, or "The Chief" as we call her. It wasn't really our place to go ask, right now, and we would certainly not go up to the bridge, so we figured we'd have to find out what had happened through the grapevine, which is what happens most of the time for lackeys like us.

After dinner, The Chief had us meet her in the office, which isn't that unusual, because we usually go there to discuss the samples we've gathered, or to discuss any significant findings, or to hear about the plans for the next day. This was not a typical meeting, though. She had a lot more to share with us about the "Man Overboard" incident, but also some weird anomalies. The Chief was always very open and friendly with Sven and me, so she laid it all out.

This will all sound strange, especially since most of these guys were seasoned sailors and had seen everything on Lake Superior, I thought.

The Chief sat in the big desk chair near the PC monitor the captain likes to use, and we sat at the stations that had the laptops. There is a U-shaped desk surface that has three small carrels.

She knew we'd already figured out that the "Man Overboard" thing was kind of strange. She didn't think she'd ever encountered anything like it before, especially not with this captain and mate whom she'd sailed with many times. In fact, she'd sailed with most of this crew, off and on, for more than six years. There'd never been a real "Man Overboard" before, and they would not have called it if they hadn't seen something. They're very level-headed.

She told us that when she got up to the bridge, they were pretty shaken up, and she'd never seen them like that. What they saw is too weird.

She reminded us how calm the water had been and that we were headed eastward away from the sun, so it seems unlikely it was some sort of optical illusion or light aberration. But they swear this is what happened; they saw someone on the water. I mean literally on the water. Walking toward the vessel! They both saw it, and the person didn't just sink into the lake or fall, but just faded and disappeared like smoke: no splash, no waves. By the time everyone had responded to the alarm, the ship was already drifting over the place where the person had disappeared, and they could see there was nothing there. Not even a ripple. That's why they didn't do a search, and that's why they didn't know what they should say to everyone. It's really strange. I remember we circled again, but the alarm had been discontinued. The captain relieved us of our stations.

That wasn't all. The Chief also took time to show us some of the temperature, turbidity, and D.O. (Dissolved Oxygen) data we were getting from the hydrolab. I had wondered why we kept calibrating and rechecking the instruments two or three times a day ever since we shoved off. She said the depth and surface temperatures had not varied more than a degree or so since we had left Ashland, Wisconsin, and she said this time of the year you can expect wider variations as we move across the lake. A little later in the season, we can expect the lake to become isothermal nearer to the turn over. She's a marine biologist, but she also has a solid background in limnology, so she knows when the lake readings are not what they should be.

This account won't go too far into the science, but Lake Superior is dimictic, meaning it turns over or mixes twice a year; once in spring, and then again in fall when the water temperature hovers around thirty-nine degrees. We expect to see some uniformity this time of year. But not like this. Below six hundred feet, the lake is always thirty-nine degrees, and water is heaviest at that temperature, so to oversimplify, the heavy water stays on the bottom until the water above becomes thirty-nine degrees; then the heavier water above also starts to sink, causing the mixing or turning over of the lake. In a small lake where the bottom temperature stays warmer than thirty-nine, this turnover can be dramatic when the surface reaches thirty-nine and plunges to the bottom causing obvious turbidity. But we would never expect that violent turnover with Lake Superior. In the big lake, the water turns over in columns, like vertical streams, mixing and churning over time until a uniform water temperature or an isothermal state around thirty-nine degrees is achieved.

The strangest finding, she said, was that the hypolimnion, or lowest layer of the lake, has warmed to forty-two degrees and the upper layers are now uniformly around forty-three. The deep layer is *always* thirty-nine degrees. It's as though the lake is warming from the bottom to the top! You would have to have precisely the right weather conditions for an extended period of time, plus some force causing warming from below to create a phenomenon like this. That seems impossible because there has certainly been no magma activity in the region for about a billion years––literally, and there is certainly no infusion of warm water from anywhere else. If there had been warm water coming from somewhere else, it would not displace the cold, heavier water at the bottom of the lake. That colder water would still sit there as the warmer water comes in.

Imagine what would happen if the lower layer of Lake Superior were suddenly to become uniformly warm and the top became uniformly thirty-nine degrees. It would be a cataclysmic turnover!

While we were out there, The Chief got on line with one of the limnologists at the Great Lakes Science Center in Ann Arbor, who confirmed they were getting these kinds of readings from the buoys and their other static stations. They couldn't figure it out either.

§ § §

Ron put down the report and ran his hands through his hair. "The Baikal Phenomenon," he said to himself.

Bookshelves lined the room, including the south wall and between the windows on the west. Among the books sat a sextant and a bronze compass glinting in the late afternoon sun slanting into the room. A minutely detailed schooner model sat high on one of the shelves. Scattered among the books were other nautical bric-a-brac and geological specimens, some serving as bookends. Several framed photos leaned against books.

Ron looked to the upper corner on the east wall where old leather-bound books sat tattered and dusty. Several of these books had ragged bindings, the titles and authors obscured. Some of these books had been given to him by his father, who had received them from his father before him. He stepped up to the shelf and ran his finger across several before he pulled out two of the most frayed and delicate; one with the binding too worn to read and the other with no writing on the binding. The second book had deckle edges on the pages of a type that indicated the book may have been printed on handmade paper. It was one of Ron's most treasured and probably most valuable books. None of his antique books on the east wall would ever be appraised; he never loaned them to anyone, and rarely let anyone look at them. Another small, precious collection was kept in a safe in his bedroom closet.

He stepped back and put a finger to his lips as he tried to read the bindings, then selected a third book from the shelf.

Tucking the books under his arm, Ron scanned shelves that held a vast collection of the lore, science, and culture of the great lakes--*all* of the great lakes. Not only in North America but around the world—from Lake Victoria in Africa to Titicaca in South America and Baikal in Russia.

At his desk, Ron slid the three books aside and sat back in the deep chair in front of the oak desk to return to Samantha's account. He continued to read through her brief sketch of some of the scientific aberrations, then came to her account of the final night, and the harrowing day before harboring at the Soo:

§ § §

We were all sort of spooked after hearing about the sighting of someone walking on water, so we turned in late. We anchored on a shoal that was well out in the middle of the lake. Closer to Caribou Island than Grand Marais, we were still out of sight of land. It was a gorgeous, calm, clear night where you could imagine the stars as a great dome and the lake underneath as a great bowl reflecting the stars across its quiet surface. We saw a glow of northern lights along the horizon. They were not real bright but still beautiful. Oddly, there was also a red and blue glow, south of us, that hovered closer over the lake and wavered and changed like the Northern Lights. We all saw it and thought it might be a big fire or something along the south shore, but I swear I could hear a distant crackling or rumble coming from that direction across the lake. It was spooky. We were way too far away from the southern shore to hear anything from there.

I'll report what else I witnessed that night straight out and try not to edit it, and I'll let other people decide if I was crazy, or if some of us were crazy or stoned or whatever. I just have to write it down.

That night, everything was stowed and seemed routine.

I don't think I was asleep more than half an hour, and it was probably eleven-thirty or midnight. I awoke when someone whispered next to my face in a thin, raspy voice--"Co-o-ld." It scared the crap out of me, and I sat up and looked around. The Chief was in the other bed because we shared one of the two double cabins. She was still sleeping. I heard a voice again from down the hall in the direction of the galley. Everything is really close, of course. You can hear every time somebody uses the bathroom at night. No privacy. The mate and engineer shared the other double bunk across the hall on the starboard side, and Sven and the rest of the crew shared the two small double bunk cabins toward the bow. The captain had a small single cabin below the bridge and off of the office area.

This time, the voice was very faint. No one could hear it unless they had been listening. I got up, quietly got out of my cabin, and headed for the galley. I figured it was one of the guys on anchor duty. He must have had some trouble or something. All of the boat's crew had to take two hours of anchor duty whenever we were anchored offshore in the vessel. Also, on a small boat with eight people, it wasn't uncommon to hear someone talking in their sleep. I thought maybe someone could be sleepwalking.

"Co-o-ld." I heard it clearly this time as I stood in the passageway. It was definitely coming from the galley.

But even though I could tell where it was coming from, it still sounded like it was farther away. It could have almost been coming from outside the ship. "Co-o-old, so-o cold," I heard it say just as I came into the galley. It was dark except for a dim light kept on near the sink. I could see two of the burners were lit on the stove, and it provided enough light to show the cabinets and fixtures and––I took a deep breath. Someone was huddled near the burners on the stove, with one of the canvas covers from the main deck wrapped around their shoulders.

"Cold. So co-old." The voice was dead and scratchy.

"Are you all right?" I was scared because I was sure it was one of the guys. Then he looked at me. I'm not kidding. I know what I saw. He was sitting in one of the galley chairs pulled up to the stove. The canvas slipped down over his right shoulder. The hand that held up the canvas on his other shoulder was marbled white, and I stared into this face. It was both horrific and sad. So sad! This was just a kid, probably seventeen or eighteen with a tousle of wet, black hair, a frayed flannel shirt, and ripped bib overalls with the right strap broken and dangling. He was so sad, but his face had that terrible, white-marbled hue. His eyes were sunken and cloudy, and he kept grasping at that scrap of canvas with his withered hand. It was horrible. I'll never forget it.

I was too frightened to scream.

"So-cold—it's-so-cold..." he said slowly. It was insane; it wasn't real. I had no idea what he was or where he came from; I just knew this wasn't some kid who had swam twenty miles or more up to our ship. Jeez, I was scared. I was too afraid to go near him––or it, or whatever he was.

"Co-old," he hissed.

I rushed back toward the cabins to get The Chief or somebody because I was scared shitless and didn't know what to do, but when I stopped, turned around again, and looked into the darkened galley, he was gone. The canvas was still on the chair, the two burners were still turned on, and the chair was still by the stove. There was no way he could've gotten from that chair to the door and out to the deck in the two seconds I had stepped down the passageway. No way. And I never heard a door open, and he was nowhere in the galley or lounge area. He was gone--disappeared.

I rushed up top and saw the mate was on anchor duty. He was sitting in the cabin reading, so he hadn't seen anything, and I didn't even bother to say anything.

I came back down and got a glass of water. My hands were shaking so badly that I had trouble turning off the stove. I sat at the table thinking: *What the hell just happened?* It's a good thing no one else came through the galley on duty, or to get a snack or a drink, because they would've thought I was totally nuts. I can't explain what I saw or who or what that was. But it sure as hell fit in with everything I heard the next morning and with everything that happened the next day.

§ § §

I hadn't slept a wink and the alarm went off at five-thirty because we had to take some early samples. When I rolled over, I saw that The Chief's light was on above her bed and she was gone. While I was still lying there, she opened the door; the light from the passageway was daggers. She was already showered and dressed.

She fluffed her hair with both hands and saw I was awake, "You had a hell of a night, too," she said. "Just like everyone else."

Several of the other people on the boat had seen and heard strange things. No one could figure out what was going on. Everybody talked about it at breakfast, and you could hear snippets of conversation as we started the day. Some thought we had carbon monoxide poisoning, which didn't make sense because we have alarms and they were all checked. Gas from the refrigeration unit was discussed, but that wouldn't make everyone nuts.

A couple of the crew said it was just a plain old, nautical haunting. One of those weird things that happen to people on ships. Like the Bermuda Triangle or something.

Ivan, one of the hands, didn't help the mood much, or my nerves at all, when he explained his theory. He said sometimes a small ship anchored out here is just like a piece of bark on a pond, and all of the spirits come clinging like spiders. Jeez!

Two of the other crew members had seen people walking through the boat from one side to the other, through the bulkheads, as if it were the most natural thing in the world. They brushed it off as dreams or bad food or something. Nobody saw anything as weird as I did, especially when you consider what happened later when we were bringing in the nets.

At breakfast, the group laughed nervously as they listened to what Sven had seen. He said that he had turned over in bed and was staring into the face of a bearded man. Chunks of beard were missing, and his gray flesh and dead-fish eyes made him look like a zombie. But this zombie was trying to talk to him in Norwegian! He'd convinced himself it was a nightmare. It wasn't something we wanted to hear over breakfast.

No one had slept well, and even the crew members who didn't see or hear anything awoke looking haggard and tense, like they had some half-forgotten nightmares stirring their thoughts.

That morning was strange. Everyone seemed spaced out from the sleepless night and was walking around like we were all Norwegian zombies lost on our little boat. But things improved by mid-morning. We had work to do. So, most of us were able to lay aside our weird night to "focus on the task at hand," as The Chief would say.

Despite the uneasiness on the boat, the lake was showing us its finest face that morning. The sun rose in reds and purples, and the surface was soon sparkling with greens and blues from water to sky. No one could have anticipated what would happen next.

We were reeling in the nets on our mid-level trawler to gather the morning samples when all hell broke loose. The nets roll onto a large spool under a rig at the back of the boat. Weights are reeled in along with the otter board that runs in front of the net to keep the mouth of the net open.

We had already pulled in the nets from the medium depth and had redeployed the nets to take some deep samples. We began to reel in the deep nets, and the first thing we noticed was a really foul stench. It was so bad that I thought even Ivan was going to hurl. We were looking around the side of the boat, thinking we'd run into a moose carcass or something. That sort of thing can happen out there.

The Chief saw it first. I could not imagine her sounding like that. "Oh, my God, look! Stop the nets! Hit the— the.... Stop!"

All the anxiety from the night before spiked us again. I think her panic made everyone else freak out because no one bothered to run to the controls; we all ran to the back of the boat to look at the nets. Something big was snagged in the nets and getting dragged toward the boat. One time we had a log caught in the nets, but we saw it on time, so it never got to the boat. This time no one hit the kill switch for the spool because we were all in shock. We'd never seen anything in our nets like this. A ragged gray arm was protruding from a mass, and it twisted and splashed as it skimmed the water. Caught in the nets, it was heading for the boat. The Chief saw it first because she was on the rig.

"Stop the net!" she yelled again. She could've shut it down, but she was frozen in place, like the rest of us, and must've forgotten she was the one near the kill switch.

For the rest of my life, I'll never forget what happened next. In seconds, the corpse was hauled in. It flopped over the back of the boat, and before we could do anything, it was rolled right onto the spool. God, it was awful as the thing wound around and the bones cracked. Gray, horrid liquids splattered on the deck. I distinctly remember the thick black hair as one more turn on the spool crushed his head. The engineer finally jumped down and hit the switch, but by then, it was an indescribable mess: the net, the corpse, the clothes––a frayed flannel shirt and ripped bib overalls.

I can't tell you what it was like to have to unwind that corpse from around the spool and get it into a bag. The putrid odor was horrible, but fortunately, we had the gloves and gear to get it taken care of. But, eventually, I couldn't handle it anymore. I was gagging. So, The Chief, the captain, and the engineer finished up, hosed everything down, and double-bagged the body and put it in the cooler.

It's so strange. I remember at one point turning my head, looking away, as we were cleaning up all the horror and gore. I looked at the sky and across the lake toward the rising sun, and I noticed the entire surface from our ship to the eastern horizon was shimmering like bright, white sparklers: fantastic. I'd seen this dazzling glitter before, but today it was almost—I don't know how to say it––mocking. It was very strange. Was it the lake or was it just me? I know the lake is severe, cold, dangerous, and deadly, but it had never seemed so sinister. There may be something at work here, after all, but it is not the lake itself; it is something more. Something...deeper.

§ § §

We radioed the Coast Guard, finished up the experiments, and headed straight for Sault Sainte Marie so we could dock and spend the night anywhere but on the ship.

The Coast Guard met us south of Ile Parisienne in Whitefish Bay and we transferred the body. They were pretty tight-lipped, but the captain said this wasn't the only incident like this recently.

As we found out later, and as it came out in the press, the body was thought to have been in the lake for more than fifty years, probably a lot more, and had been preserved on the bottom in the constant thirty-nine degree temperatures just like being in cold storage. But no one has been able to figure out why it would have floated up to our nets, and it doesn't account for the other corpses they say have started showing up around Lake Superior. Could it be the warmer water at the bottom? It certainly doesn't explain the strange things that happened that night on the boat.

We left Sault Sainte Marie and sailed straight through to Ashland. We had a debriefing meeting, and there will likely be another report by the time this is all done. I just wanted to get everything in writing while it was still fresh in my mind.

CHAPTER 13

SHIRLEY'S CABINS

"WE MOVED HERE IN 1976. I was only twenty-two, I think, and Bill was twenty-three. We already had Jon and Becky. They would've been only three and one, then. I thought this place was the end of the world, but it was all we could do at the time." Shirley stretched out her thin hand and flicked ashes mostly into the tray as her oxygen tank hissed.

The agency had a contract to make home visits for a behavioral health evaluation based on referrals from visiting nurses. It worked well for Adam. He could take care of some of those time-consuming home visits while therapists who had regular clients could continue to see their clients at the clinic. Along the highways, dirt roads, and two-tracks of Chippewa County, he was able to cover a lot of territory––on the road and in his mind. He went looking for the lost and lonely amid a population of less than forty thousand, who were folded into forests and rivers, swamps and valleys knit together by twisting trails and scenic highways covering an area larger than Delaware.

Shirley was homebound with chronic obstructive pulmonary disease and a bone disorder. Nurses monitored her health, checked her blood pressure and oxygen levels, and faithfully chanted their quit-smoking invocation. They became concerned that she was becoming demented. If she could not take care of herself safely, *apart from smoking while using oxygen,* she would lose her ability to stay in her home.

Adam agreed that the interview would be easier in the home, but now he had second thoughts as he kept a wary eye on her cigarette and the hissing tank. The house was small and neat, filled with the smell of cigarette smoke and fried breakfast.

She paced her words to stay ahead of her shortness of breath. "It was all we could do 'cause Bill was still messed up from the war in Viet Nam and couldn't hold a job." She took a breath. "We figured the place was cheap enough and the cabins would give us some income while we got on our feet. It actually worked out pretty sweet. Billy took care of the cabins, avoiding any contact with people as much as he could, of course." She looked at her cigarette and smiled. "And I took care of the booking and did all the face-to-face stuff. We both did the cleaning, but we hired help when we needed it. We were proud of our place, still are, and we raised four kids here ta boot." She took a slow drag and set her hand near the ashtray again. "Danny, our youngest, teaches in Newberry, and he still helps out a lot. I hired Sheila from Hulbert to take care of the day to day, but I still do all the booking."

She looked out the kitchen window across Whitefish Bay. The sash was open a few inches despite the cool day: a smoker's courtesy, but also relief from the claustrophobia of COPD. The bay was hung with gray sky, and waves were restless ahead of a moderate breeze. Shirley's thin frame sat slumped in her wheelchair, pulled up to the kitchen table. Dressed in sweat pants and an orange sweatshirt, her gray, scraggly hair was held back on the right by a purple barrette with a bunny on it that was probably found in a cabin. She reached for her cup.

"Would you like more tea, Dr. Knowles?"

"You can call me Adam. No, no, I'm fine." He looked again at the proximity of the cigarette to the oxygen tubing and hoped the oxygen was set low enough so he didn't have to deal with a flame thrower.

After a while, she began again. "So, you didn't drive all the way up here to learn about the history of Shirley's Cabins, I'm sure. The nurse told me you'd be coming here to decide if I was crazy or not because she thought I had started ha-*loo*-cinatin'." She cleared her throat gruffly.

"Yeah, I guess I have a few questions," Adam replied. "I want to help, if I can. The nurse was concerned about you. Since you mention hallucinations, I just have to ask: *Are* you seeing things, and what sorts of things are you seeing?"

"Okay, good. Looks like you're not one to beat around the bush, and neither am I. I'll be straight with you 'cause you seem like a nice guy. I think the nurse thought I was a little screwy, and I even think Sheila, my helper, thought I was going off the deep end." She snuffed out the cigarette and sat back with her elbows resting on the wheel-chair's arms.

"What I came here for was..." Adam began.

"Let me finish." She held up her hand. "I want to lay it all out the way I see it, 'cause I think you're going to get me off course by asking too many questions. I'll save ya some time and you'll be back in the Soo by suppertime." She smiled and took a breath. "You are here to find out if I'm nuts, and I can give you the answer you're here to find out: I'm not nuts and I don't have that old-timer's disease, either. I really think something is going on. I tell ya, I went through hell with Bill and all his war crap, and I sure as hell know crazy when I see it." She looked Adam in the eye, then out the window to where two of six cabins sat near the shore. She pointed with a long, thin finger.

"It was right out there about two weeks ago toward evening. It wasn't dark yet, more like late in the afternoon about four-thirty or five. The sun hadn't even set, yet. This guy, I swear to God, walked out of the water, like he'd swum right up to the beach, but he wasn't swimming; he was walking: straight up. And he came right out of the water. It looked scary as hell 'cause he was fully dressed and he didn't look left or right; he just walked on down to Cabin 3. That's what made me just about shit--'scuse my French--I recognized that guy!"

"Was he staying here?"

"Ha! Yeah, he was staying here. About twenty years ago!" Her right hand clasped her left tightly. She nodded. "He was the guy that left in one of our motorboats and never came back. I mean *never* came back. We thought he had stolen it and gone back to Toledo, where he was from, but he never showed up there either. So they figured he'd drowned. I always thought maybe he just took off some-where—ran away—because it was weird that they never found the boat or anything else, like even a paddle or a cushion." She waved her outstretched finger around, pointing at the dock. "I had everything marked with our name and phone number 'cause someone was losing something all the time, and it would float in somewhere's a couple of days or months later. I actually got a cushion back from a guy up by Wawa one time!" She covered her mouth with a balled-up tissue and coughed.

She grabbed her cigarette pack and stared at it while she flipped it end to end on the table. "Anyways, this guy had been staying here for a few days, and then he disappeared with our boat. He'd been here a few times before. Always alone."

"What did you do?"

"You mean when he left or when he came back?" She laughed hoarsely, coughed, then laid her hand on the table, leaned toward Adam, and grinned.

"Well, uh, when he came back, I guess." Adam smiled thinly, brows raised in anticipation.

"After I seen him, I got my walker and trudged down the walkway here and toward the cabin. Just then Sheila was coming out of Cabin 4. No, no, it was Cabin 5, and I yelled at her and she came across and met me. When I asked her, she said she hadn't seen anything 'cause she was in the cabin, but I asked her to come with me into 3." She took a breath. "When we went around to the front, she pulled out her key and helped me up the step onto the porch. The door was locked, so she opened it."

"And nothing, right?" Adam said as he opened his briefcase to take out his tablet. Based on his experience, he felt he knew where this story was going. He clicked on his tablet and looked up at her; she was staring at him with eyes narrowed.

"No! Dammit! There he stood in Cabin 3: Peter Lane, the guy who went missing twenty years ago! Sheila saw him. He was the same guy, the same age. He looked at Sheila, he looked at me, and he looked around the cabin as if he realized where he was, and what was happening. He was, I don't know, kinda sad, confused, anxious." She looked blankly at the table a moment. "He turned around all of a sudden, and just headed south, right through the door at the back of the cabin and back home. He just walked right into the woods over there and was gone."

"So, Sheila saw him?"

"Sure, she did, but Sheila is a bit, how would you say--simple. She would never put it together. She probably didn't see him walk through the back door. But the guy walked right into that brush, and not even a leaf stirred as he slipped in. You could see it out of the back window of the cabin. How'd some guy end up in a locked cabin in the middle of the day with all of us around? Nobody would be in there. I saw him walk out of the lake and up to that cabin. I remember the guy! How could I forget?"

"I honestly don't mean to doubt you, but you're *sure* this was the guy?"

"Sure's hell! Same guy, same cabin, same age, even." She drew her hand across her mouth. "An' Sheila saw him, too." She clutched her cigarette pack. "Do you think I'm nuts?"

"Shirley, I don't think you're nuts. You've probably heard what's going on all over, too, and I...."

"Come on; take a little walk with me. I keep a nice place and I like to show it off."

Before Adam could offer to help, she swept the walker near and stood in one, smooth maneuver. The tank and tubing were already attached to the walker, so before Adam could gather his things, she was headed for the door.

"Let me get that for you."

"Got it," she called over her shoulder as the walker was rowed out the door and toward the boardwalk that led to the dock.

The dock was built over a narrow crescent of beach. Choppy waves gurgled under the gray-green wooden deck and slapped clear and cold against the sand. A rock barrier cut down some of the force, but a steady breeze kept the waters in constant agitation. All the swimming gear and boats were long ago put up for the season, except for one decrepit rowboat that bobbed in the waves on the dock's south side. She slowed and scraped her walker the last couple of steps to the boat and paused to catch her breath. Adam resolved that there would be no way he would consent to an offshore tour of the property. He was about to speak up when she broke in.

"The last few days, the water has been low. It seems like something is sucking all the water out of the lake. I don't know what the hell that's all about." She looked down. "Well, there she is."

"What is it?"

He stepped beside her and looked down at the boat—flaking paint and worm-eaten wood. He felt the small hairs at the back of his head stand up when he noticed the waterlogged cushions and rusty motor sagging from the stern. Even the chipped, red gas can sloshed in the back under a broken seat.

"Holy shit! I mean...."

She smiled around an unlit cigarette and looked sideways at Adam. "That's exactly what I said when I saw 'er tied up here."

CHAPTER 14

THE SHORE

THE HIGHWAY WINDS WEST FROM Sault Sainte Marie, through the village of Brimley and the tiny Native village of Bay Mills with its glaring casinos and humble homes stacked with the rigs and paraphernalia of fishermen. The lake lies brooding as it peeks and glimmers between scrubby cedars, broken piers, and shoehorned lake homes that stand in varying states of repair.

Following the lakeshore, wider views of the lake appear. The Iroquois Point Lighthouse stands at the site where a decisive battle took place; the Iroquois from the eastern regions of the continent circled around the sand dune bluffs overlooking Monocle Lake and Spectacle Lake in an attempt to displace the Ojibwe on the shore. The Ojibwe had likely displaced the Menominee, who had displaced some other tribe that had claimed the shores of Lake Superior thousands of years ago when the mile-high glaciers ebbed from the warming earth.

Wide beaches line the shores that sweep to Whitefish Point, including the serene stretch from Sand Point to the Shallows, and onward across the mouth of the Tahquamenon River and on up to Paradise. The beaches that lie along Whitefish Bay can be warm enough to swim at by mid to late summer. But those beaches that lie on the southern rim of the bay face the northwest winds, which can stack up waves and rip currents on a warm summer day. Here, on one particular beach, Adam and Julie had met tragedy several years before.

Returning south from Shirley's Cabins and other home visits, Adam stood there, at the very spot where they had sat that day. He looked north beyond the great, gentle arms of tree-lined dunes that wrapped the bay to the west until the shore blended with the lake near Paradise. And he looked to the east where high bluffs opened to the great Saint Mary's River, and swept to infinity along the rocky Canadian coast to Agawa Rock. Near the shore the lake rested, almost reverent. Whitecaps bobbed miles out in the mouth of the bay, and beyond the bay, only blue-black water spread to the horizon.

The feelings were too harsh. Emotion crashed over Adam from head to feet while it clawed and insinuated itself into those deep areas of his heart that he had dammed and sealed off so efficiently. He'd fled. He had ignored and impounded grief that lay moldering like sweet carrion. He had arrived at this beach with trepidation but was determined to complete this stark task and find a path that would lead his life out of this dim valley toward a resolution. And maybe, a new intention for living. But it was too harsh, too much to bear. He slumped down on the damp sand, his legs crossed, and wept—deep sobs and struggling breath. The sun seemed to pause as it wavered just above treetops lining the west shore, then slipped solemnly into golden pink radiance, pulling a gray-blue blanket over water and sky.

Light was chasing away toward the horizon. He stood, slipping his hands into his coat pockets, realizing how cold and empty he had become. There was no more to do here, no more subtle message to extract from this stretch of beach, and no chance to realize his deep, unspoken dream: that somehow, in some realm or some shadow of existence, he could glimpse her again. But he knew now that she would not come to him walking across the water. She would not whisper to him from among the birch and balsam where thick, cool moss and ferns, scented in wintergreen, had made a fleece for their passion. She was gone. Lost to the lake.

Adam shuffled along the darkening beach toward the small parking lot a half mile to the west. He looked one more time toward the lake in meager hope, then turned, silently closing a door inside.

He trudged through the sugary sand to a small, paved parking lot. The lot was large enough for only eight or nine cars, but there was only his car and one beat-up white pickup truck that was spotted with rust like a Guernsey cow. The truck had not been there when he arrived. It made him a little nervous, so he decided to hustle to the car and get out of there.

"Adam." He heard the hushed voice. He turned, but it had been so low and quiet that he thought he may have been mistaken. He went back toward the car. "Adam." He turned to see what looked like a haggard old man, his hand on the truck, edging his way around to the front of the pickup, dressed in clothes from another era with a long, ragged coat and frayed, wool pants. Adam backed closer to the car door and shuffled his keys. The man let go of the truck and thrust his hands into his coat pockets.

Adam was edgy, considering all the weird things happening. He also feared it could be any number of former psychotic clients. Or one of James Graves' minions stalking him.

"Adam, you don't have to go," the man said again in a quiet, gravelly voice. "I thought I'd find you here."

The person sounded familiar, but he did not sound particularly threatening or even too crazy, so Adam turned, still holding his keys. "I'm sorry; I just don't recognize you. Can I help you?" His voice was still shaky from emotion, and possibly from fear.

"Adam, it's me." He had a crooked smile. "Cam."

"Cam! Cam?" Adam didn't move. "Jeez, you sort of scared me. I—I would've *never* recognized you." He didn't know what to say.

Adam hesitated as he looked at his old friend. Cam was unrecognizable, with long, black hair and a beard flecked with gray. He was about the same age as Adam, had been tall and muscular, but now looked old and withered. Adam approached Cam near the truck. Cam held out his hand slowly. Adam was about to lean in for a quick embrace, but Cam dodged. Adam patted his shoulder awkwardly, shook his hand, and stepped back, trying to ignore the smokey, sour odor.

"How did you find me?" Adam asked

"Well, the Indiana plates helped," he said haltingly, "and I talked to Ron to tell him I was coming back, and he said you were going to be along the lake so...I figured this would probably be the best place to find you." Cam looked down; he cleared his throat, but he was still hoarse as he continued. "I'm sorry. Really. This was not a good way to meet. I'm really sorry." Cam turned side to side, looking at the darkening lake with his hands in his pockets, feeling awkward.

Adam sensed Cam's discomfort and realized this cursed stretch of beach was not a good place to talk. And there was so much to talk about. "Cam, why don't you follow me? I was going to stop at the Fish Shack in Brimley 'cause I could use something to eat. And I haven't had a chance to get any fresh whitefish since I've been back. Follow me in the truck and I'll get a chance to pay you back for that dinner you bought me."

"What dinner?" Cam smiled and huffed. "Oh, I get it; that's how you tell me you want to buy a meal for that nasty-looking homeless guy."

"Yup, you're still sharp as a tick, uh, tack." Adam tried to use an old quip.

"Okay, I'll let you buy––this time," Cam said with a forced grin.

§ § §

Adam waited to be sure Cam's truck started; then he turned east out of the parking lot, following the winding highway through Bay Mills to Brimley. Seeing Cam again lifted him from his grief for the moment, and refocused his thoughts onto the present. But Adam was definitely concerned for the man who had played such an important role during the most critical part of his life.

With a smile, he remembered meeting Cam on the first day he started work at the agency. He had thought Cam must be one of the clients, someone who'd wandered into the breakroom.

"Can I help you?" Adam had asked, even though he'd only been working there about four hours.

"No, but can I help *you*?" Cam smiled with that conspiratorial grin that made it look like nearly every human encounter was an adventure for him. He looked like a happy kid who was just told an adult would willingly play with him. Every new person was a chance for Cam to make a new best friend.

Cam sat down at Adam's table and put both elbows on it; he folded his hands and leaned forward with a stern gaze. "No, seriously, can I help you? Are you in pain? What are you abusing? Who are you abusing? Who do you *want* to abuse? Are you abusing yourself?" He maintained his straight face and intense gaze for only a couple of seconds before breaking into that laugh: head back, mouth wide open, his full lips and large teeth the caricature of a big smile.

"Who the hell *are* you?" Adam grinned. From that moment, their relationship never changed. They were never afraid to give offense to each other, while never actually giving offense—rarely serious. They became closer than brothers.

That first morning, they joked and laughed, and because they shared the same sense of humor, slipped into an exchange that made them late for their next appointments.

Over the year, their relationship evolved. They hiked, kayaked, and did some hunting and fishing together. The social circle at the clinic seemed to revolve around them and what they were up to.

Then came Julie. She was Cam's friend. She had grown up with Cam in Newberry; they dated a little in high school, hung out with the same crowd. Now she needed help after losing her father. She also had a history of some mild depression and anxiety, so Cam steered her to Adam, who was more than happy to help any friend of Cam's.

The therapeutic relationship was pleasant and productive, and Julie's therapy and recovery were routine. They both admitted to each other later that the attraction was there from the beginning, but they had kept a professional distance throughout her brief therapy.

Months later, Adam ran into Julie at a barbecue at Cam's house near Brimley. They started dating. Adam was suspicious that Cam had played matchmaker a little, but their relationship clicked and things moved quickly from there.

Cam moved into the background, but the three of them still socialized and even double-dated with one of Cam's girlfriends. The guys still shared outdoor activities, but Julie would join occasionally. Over time, they moved apart. But Cam had been Julie's friend, too, so it seemed Cam would continue to move in and out of their life somehow, and he seemed to show up at odd times even when Adam was not expecting him.

Alcohol was a bigger item in Cam's life than Adam's, and sometimes Cam's chosen activities involved a lot more drinking. Adam and Julie started to avoid these activities, and that pushed them further away from Cam. None of them was happy with this situation. Adam and Cam missed each other's friendship and humor.

Then came the rending tragedy of Julie's disappearance, and it seemed the men's relationship had finally lost traction, rolled freely down the hill, and crashed into pieces. They never saw or heard from each other again.

§ § §

Cam's old Chevy pickup rolled into the parking lot about two minutes behind Adam, crunching over gravel with its left headlight jiggling and flickering like a crazy eyeball. Cam pulled into a spot next to Adam's car and shut off the engine, letting it sputter and pop until it finally quit. He got out and slammed the door with a rattle.

"Is that the same truck you've always had?"

"Yeah, it had 212,000 miles on it when the odometer quit," he said with a half-smile.

They climbed the wooden steps. Adam held the door for Cam, who hesitated for a minute before going ahead. "This'll be a little weird for me, you know. I used to hang out here sometimes back in the day before I quit drinking and stuff."

"Well, consider it therapy then," Adam said.

The lights were low, and mostly the regulars were in attendance. It was a weekday night. The Fish Shack consisted of a single long room with a bar taking up about half the length on one end and a dining room on the other. Tall tables with high-back stools stood near the bar. The dining area was set with rugged pine tables and chairs, and a stage angled in the corner that held a small drum set, two mic stands, and shabby black speakers.

The bartender had a blank expression as he looked back down the bar for empty glasses. As his head swiveled toward the door, he did a quick double take. It was either recognition or curiosity as the odd couple entered the bar. He didn't really care to know, so he looked down the bar and turned his back to shuffle away.

The place was well kept—clean, and roomier than it appeared from the outside. Patrons congregated in groups of two to four with a total of ten or twelve on board tonight. The better oiled in the room would call out from one little group to the next, or sidle over to the other bunch to repeat a joke or make a clumsy play for a younger woman. It was all harmless, and everyone pretty much ignored the two men who had entered, even though, if they'd recognized them, every local would have known their story.

Adam led them to a table in a back corner. The waitress was young—a large woman with black hair pulled back in a long ponytail. Her apron was snug over a polo shirt and jeans. White sneakers seemed small below her tired ankles. She took their order, nodding silently, seeming to write out every word they spoke on her little pad, her lips tight in concentration.

When their drinks were served, Adam tried to turn the small talk to humor but with little results. It all felt unfamiliar and tense. After a surprisingly short time, the food arrived—big slabs of whitefish that only hours earlier had been swimming in the lake. Served on a platter, the fish was coated with the thinnest crunchy batter and mild seasoning, surrounded by mashed potatoes with gravy, a paper cup of coleslaw, and a roll. The server slapped down the receipt, told them, "Just pay at the bar when you're all done," and walked away. The men made eye contact; Adam raised his eyebrows and Cam smiled.

"That reminds me," Adam said, "someone at the clinic was asking about you."

Cam nodded slightly, unwilling to take his attention away from the feast before him. He'd already consumed half a roll and a generous portion of fish.

"Remember that hard-nosed office manager, Shelly..." Adam started to say, then covered his mouth, nearly expelling a large chunk of whitefish, while holding his other palm toward Cam. "Don't say it. Don't!"

"Shelly Radantz?" Cam said flatly while leveraging a big fork of mashed potatoes.

Adam gulped, forcing down the fish, still covering his mouth. But it was too late. Adam snorted loudly, then like a dam of emotion breaking, there followed an explosion of laughter. He rested his elbows on the table and pressed the heels of his hands into his eye sockets as his shoulders shook. "Gen--Gen--GENERAL RAT'S-ASS!" Adam blurted out. Cam looked around nervously with the smallest grin. The rest of the bar probably thought Adam was stoned or drunk; even the bartender and the stoic waitress looked over. Adam stopped laughing, looked around the bar sheepishly chuckling, and felt immediately embarrassed. Cam made a sideways smile that seemed more like sympathy to Adam's embarrassment.

Adam stammered and scratched his head. "S-sorry. Well, that was awkward. Sorry. Well, yeah, I guess we have some catching up to do. That was crude and stupid. Gods. You'd think I'd know better." He stared at his plate. "It's been a very weird day. My feelings are...I don't know, shot to hell." He sniffed, shrugged, and grinned. "Ya think I need some therapy?"

Cam looked down and smiled. "We all have things to deal with now, don't we?"

They finished the meal with small talk, but Cam was not ready to open up, and Adam was not ready to push him. Cam thanked him for dinner and looked around like he was ready to leave.

"You're really leaving the cabin. Where will you stay?"

Cam made circles on the table with his finger. "I don't know. I thought I was going to get back to town earlier than this, today. I will probably get hold of Ron."

"He told me you'd contacted him. Was that supposed to be confidential?" Adam would not tell him that he had heard his message on Ron's office phone.

"No, I would expect him to tell you that much. I think he knew I was leaving the woods."

"He knew you were leaving for sure?" Adam tried to remember what he had heard on Ron's voicemail.

"Yeah, you know Ron. He helps me out a little once in a while, but I made him promise not to tell anyone. I didn't want anyone to know I was coming out of the woods--yet." He looked up at Adam.

Adam was uncomfortable. What Cam was saying was not the same thing Ron had said. He was worried Cam was imagining that he had, somehow, given more information to Ron. According to Ron, Cam had not spoken to him much. Adam had heard the brief voice message, and he was sure Ron would not be ready for Cam to show up at his door. Adam was silent for a while, then began to reach across the table and stopped. "I'm glad you found me, Cam."

After a pause, Cam said, "Yup, me too."

Adam remained silent for a while, then offered, "I have an idea that may work for you."

CHAPTER 15

AT THE INN

ADAM SAT IN HIS CAR, contemplating again the old inn—the broad, dark porch, the two towers, and several dormers with black windows receding into darkness.

He waited for Cam to arrive while still feeling embarrassed by the reunion at the bar. It was obvious that Cam was deeply troubled, and Adam had handled the situation miserably. One nagging, tiresome burden of the past several years had nearly been wrapped up in a neat, little circle. But he had blown it. All his training and experience were useless. He would not be surprised if Cam had turned around and headed back to the woods, declining his offer to stay at the inn.

Adam had called Maggie before leaving the parking lot at the Fish Shack, and she had agreed to the plan without hesitation. She told Adam she had probably met him once. It seemed to be in Ron's nature to bring people together. Cam had been among many whom Ron had introduced to her over the years.

Maggie's shadow appeared at the door, swayed, and moved away.

It was several minutes before the approaching rumble and wheeze of Cam's truck ended in the street in front of the inn. Half a minute passed until his door screeched open. Adam watched in his rearview mirror as the hermit stood in the dark with his hand resting on the hood of the truck looking toward the inn. *Slow. Take it slow*, Adam reminded himself, and he wondered if this was going to be more than Cam was ready to handle. He eased his door open and stood looking back at Cam, who shrugged a duffel bag over one shoulder and stepped toward the inn.

Adam came beside him and put his hand on his shoulder, then withdrew it cautiously as Cam smiled weakly. He patted Adam on the back as they approached the door.

Maggie was gracious as usual, even though Cam looked and smelled like smoked bear when he attempted a sudden, awkward hug. Adam knit his eyebrows—*What's he doing?*—as he met her stare over Cam's shoulder. She was wide-eyed with a straight smile as she quickly returned a cursory hug. Adam shook his head and smiled at Cam's attempted normalcy.

Maggie invited them into the sitting room. As they entered, she offered tea or coffee, but they both declined.

She took one of the stuffed chairs while Cam sat in the middle of the couch, leaning forward, hands folded, forearms across his knees. As he stepped to the fireplace, Adam noticed Cam's trembling, folded fingers. He bent down, crumpled some paper, and snapped kindling to start a fire.

Despite his nerves, Cam opened up to Maggie in a way Adam could not have anticipated––or accomplished. Her skills as a therapist were apparently better than his, and soon Native ghosts and long dead trappers were analyzed and examined while Adam piled sticks and logs on the fire. He took the other stuffed chair and marveled at her incisiveness and concern. Maggie unwound layer upon layer of Cam's visions and stories, which he unburdened to her like raw confessions until he seemed relieved of his anxiety in her careful hands. Here was Maggie's true gift on display, Adam realized. She was able to interpret and incorporate these apparitions like no one else.

With careful detail, Cam described the man he'd seen on the trail yesterday. "He seemed like he was suspended above the trail. Then it seemed like he stepped down and started walking toward me. Was it just me? Was I seeing things all messed up like that?"

"Marion McCloud," Maggie said, her elbow on the arm of the chair and one finger pressed to her temple. "I think it was around the turn of the century or maybe even in the 1890s. He used to take the mail from the Soo to Iroquois Point and on up to the rescue station by your cabin at Vermillion back in the winter. That would be before they had roads up there. He could do sixty miles in two or three days—four days in bad weather—then turn around and come home. I think he did it every couple of weeks or every month. He wasn't the only mailman like that. You could write a book just about those mail carriers back in the day." She looked from Cam to Adam and back. "He was never found. The mail didn't arrive at the rescue station for a few days in March, so they searched for him for a long time. He had a cabin midway near the Shallows, I think." She smiled. "Some thought maybe he went off on a bender or something or shacked up with an Ojibwe girl, but most people knew he wasn't that sort of man." She grasped the ends of the chair arms and leaned forward. "It was an early spring that year, so they think he probably drowned trying to cross a swollen river and was washed into the lake, or maybe he was trying to take a shortcut on rotten ice." She looked at Cam. "I'm sure that's who you saw."

Cam shrugged his shoulder. "So, um, why was he hanging in the air like that? That was the part that was so weird. Then he just walked past like a regular old guy in old clothes." He looked down at his old clothes, smoothed his pant legs over his thighs, and smiled.

"It's that loop thing I was telling you about earlier. Adam and I discussed this, too. That's what these––we might as well call 'em ghosts––are that you were seeing in the cabin," Maggie said. "Sometimes, they seem to come back into our world on the same plane of existence on which they left it."

Cam raised a brow. "But I thought you said he drowned. He didn't leave the world walking on top of the ridge."

"No, they usually don't come back at the same place they left. And when they return, they are sometimes slightly out of sync, or displaced from this world." She shrugged. "And they will make a little adjustment. I don't know if they are adjusting from another dimension, another plane of existence, or maybe it's simple—that path on the ridge was a couple of feet higher when he walked it; now it's eroded away. I really don't know." She shrugged as they turned to watch the fire.

She spoke while still looking at the flames. "I think the other ones who appeared in your cabin had drowned, too, but were never recovered. These spirits were leaving the lake when you saw them. That is what everyone is seeing. That has to be what's happening." She smiled and turned to Cam. "But I think Marion the Mailman was different. He wasn't leaving the lake when you saw him. Maybe he was just taking a little detour and following a path he'd taken over and over for much of his life." She paused. "You see a lot. I think you're a pretty sensitive, young man."

He looked at the fire with a faraway smile.

§ § §

Cam was introduced to the kitchen and the small dining area. When they stepped into the hall to take the servants' stairs, he stopped.

"What the hell's that?" He turned toward the short dark hallway. "Oh, sorry, Mrs. Stewart. I mean, what *is* that?"

The big arched door to the infirmary stood shadowed on the left in the hallway.

"The old Fort Brady Infirmary is attached to the house. We don't use that," she answered, but said no more.

He turned back to her, his eyes wide, said nothing, and started up the steps. Adam glanced at Maggie and shrugged.

The room down the short hall next to Adam's room was much smaller. Maggie flicked on the light in the room. Cam stuck his head in. "Is that the bathroom?" He pointed at a door on the back wall.

"No, I'm afraid this room doesn't have a bathroom. It's right here across the hall." She pointed at an open door. "That door in your room used to go to the infirmary, too, but it's been blocked up for...."

"I'm sorry, Mrs. Stewart; I really am. You've been so kind, but I don't think I can sleep near that door. I just...."

"No, no, don't mention it. There's another room right down here across the hall. It's even a little bigger, but it's a little farther from the bathroom. Those two rooms share that bathroom. No problem, really."

He continued to stare at the infirmary door at the back of the bedroom as he turned to leave.

"Will you be okay?" Adam asked Cam.

"Yeah, I'm really sorry. You guys have been so nice. I—I just have to.... I'm sort of treading water a bit, and I need to have—I mean I...."

"No problem. I understand. Whatever you need. Seriously," Adam assured him, but he wondered again if this was too much for Cam.

Entering the next room, Cam looked around and smiled. "Okay. Shower, clean clothes, uh, sort-of-clean clothes," he said, holding up his bag, "and a real bed. What can I say?"

Maggie rested her hand on his shoulder. "Let me know if you need anything. I'll be upstairs." She winked at Adam; he mouthed, *Thank you*, and she left.

"Hey, I have a big T-shirt and some old sweatpants if you want them," Adam offered. "They might be a little small."

"Well, yeah, actually I only have a shirt and jeans in my pack. And they're not the best."

§ § §

Adam lay for a long while staring at the ceiling. He felt relieved by Cam's improved mental status and his connection with Maggie, but he was trying to figure out the––distance—this hesitancy that Cam displayed. He hardly made eye contact with Adam for more than a fleeting moment, he spoke little of the past, and there was no mention of renewing their friendship or even asking about what Adam had been up to the past couple of years. And there was hardly anything Cam would share about his life in the cabin.

Adam heard the bathroom door in the hall open and close a couple of times, and the shower was still running when Adam fell asleep.

§ § §

"Goodnight...Adam." Thin and far away. Dreamless, he thrashed awake, and blinked in the dark, the voice reverberating and fading like a bell.

With both hands, Adam rubbed his face, pressed the knuckles of his index fingers into his eyes, ruffled his hair, and threw off the covers to sit at the edge of the bed looking out the window; 1:15 the clock glowed. The night was deep and quiet.

A distant streetlamp grayed the top floor of the infirmary. In the farthest arched window, a light flared. Sudden, like a single match, then gone; unmistakable. Possibly a reflection from the street, but that did not seem likely.

A muted whining squeal came from deep in the infirmary, fine and wavering. A creaking door? Sliding furniture? A voice?

Adam rose to stand near the window. The multi-paned glass windows of the infirmary were matte black, reflecting nothing. Wavering briefly and more distant, the eldritch squeal recurred. He felt a wave of tingling fear crawl up his back.

His hands fumbled as he pulled on jeans and a shirt. He opened his door slowly, then returned for his phone. He looked around briefly for a candlestick, broom, or any sort of weapon. Seeing nothing handy, he slipped on his leather loafers and went into the hall. It crossed his mind to call Maggie, but he decided not to. Down the short hall to the first bedroom that Maggie had shown Cam, he entered the room and hurried to the door leading to the infirmary. The black glass knob turned freely, unconnected to the mortise assembly. He pulled on the knob, but the door was sealed tightly and did not rattle.

After going quietly down the servants' stairs, Adam turned left at the bottom and stopped. Low light from the kitchen shown down the short hallway to the great wooden door of the infirmary. It loomed in shadow, and stood open a few, dark inches. Again, he thought of getting Maggie, but he changed his mind and approached the door. He shouldn't go in there; *no reason to go in there*, he tried to tell himself. But his curiosity was ripe after the events of the past week, and maybe he felt a vague sense of responsibility—a need to protect Maggie and her home. There was more. He knew there was more. Maybe he was still looking for something or someone he was unwilling to let go of.

Adam held his phone in his left hand, creating an anemic light that preceded him as he pushed the great door open. Cast-iron hinges were surprisingly silent. He entered.

Stones pushed through broken plaster along the wall on his left where two windows were outlined in grimy light. The back wall had a door at the center, and several dusty captain's chairs sat randomly along the walls. The cool air smelled like damp masonry and mold.

As though standing between worlds, Adam turned to look back in the inn where a stately hall waited dark and silent and a clock ticked near the kitchen.

The floor crackled with gritty plaster under his shoes. He waved the light to his right where a wooden-spooled cashier window was set in a light-green, tiled wall. He realized he was standing in what must have been a waiting room or lobby for the old infirmary. Next to the spooled window was a wooden door inset with stained glass depicting the Rod of Asclepius. The head of the snake was large and out of proportion with dripping fangs. Under this was inlaid *Primum Non Nocere*: First Do No Harm.

Why wouldn't the Stewarts have used this as part of their inn? he wondered.

The knob turned easily on the stained-glass door, and Adam led with his phone into blackness. Through a small vestibule set with shelves was an open door that led into a dormitory so large his phone scarcely lit the back wall. Another set of arched windows lined the wall to his left while similar windows, empty, bricked over, lined the side toward the inn. On the back wall was a large door, almost identical to the one he had entered from the inn. The light was too weak to see clearly from that far away. Angled heaps of old furniture and beds were pushed together in dark corners. Hewn beams crossed the ceiling.

Returning to the waiting room, Adam walked to the other door, across from the entry. A wedge of plaster dust had been swept on the floor where the door had opened into the room and closed. He eased the door open.

He faced a short hallway with a window on the left and another window at the end of the hall. The short hallway closed around him, and the windows seemed to lean in as he scuffed through fallen plaster to steps that led away to the right.

The short flight of stairs was deeply worn. There was a landing, and he assumed, another flight that would lead around on the right. It was impossible to tell in the dust and plaster if anyone had gone this way. His light was trembling as he looked down the hall, then back up the steps. *Why am I doing this? There's no point in wandering around here tonight. Come back in the morning. Maggie won't have to know.* Then he remembered the voice: "Goodnight...Adam." *Who are you really looking for?* he asked himself.

He inhaled, let his breath out slowly, and took the first step. The step creaked. It was followed immediately, right above him, by the whining moan. It reverberated on stone and brick. He paused, then carefully took the next noisy steps up to the landing. Slowly, he moved the light around the corner and moved toward the next flight. He stopped.

At the top of the stairs near the ceiling of the second floor, a light glowed and wavered. At first, he thought it was a reflection or a plume of dust. It widened to a shimmering veil that fell slowly and began to roil—a mother of pearl sheet from ceiling to floor. The edges glimmered and dissolved as the center rippled into a jagged tear, opening to ultra violet, dark purple recesses like a tunnel. There were whispers of music, singing and soft chanting, high and beautiful, from far in the depths. The veil was writhing and changing.

Adam did not breathe. Behind the changing surface, a figure emerged. No, only a hand and the outline of a head. He must be imagining it—making up a form of someone who was not there. The figure receded but soon reemerged, closer. He could make out a shoulder, a woman's head. It was reaching, hands spread across the veil. He knew her. He reached out, and rushed up the steps, but the shimmering window formed prism ripples, the rings spreading, fading--gone. He stumbled through a fading mist that felt like tingling droplets on his flesh.

Emptied, tormented by what he saw, *whom* he thought he saw, he stood at the top of the steps on the second floor, his head down, eyes tightly closed.

The high, keening wail was heard again from somewhere nearby. He turned his head rapidly, trying to locate the source.

The second floor was similar to the floor below, with a single window at the end to his right, and windows leading down a hallway to his left. At the end of the hall, toward the inn, was a doorway he assumed would be the door into the bedroom Cam refused to take.

Adam tapped off the phone light, not sure what he was looking for—possibly another fading glimmer. His eyes adjusted by degrees to see three weak arches with mullioned shadows sketched by streetlight on the wooden floor along the hallway.

Two doors were along the hallway. A whimper came from behind the second door. The phone shook in both hands as Adam fumbled for the light, again. He edged toward the door, leaned his shoulder into it, and creaked it open to see a small room.

"Who's in here? Are you okay?" He didn't realize he was whispering.

Muffled sobbing.

"Hey! Who's here?" He led with his phone into the room and swept right to see a dusty oak desk and broken chair. A metal file cabinet sat in the corner behind the desk.

Sniffling.

Adam raised the phone and shone it over the desk onto the chair. Horsehair was sticking out of the cushion, and the light cut between slats in the back of the chair.

Beside the file cabinet in the corner was a man crumpled and shaking, his left hand over his face and his right hand bracing the floor. His short black hair was damp and ruffled.

"Who are...?"

"I-Am-Death." The man sniffled. "I am death," he whispered slowly.

Fear was rising, cresting to panic, and Adam could feel quivering in his arms and legs. He tried to steady himself, to calm down. From somewhere, crisis management skills or some forgotten training kicked in. "I--hey—I can help you. I will call.... I mean, tell me what you need."

The hand slid down to reveal a face bloodless and gaunt. A frozen moment passed, then Adam gasped. "Cam? What the...? What's the matter?"

He had cut his beard and hair—badly.

Staring blankly at the light, Cam ratcheted his head lower until his chin rested on his chest. His eyes widened; then he flung his head back, smashing on the plaster wall behind him with a splintering crunch. He lowered his head slowly again, then smacked it on the wall. His head bobbed down, and a dark, red stain had appeared on the dirty wall.

Throwing his lit phone on the desk, Adam lunged. He wrapped his arm around the back of Cam's neck and pressed his other hand to the broken man's forehead. "Cam, stop! Stop, Cam. It's me, Adam. It's okay. It's okay," Adam said soothingly.

Cam's chest heaved as he sobbed.

"Adam!" A woman's voice called from the other side of the desk. Holding Cam's head and neck, he turned and squinted into bright light. He could not make out a form beyond the light.

"Adam! What is going on? Adam are you, okay?" Maggie stood in the doorway, wearing a robe, holding a flashlight and kitchen knife.

§ § §

With his poorly shaven face, his crudely cut hair wrapped in a bloodied dish towel, Cam looked thin, wasted, and battered sitting at the table. He stared at the kitchen floor with his hands in his lap.

"We're going to get help, Cam. We're going to help you," Adam offered.

Maggie stood near the sink, arms folded, looking worried. "Is there anything I can do?"

Adam looked from Maggie to Cam. "No, they should be here, soon. We just couldn't risk taking the car because he's too...." He carefully laid his hand on Cam's shoulder. "I'll call ahead to the ER for you, Cam. We'll get help and go from there. Okay?" Adam said.

Cam said nothing.

"Cam, can I call anyone for you, dear?" Maggie asked.

He closed his eyes and shook his head once quickly.

EMTs arrived with lights, no sirens. They talked with Cam gently but got little response. Adam filled them in and followed them onto the porch as they walked Cam slowly to the ambulance. He offered no resistance. Maggie touched Adam's arm and hugged him.

"I'm sorry," Adam said.

Maggie only shook her head.

While Cam was helped into the ambulance, Adam called the hospital and gave them as much information as he could; his frosted breath haloed in the porch light as he talked.

Deb was the triage nurse; she had worked in the ER a long time; she remembered Adam, and knew Cam. She was concerned and helpful, and promised to call Adam back if they needed more information.

"Are you sure I don't need to be there?" Adam asked.

"No, the psychiatrist, Dr. Patel, has been on call. She's actually here seeing another patient. You know how busy we've been," Deb replied. "I'm sure she'll see Cam as soon as he gets here. I don't think there will be much for you to do. And besides, it's late. Get some sleep and take care of yourself."

§ § §

Adam and Maggie walked slowly into the house. Adam continued down the long hall, the floorboards gently moaning. Halfway down the hall, near the main staircase, he turned as he heard Maggie lock the door.

"Is there anything I can do? I'm so sorry I got you messed up in this," he said.

Maggie walked slowly toward him, then paused, inhaled, and nodded toward the sitting room. "Come in the sitting room with me," Maggie said. "I need to make a little confession."

Adam raised his eyebrows and followed.

She motioned for him to sit next to her on the couch. The fire had died, and the room was only lit by the stained-glass lamps. She tucked her hair behind her ear and cradled her hands on her lap.

"I'm sorry about Cam. I hope he'll be all right," she began, then inhaled. "You probably figured out by now that there's more to that old infirmary than I told you. I'm sorry," she said.

"I guess I wondered why you never did anything with it."

She sighed. "Well, I'll tell ya." She patted her hair. "I was not completely honest with you. I didn't want you to be all upset, just moving in here and all."

He nodded.

"A year or so after we moved in here," Maggie said, "Leslie wanted to make that infirmary into rooms and maybe even a banquet hall. Like I told you before, I didn't like it and he knew why." She rubbed her hands together. "One evening after dinner, he went in there. He said he wanted to take some measurements. It got late and he hadn't come back, so I went in there to see what he was up to. I wasn't too concerned because he was a man who liked to take his time and do it right. And he was also a man who could get mighty distracted and wander off on some detail or open a door and get lost somewhere." She smiled to herself, then suddenly stood, and walked toward the library. Adam waited, not sure if she had been overcome with emotion.

Maggie soon returned to her chair and held a framed photo for Adam to see. "This is my Leslie." She lovingly moved her finger across the photo of a balding man with wisps of gray hair sprouting freely at the sides of his head. A big, genial smile crossed his broad features and his eyes betrayed mischievous humor.

"Anyway, I went back there looking for him, and he was sitting in one of them dusty old captain's chairs, staring ahead. I walked up to him slowly, and I don't think he even knew I was there. Then he said...he said...." She shook her head. "He said, *'They are all hurting; they are all in pain. They are all hurting; they're all in pain.'* I'll never forget it. He was lost. I led him out of the infirmary. Heaven knows I was scared witless; I thought I was going to have to call his doctor or something. I'd never seen him like that." She looked at Adam, worried. "I led him into the kitchen, we sat at the table, and he came around."

"What happened? Did he say?" Adam asked.

"Terrible," Maggie said. "He saw terrible things. The infirmary was full of broken souls."

"What did he mean?"

"Let me explain because I was actually foolish enough to go back in there with our little troop of ghostbusters. I can't believe I did that." She slid to the edge of the couch and leaned toward Adam. "I told you about how some persons, when they pass, may leave a fragment caught in the door if their death had been unsettled. It seemed as though the infirmary was attracting *whole lives* that had been unsettled; that needed to be--how should I say this?--fixed. They were drawn to the infirmary in the afterlife just like sick people had come to the infirmary in life. When Leslie said 'broken souls,' he was right. It seemed like the apparitions were people who had been broken in life. People with terrible regret—horrible pain. People with gaping holes in their souls. They were damaged, or had damaged themselves, somehow." Maggie looked down and shook her head. "I don't want to even tell you what we saw in there." She rubbed her hands together nervously. "But I don't need to explore it any further. I can't handle this stuff anymore." She wiped the corner of her eye. "We closed it up, and I never went back, and I never let Leslie go back."

"I'm sorry," said Adam. "It must be hard to live here sometimes. I mean...."

"No, not as long as I keep it closed. Like I said, the house is quiet, and I just ignore the infirmary."

"It must've been terrible for your husband. Was Mr. Stewart, should I say, was he like you? I mean, could he...?"

"No, not at all," Maggie replied. "That was the tragedy of it. He wasn't clairvoyant or anything. He never really got over it. He carried it with him to his grave. He had never seen ghosts and never did again." She pushed the cuff of her nightgown up her arm. "I wanted to tear it down, but after talking to the historical society I changed my mind, and I just had someone bolt it shut. Someone else can deal with it someday. I want nothing to do with it any more. I cannot imagine how that door was opened or how your friend, Cam, got in there."

"What a night it's been," Adam said. "Again, I am so sorry I got you messed up in this and you had to open up all that stuff about the infirmary. It must be painful."

"Don't mention it. Anybody would've done the same." She clutched her robe as she stood up. "You try to get some sleep. I'll lock up. And by the way, Adam...."

He stood and looked at her.

"You did the right thing," she said. "Bringing him here was all you could do. You tried to help him."

Adam nodded and walked down the hall to the foot of the main staircase. Looking up into darkness, he laid a hand on the thick bannister, and stepped slowly onto the first step. "Goodnight, Maggie," he said, looking back. Then he ascended the staircase. It creaked and groaned until he reached the top where the hall was dimly lit by the open door to his room.

Adam stood next to his bed, reached to turn back the covers, then stopped. The dream catcher from the casino lay on his pillow. It must have been knocked off the shelf when he got up, or maybe he tossed it there when he quickly dressed to go in the infirmary. He was too tired to care about it, so he laid it on the shelf above his head, slipped into bed, and turned out the light. He knew he had to get up for work in a few hours, and he would probably be lying awake a long while.

CHAPTER 16

WHITE PINE

ADAM WAS AWAKE WITH HIS eyes still closed. He had been blissfully awakened by the aroma of white pine—sweet, spicy, infused with the scent of warm air and open forest. Fluting bird songs quavered, echoed, and rose to a harmonious trill that reverberated as if in a canyon.

He opened his eyes to a great forest; columns of nut-brown tree trunks, widely spaced, rose to a canopy far above that swayed and sparkled like an inverted, green sea. The forest floor was an unbroken mat of deep moss—cool, soft, and covered in patterns that shifted in the diffused light.

He did not remember driving, walking, flying––or dying. *This could be dying,* he thought. As he lay there, the warmth and beauty washed over him, the canopy shifted and shimmered, and great limbs waved and bowed.

Adam was content to stay and relish this feast of the senses. He felt no inclination to explore or discover.

After a long while, lying on the velvet moss, enthralled by the concert of bird song, he noticed a deep, hollow rumble. At first, he thought it might be thunder, but too brief. Seconds later, the sound repeated; then, after a time, came another beat in a very slow, even tempo. Swelling and fading, he realized it had been in the background a while, unnoticed. The tempo increased slowly until it sounded like very deep drums—a large timpani that carried far through the glen with a rhythm as steady as a heartbeat. BOOM, boom. BOOM, boom. BOOM, boom. Far away but approaching. An occasional flourish interspersed with higher tones from smaller drums.

Adam sat up.

The drums paused for a moment. Horns blew distantly, echoing spectacularly through the forest. Long, throaty blasts that quivered and grew. The deep drums again, closer. A flood of higher melodic rhythms pealed in; small toms, warm wooden tones hit with mallets, joined by Asian bronze, and marimba-like timbre. The rhythms became wildly complex and sustained. Layered in with all this was a constant, clear, musical jingle or rattle.

Adam smiled. *What a strange, vivid dream this is*, he thought. Again, he tried to remember if he could have traveled somewhere, but he knew there were no stands of massive virgin white pine like this anywhere. He'd seen the great virgin Estivant pines of the Keweenaw Peninsula—that cold, rocky finger hooking far into Lake Superior, strewn with ghost towns, empty mines, and legends. Many of the Estivant Pines were aged and battered, lonely among low brush, weeds, and young trees.

Here was a vast expanse with nothing but native white pine standing above a floor of moss. The white pine was sacred. The tallest tree along Lake Superior with crowns reaching to heaven.

The music swelled. Pipes and flutes were added. Flowing into this chorus, another melodic thread droned like an ancient Mandarin two-string. Adam thrilled at the sounds that filled every space of infinite forest. Giddy, his eyes darted from glade to glade to find where it was coming from. Finally, far in the distance, around columns of trees, he saw a strange procession winding its way toward him. At first, the figures were hard to discern.

Suddenly, all music stopped except for the rhythmic jingling: crisp and tonal.

When Adam saw the procession come near, he knew he was not in any world he would have ever known. He thought at first that the approaching folk were simply dwarfed by great trees and broad forest. He soon realized they were, indeed, very small people.

Three men and two women, dark-skinned and bare to the waist, became visible. With features ancient, Native, or even Asian, and in ornamented dress, they had a mystical bearing. Adam struggled to gain perspective amid a forest of giant trees, but he was certain these people would barely reach his waist.

The men wore elaborate headdresses woven of feathers and bits of reddish fur that sprayed from their heads and swayed as they walked. Long, broad loincloths made of white leather, intricately beaded, reached below their knees. Silver and gold threads glistened.

The women wore large headdresses with long feathers set in a woven crown on black hair plaited with beads and copper discs cascading to low slung, white leather skirts covered in silver cones. The rhythmic jingle Adam was hearing came from the silver cones that swished as they walked. Around their necks, the women wore white leather chokers adorned with red stones and green-tarnished copper. From these collars hung intricate plates that spread nearly to their breasts; the plates were made of bits of polished copper, mother-of-pearl, and beads of many colors. It was a magnificent appearance: savage, angelic, and utterly human.

Their faces were serene, uplifted, and serious, yet wholly pleasant. Their level gazes fixed on Adam as bare feet trod steadily and si-

Craig A. Brockman

lently on damp moss. The drumming and music had stopped, so only the jingle dresses shuffled rhythmically as the people walked to him.

Adam rose to his knees as they approached. They were, in a sense, terrifying––primal and fierce—but he did not feel threatened. They held no weapons, and their countenances were utterly passive. None of them carried instruments that would account for the music, except for one man, who carried a small drum made from what may have been the crown of a skull. The music had not come from this little band, but had welled up from the forest and from other unseen entities.

They walked boldly up to Adam as he stayed on his knees. Their faces captivated him. He saw features that spanned continents from Mongol to Mayan, with bodies dark, sculpted, lithe, and beautiful— animal-like in physicality, fierce in humanity.

They made a semicircle around him. He stood, but somehow, it felt a sacrilege to stand in their presence. No one appeared to be the distinct leader as Adam looked from one to the other. *I'm dreaming! But how can this be a dream? Watch. Watch and pay attention!*

They began to speak softly, but Adam was not sure if they were talking to him or among themselves. The dialect was musical, like the birds. Although he tried to understand what they were saying, it seemed to be a language long lost to history and totally beyond his comprehension. They talked for a short time until one of the women reached out her small hand confidently, palm down to take his hand. He reached forward and took her hand, which felt as small and soft as a kitten's paw. The group turned and began to lead him in a different direction from where they had come. Adam realized that trying to speak to them or ask where they were going would be a foolish waste of time.

He took small steps to keep up with their gait. The jingle dresses formed a rhythm. When the group paused, the man with the small drum made a series of complex beats. They waited. From the forest canopy and from around the columns of trees, the large timpani boomed. Higher percussion rattled and thrummed. An invisible cue brought in the pipes and flutes, and they were followed by the droning strings. In profound wonder, Adam smiled, gazing upward to the canopy. Music and rhythm was coming from everywhere. He could not help but step to the beat as they led him through the forest.

Soon the trees thinned. Instead of forest, Adam saw patches of deep blue ahead, but he could not tell, yet, whether it was sky or water. They emerged from the forest to the edge of a high cliff above still waters; crystal blue spread to a seamless horizon of sky. Two eagles circled high above. Beauty and stillness washed over them as the small band that led him to the cliff looked across the water in serene respect. He was too enraptured to notice the music had stopped.

After standing motionless for a while, the woman let go of Adam's hand and the small people stepped into a line along the cliff. They stretched out their arms, and the women began speaking in cadence; it was poetic and beautiful, words rhyming and intertwining until phrases lifted into song. Adam didn't know why, but as their voices chimed and harmonized, and the tone grew tranquil and sad, his eyes were moist. Images surged in his mind.

Adam understood not a word, but by their voice and cadence, their intensity and passion, he saw visions: panoramas, a great pageant. He could see the span of an ageless continent: ice cliffs glistening to the sky retreating before scattered peoples in ragged hides. Great hairy elephantine beasts lumbering to their deaths. Hulking predators, fangs and claws against flint and stone, spears and arrows. These wild people sang of armies of warriors, red from battle, torn and flayed on the field. Women and children captured and bartered, raped and battered. He saw great ships and guns, cannons blazing, sails swaying in the bloodied sun.

Raising their small arms higher, letting them sway, they continued to sing, and Adam heard in their song the Great Human Story: the culmination of tens of thousands of years of migration from continent to continent. He could envision the scattered bands and lost hoards moving into the Middle East, other tribes branching into Europe, while intrepid hunters spanned Asia and crossed the Bering Land Bridge on foot and paddled across oceans to this continent. The arms of humanity spread around the earth until East and West were no more, and the far flung, most divergent peoples—the Native and the European—came face to face on the shores of the New World. The circle was complete.

In their song, ancient cities rose out of jungles; then there were cities on plains, cities on mountains and shores; soon, the cores of these cities were decaying, their millions of inhabitants writhing with anger, greed, and death. Streets were running with blood.

The small men joined the song, which grew deeper and droning. All voices harmonized and grew louder in fervor. Adam heard a new song. Somewhere in the refrain, he heard of power with justice, truth overcoming hate and vengeance. Restoration occurred, and finally, the purge of injustice.

Their song became low and lovely; going home, the faces of family, suckling infants, strong children, the wisdom of the aged, harvest and peace, sun and rain. The song grew quieter until it dwindled and died. Adam had not realized he was no longer standing but kneeling, his face washed with tears.

After several breaths, Adam heard the small people begin rhythmically whispering, no longer singing. This grew full-throated as they raised their arms higher over the lake. The women's dresses softly jingled with the growing intensity of their incantations.

Adam looked across the water in the direction of their gaze. The water was no longer still and flat but crossed with choppy waves and vague swirling currents. He could feel the power and intensity of the lake surging below them. He stood again. At the peak of their calling, he could see, perhaps a mile away from the cliff, the lake swelled to a great mound that shuddered, grew, then receded. It rose again, but now a hundred yards closer. When the water crested, it formed a great wave that crashed as a white wall. Closer and closer it came, mound upon mound, wave upon wave until finally a great swell formed only a hundred yards from the cliff. Adam gasped and jumped back as massive spines rose from the lake. A tremendous, green, shiny back slid underwater, breaking a great wave that rumbled in the bay. The people stopped speaking and lowered their arms.

A massive creature glided under the surface with spines forming boat-sized Vs in the water. At the foot of the cliff, it slowed, and the wave it was forming crashed below them and broke against the cliff. Adam inched forward and looked slowly over the rim of the cliff far down to the water below. From deep in the lake, he saw eyes: yellow and cat-like, peering up through clear water at him and at the little band at the edge of the cliff. A head like a lynx, large as a schooner, began to rise from the water. On each side, great horns, larger than mastodon tusks, shed the waves. Terrified and confused, Adam tried to step back, but the men, smiling, took his hands and urged him forward again.

Rising, the beast blew showers from its feline nostrils, and came nearer to the edge of the cliff, casting a brutish odor of lake bottom. Adam was becoming frantic, but the small people were calm. The man with the drum once again beat the complex pattern. Once more, from behind them and from the trees, came the orchestra of deep drums, flutes, and drones. As the creature rose level with the cliff, Adam took in the massive horned head and pointed ears. The yellow eyes blinked. Wiry hair gradually transitioned to scales. A row of tall spines down the creature's back led to a long serpentine tail that wallowed in deep, clear water. When it snuffed a wet gust, Adam flinched.

"I'm dreaming; I am dreaming," he had to tell himself as he put a hand to his forehead and looked around at the clear sky rimmed behind him by tall white pines. *What is this? Where am I?*

One of the women turned to him with her tiny hand pointing and spoke in her sweet, wavering voice. "Mishipezhu," she said. "Mishipezhu."

The music stopped, the scene froze, and then all dimmed to blackness.

Mishipezhu.

CHAPTER 17

A MEETING
PART 1

T HE DRAWING ROOM HAD BECOME his own private escape, Adam thought, as he stretched on the couch, staring into the fire. Though the weather had turned unseasonably warm after the early snow, Maggie liked to keep a fire lit. Low light was cast from the stained-glass shade and from yellowish prisms that shown through the ornate, leaded glass pocket doors, separating the drawing room from the library. Patterns mixed with flickering firelight and scattered the walls. Maggie's right arm was wavy and contorted through glass as she scrolled with the mouse and shuffled papers at her computer monitor in the library.

It was quiet. Adam had awoken from his strange dream that morning to find the dream catcher once more lying on his chest. When he got up, he set it thoughtfully on the shelf again and went through his day. He was able, due to years of experience, to put the dream away on a shelf, too.

After the fright with Cam, the phantasm between two worlds floating in the infirmary, and having that vivid dream, it had, thankfully, been a fairly typical day at the clinic: listening to his clients' feelings of anxiety and their encounters with strange specters.

Despite Adam's efforts, the compelling memory of the dream had whispered in his thoughts and followed him like a shadow, until Ron had caught up with him and managed to extract a few details of what he had seen in that forest. It didn't really help to talk about it. Adam would start to describe it, but then words would fail.

He jumped at the blast of the fire alarm/doorbell.

"I've got it!" Maggie said from her desk. Adam sat up, reached for a newspaper from the end table, and slid to the end of the couch near the light. He looked up. *Oh, damn, it's Ron!* he remembered. He had sunk so deeply into his island of serenity that he'd completely forgotten Ron had planned to stop by to continue the conversation they'd started at work. Ron had not elaborated, but he wanted to lay out some other ideas. Adam wasn't sure if Ron wanted to talk about the dream because of what the dream contained or because he was finally certain Adam had dropped completely off the deep end.

Adam heard Maggie's deliberate steps out of the library and down the hall toward the front door. He decided to stand and peer out the sitting room door into the hall so he could greet Ron. Maggie looked left and right through the glass panel on the front door until she unlatched the dead bolt and swung it open. There was no one.

"James Graves," Adam hissed to himself and backed into the sitting room out of sight.

Maggie leaned farther out the door, and suddenly, a slight, young woman appeared from the side.

"Sorry, Mrs. Stewart; I was reading the plaque here under the light. I've never been here before and.... Oh, I'm sorry; I'm Gracie

Bird." She offered her hand. "I was wondering if Ron Jarvin got here, yet. I was supposed to meet him."

"Gracie?" Adam nearly slipped when his socks crossed the hall's polished wood floor. She looked different without all the makeup, and her long hair framed her bright face. He was suddenly feeling very foolish in his flannel pants and lint-spotted sweatshirt. "Well, uh, what are you doing here? I mean...."

Maggie stepped back from the door. "Come on in. I was just going to get some tea; then I'll leave you folks alone."

Gracie looked from Adam to Maggie. "Actually, I think Ron would like you to join us, Mrs. Stewart. We may have some questions for you, too. Didn't Ron talk to you?"

"Well, yes, he did," Maggie looked a little confused. "He said you might come over tonight, but I didn't think I was to be part of this meeting of the minds."

Gracie let out a musical laugh that caused Adam to smile. "I don't think," Gracie said, "that you would call this a meeting of the minds. No offense, Adam." She laughed again.

"I'll get tea." Maggie looked from Adam to Gracie. "Would you like anything else? Coke? Water?"

"Tea sounds wonderful, Mrs. Stewart," Gracie said.

"Call me Maggie. I'd be much more comfortable with that."

"Okay. Maggie it is."

Adam returned to the drawing room and Gracie started to follow. "Wait; I'd better take off my boots." She stepped to the mat near the door and leaned over. Her long, black hair, free from the bun she wore at the casino, swished at the elbows of a jean jacket as she unlaced and removed the clunky boots under her long skirt.

Adam watched her and smiled. "I don't get it. You talked with Ron today?"

Gracie grinned, and Adam stepped back to allow her into the room. "Yeah, he called me this afternoon." She leaned in to look around. "This place is amazing. Beautiful. O-o-oo, a fire and every-thing. This is so nice!" She quick-stepped up to the fire and spread her hands.

"Yeah, I can't believe I landed here. The longer I'm here, the more attached I get to the place." Adam eased into the leather chair, looked down at his flannel pants, picked bits of lint from his shirt, and looked back at Gracie. "I'm sorry. I totally forgot that Ron was coming over tonight." He paused. "And I had no idea you would be here. That night at the casino was, I don't know, so strange. Weird."

Gracie walked back and sat on the couch near Adam's chair. She engaged his stare as she said, "Yeah, I was going to check up on you to be sure you kept the dream catcher and that Graves left you alone, but...I didn't want you to get worried." She folded her hands between her knees and looked at the rug. "I knew more was going on when Ron called me and told me a little about the dream you had last night." She scratched her head with one finger. "Sorry for invading your space, but this is the kind of stuff Ron and I have talked about. We will explain––or Ron will explain." She swept her hand in the air. "And with everything else going on, I agreed with Ron that it was about time we all got together. Ron knows this stuff, and I know there's so much more that could be happening. I think your dream was a turning point. For me, anyway."

Gracie looked around the room and then at Adam. "I'm sorry; this is a lot to digest, I know." She held her serious face a moment, then grinned. "How long have you been here?"

Adam was staring at her and held out his hand to pause. "W-wait. I need to back up. I don't know where to start. Like I told you at the casino, I'm out of the loop more than I realized. I hope I finally get to hear from everybody what's happening here. You guys know a lot more about––about everything. I still don't get it."

Gracie continued to smile and shook her head. "Don't worry. Yes, there seems to be a lot going on, and I think you already know more than you realize, from what you've seen and heard. Ron has a few answers, and together, we can assemble some pieces––for all of us—I think."

There was a long silence. "Well…." Gracie shrugged and began in a small voice, "Well, I'm sorry; it seems like I just dropped in. I actually thought Ron would be here, already."

"No, no, it's fine," Adam said. There was another pause. "But how *do* you know Ron?"

Maggie entered with a tray followed by a spicy scent of brewing tea and something she must have heated up in the microwave. In the rattle of cups and saucers, she said, "I've got stuff to do in the library, so I'll be in the next room if you need anything."

"No, Mrs. Stewart—I mean Maggie," said Gracie. "Really, we need some of your wisdom here."

Maggie offered a straight little smile. "I'm not sure I like that word *wisdom*. Does that mean age or…does it have something to do with things I no longer know about, or I should say, *want* to know about?"

"There's a reason James Graves came to see you, you know," Gracie said.

Maggie inhaled and then sighed. "I'm afraid I can see where this is going. Are we going to wait for Ron?"

"Let's wait," Gracie said.

"You know," Adam added, "like I said, I totally forgot Ron was coming. Let me run my stuff back up to my room and get changed, now that it's going to be a formal affair." He smiled to himself, aware that both women were too polite to comment on his shabby attire.

§ § §

When Adam returned, Gracie and Maggie were sitting together on the couch engaged in conversation about Maggie's homeland, her commitment to the inherited mansion, and the history of her family and the Stewart family. Adam slipped back into the leather chair. As he listened, he was fascinated by Gracie's interest and specific knowledge, not only of the history of Sault Sainte Marie, but also of Maggie's Scottish roots. The conversation was coming around to Gracie's past when the doorbell clanged.

"That's probably our man." Maggie stood and walked out of the room to answer the door. They heard conversation between Ron and Maggie that continued as he took off his boots. He swept into the room smiling broadly, carrying a tattered canvas pack. The corner of a book stuck out of a hole, and book edges were visible through thinning canvas. He set the load down on the coffee table with care and patted the pack, smiling at Gracie and Adam.

"So, you've met. Again," Ron said. "Hi, Gracie; I'm glad you could make it."

"Of course." She smiled confidently while looking around quickly at the little gathering.

Ron slipped off his coat, which Maggie quickly snatched. She stepped out of the room to hang the coat on the hook near the front door.

"I'm sorry I'm late," said Ron. "I just had to run out to the west pier to see it."

"See what?" Maggie asked.

Ron looked puzzled. "Well, the *seiche*. Didn't you hear about it?"

"What? The saints? Or what did you say?" Adam asked.

"Seiche. The water is way down. It's amazing. The bay looks empty. The bottom is completely exposed. They shut down the locks because a ship is stuck west of the International Bridge," Ron said.

"How does it happen? I never heard of it," Adam said.

"It's a seiche. I didn't mention it when I came in," Gracie said. "It's sort of like a freshwater tide. This is Ron's area of expertise, though."

"It usually happens," said Ron, "when a small, intense atmospheric pressure system passes over one end of the lake and pushes on the water or draws it up. A long, steady wind can pile up water on one end while pulling it away from the other, too. But today, this one got crazy low."

"I noticed how low the water was on the beach, and Shirley mentioned it yesterday—that woman who owns the cabins," Adam said. "It lasts this long?"

"No," Ron said. "Usually, it only lasts a few hours, but then it sloshes back and causes high water. But this one seemed static until today when it got a lot lower here. I hear it's low, like this, all around the lake. It can only mean that water is somehow getting piled up in the center of the lake." He shook his head. "I have no idea what it means anymore. I have to talk to someone down in Ann Arbor or over in Duluth." He shrugged. "So, what have you guys been talking about while it took forever for me to get here?"

"Not much," said Adam, "but, Gracie, you were just about to tell us about your family."

"Where do I start?" She watched Maggie ease into the chair while Ron sat on the couch. "Let's see; a couple of hundred years ago, we claim that the Ojibwe pushed my ancestors, the Menominee, off this land and they wound up over in Wisconsin, which is where I was born." She looked from Adam to Ron, grinning. "That's about it, I guess!" Still smiling, she looked at Maggie and then around the room. "But just like Maggie, I think my ancestry sort of controls where I am today, and what I'm doing here now." She inhaled slowly, then said, "My mother was called Waabishki Oniijaaniw."

"The White Doe," Ron interjected with the hint of a sad smile.

"Yes. I feel a little hesitant to talk about myself like this, but I was granted her name. It's complicated, but the name was conferred on me in a ceremony when I was a little girl after.... Well, after my mother died." Gracie looked down and brushed her sleeve quickly, then looked up sharply. "But no one, particularly at the casino, can know that. They can't know who I am." It was silent for moments.

"I'm sorry about your mother, Gracie," Adam said. He hesitated. "But what's going on at the casino? Can we help?"

"It's about James Graves," Gracie said coldly. "Like you saw at the casino, I'm here to keep an eye on him and this twisted magic of his."

They waited for her to continue.

"He's a Midewinini." She shifted nervously. "Do you know what that is?"

"It's something to do with Native religion?" Adam offered.

"It has to do with *one* Native religion," Ron said, looking at Gracie. "Go ahead, Gracie; you know this stuff better than I do."

"A Midewinini is like a medicine man in Midewiwin, which is the religion people have normally associated with Woodland, Northeastern, and some Plains tribes for a long time. But it's really only been around for a couple of centuries. I think of it as, not really a cult," she blinked, "not all of it. But much of what happens at the powwows, the sweat lodges, the ceremonies and rituals, and even some of the legends have been created by this religion. A lot of people think the rise of Midewiwin could have been a response to the loss of authority within tribal leadership. And also because of disease and strife after the invasion of Europeans and their Christian religion."

"Really, I mean, I've never heard of anything like that." Adam looked confused. "I thought this stuff was all ancient."

"My ancestors were not really all that religious." Gracie licked her lips and looked at the ceiling again, searching for words. She leaned forward with her hands on her knees, folded as in prayer, moving them up and down for emphasis. "I would never disparage any religion, of course." She nodded toward Maggie. "I mean the ancient Woodland people were spiritual, but they had very little of what we would think of as religion. I think some of the spirituality that people attribute to Native peoples has been sort of projected on them." She shook her head and smiled. "I'm not going to go there. We can save that for another powwow." She smiled slyly and started again. "Anyway, people like my mother and the other leaders tolerated Midewin. Midewin was actually helpful for many and provided important cultural strength, and what would you say? Glue. But there were times when some of it was harmful." She took a deep breath. "There have been some Midewininiwag who created their own versions of the faith, and I'm afraid this is one of those times."

Ron nodded at Gracie, saying, "Her ancestors go way back to the original Algonquin nations, before the tribes were all separated, and way before Midewiwin. It's true, however, that their spiritual system would have had similarities to modern Midewiwin." Gracie nodded as he spoke. Ron continued, "These ancestors were thought of as the original keepers of the lake. And they still are today." He paused. "And that's the other reason Gracie's here, at a time like this." He reached over and tapped the books again.

"People like James Graves," said Gracie, "are here to hijack things that are happening in the lake and use them for evil. People like Graves thrive on power and control."

Maggie and Adam exchanged glances, and Adam raised his eyebrows. "Okay, I think we're still a little confused. Right, Maggie?"

Maggie gave a narrow smile, then shrugged in confusion. "You mean the ghosts and the hysteria, or whatever you want to call it? Is that what Graves is trying to hijack? I'm not sure I know what you mean by power and control. Power and control over *what*?"

"I think we can cover that," Ron replied, "and I'm interested in what Gracie has to say, too. She and I haven't had very much time to talk."

"You and Gracie getting together on this makes me more than curious." Adam looked at both of them. "What is going on?"

"First of all, Ron is well known to those of us who are connected with the lake," Gracie said. "He's the guy to ask; he's the authority when we want to know what's going on with the lake and how it relates to anything else, I guess." She winked at Ron, then looked at Adam and Maggie with her hand beside her mouth, whispering, "He's just like his father and grandfather and his de-frocked great-grandfather. But

I won't go there." She leaned back, her hands clasped around a knee, and laughed. "He comes from a long line of indecisive priests who fell in love with this lake."

"Please stop." Ron smiled and rolled his eyes, not wanting to get into the subject.

"Show us the books and we'll all see what I mean by your authority on the Great Lakes." Gracie nodded at Ron.

"I'll get to that, but before I do that, I want Gracie to tell us what she knows about James Graves," Ron said. "He is the critical issue, right now."

Gracie took a deep breath and looked at the floor. "Okay, I can say a few things. But where do I start? This will all sound off the wall to you guys." She looked up at Adam and Maggie. "Graves is not from around here. He's actually from out west and has some Potawatomi ancestors. He's trying to work his way in here, but many of the local tribal leaders and legitimate healers are on to him. That's why I got access at the casino. The leadership wants to deal with him, but he has too much popular support." She leaned forward. "It gets weirder. I can't say anything about why Duane Bird came here, and I can't say more about why I'm here." She scratched her shoulder and shrugged. "But I can say we're looking into some shady things that Graves and his buddies have been up to. Still, none of us expected to run into all this, uh, supernatural stuff. Never. Not to this extent."

"Is there anything more specific that you can tell us?" Ron asked. "I mean, we're kinda grasping at straws when it comes to Graves. I don't know what he's doing."

Gracie nodded quickly. "Sure. It's like this: to some of his disciples or followers or clients or whatever you want to call them, Graves is beginning to call himself Myeengun. He believes Myeengun was the last chief to raise the Great Lynx. It was actually his descendant, Shingwauk, who was the Great Midewinini. Graves doesn't even know *that* much. Myeengun and Shingwauk are thought to be the old ones who drew the pictographs on Agawa Rock north of Sault, Ontario hundreds of years ago. Agawa Rock is like the Stonehenge of Lake Superior, and it's had great spiritual significance for thousands of years." She paused. "Graves is up to something and, as bizarre as it sounds, it has to do with the Great Lynx, Mishipezhu."

Adam felt a sweat break out on his forehead. "What the...?" he stammered. "That name. That's what *they* said––in my dream!"

Everyone turned to Adam. Suddenly, they all jumped as the logs in the fireplace thumped and settled and a whirl of sparks crackled up the flue.

"Och, no-o!" Maggie said. She walked quickly to tend the fireplace. They watched silently. Adam blinked.

Maggie stepped back to her chair and looked worriedly at Adam.

"Adam, are you okay?" Ron asked.

Adam nodded and looked at Ron. "I guess this is where I come in. Today I was telling you a little about that really weird dream, about something coming out of the lake. I didn't remember everything, and I didn't have time to tell you everything."

Gracie raised her eyebrows. "There's more? Really? It's the dream catcher. Don't you remember? I made sure you took it so Graves wouldn't have it. That's got to be what he wanted."

"Yeah, when you told me about the dream today, it really got my attention," said Ron, "and I had to tell Gracie. Sorry I spilled the beans, Adam. What do you think Graves wanted with the dream catcher, Gracie?"

"Graves must know that the way of the Great Lynx," Gracie said, then hesitated, "is only revealed in a dream. That's what he was trying to get from you at the casino." She turned to Adam. "Tell us more."

Maggie knew nothing about the dream. She looked on with furrowed brow. "Oh, dear," is all she could offer.

Adam took a deep breath. "I awoke in the woods; well, it was an amazing forest." He went on to recount the dream until he came to the part where the tiny people came out of the forest.

"Ha!" Gracie laughed and covered her mouth, then placed palms together again, prayer-like, under her chin, her face beaming. "The Pukwudgie!" She looked around the room like *Don't you get it?*

Ron smiled while Adam and Maggie exchanged confused glances.

"The little people," Gracie continued excitedly. "Ojibwe call them pahiins, Algonquin called them the Memegwesi, and just about every other band and tribe has its own name for them. But I just like to say the name: Pukwudgie! It's more of an eastern Native term, but they were the ones you saw, uh, dreamed. They're like two or three feet tall." She put her hand out flat at that height.

Adam nodded.

"Some of the tribes," Gracie continued, "thought of them as being like gremlins or troublemakers, but the first ancient people supposedly were friends with them. They only made trouble for the tribes who came later; the tribes that displaced the first people." She kicked Adam playfully. "And I thought they would never have anything to do with Europeans. Maybe it's time to get your DNA test done!" She laughed, then grasped her knees and leaned in. "This is important, Adam. What did they show you?"

Adam recalled the rest of his dream: the music, the singing, and the chanting. He looked at each of the other three sitting in the room. He described the Great Lynx rising from the lake. "And that name: Mishi...? Mishu...?"

"Mishipezhu," Gracie said. But then she looked up. "He won't know!"

"Who won't know about what?" Adam asked. "The Great Lynx?"

"No," she said. "Graves knows about Mishipezhu, but he won't know just where the Pukwudgie come in. He won't know that only the little people master the Lynx in the dream world. Only the little people have the power to command it once it has risen. Through their songs!"

"But more importantly, doesn't the legend say that the Great Lynx will return back to where it came from?" Ron asked. "Do the little people have something to do with that, too?"

"Right. I have to believe they do," Gracie said, "and we're afraid that if Graves messes around, he could somehow interfere, and it could have serious consequences for the entire lake for a long time. Even if no one believes in Mishipezhu, it won't matter. The lake will be more deadly for a long time. The Great Lynx represents the soul of the lake."

Maggie knit her brow in confusion, Adam looked at Gracie, and Ron looked at his book bag as each of them struggled silently, trying to weigh the gravity and discern which pieces they would have to place into this bizarre puzzle.

Ron put his hand to his forehead and looked up suddenly. "How could I have forgotten? Adam, that client of yours who ran out of the office: Danny Sayles."

CHAPTER 18

SAYLES ON THE LAKE

A T LEAST I SHOWED UP *for the appointment last week so that damn parole agent will not be on my back*, Danny thought as he pulled into the parking lot at the Marina. *Well, yeah, I left in a huff, but I still have proof that I kept the appointment with that idiot shrink.*

Danny's mom was not aware that he had neglected to get his dad's boat out of the marina and put it in storage last month. She was also not aware that he took it for a joy ride now and then. In Danny's mind, it was important to burn the carbon out of the engines and maybe fish a little once in a while. This task seemed to work especially well with a few beers, and today was no exception. The odd warm day, calm winds, and sunny skies just begged for a late season day on the lake. And *then* he would put the boat away.

Danny Sayles thought of himself as an independent thirty-four-year-old who had just fallen on some hard times. But with his smarts and a little help from Mom––again––he'd get back on his feet in no time.

The 1980 *Sea Ray 300 Sedan Bridge* was a pre-owned model when his dad bought it. It was still beautiful. *Twin MerCruiser* 260 hp engines made some waves, and that was just what Danny needed to blow off some steam. He had begged his mom to keep the boat after his dad had died, and he had promised to help pay the marina bills as soon as he got a job. *Mom is still flush with all the cash from Dad's life insurance anyway,* he figured, *so she can cover the marina bills.*

Danny had little idea how to back a trailer, so they had to keep the boat at the marina until he got up the ambition to twist and tug a trailer into the water. Or he could usually make up some story so someone would help him back it up and drive it out.

Why wouldn't she want to keep Dad's boat? Besides, Danny often said to himself that the boat would be a great place to bring chicks––someday. That girl who worked at the gas station was cute; kind of young, though. But if he ever talked to her, just maybe he could show her around the boat. It was equipped with a nice galley that included a stove, a fridge for beers, and up in front were two small couches that conveniently folded out to double beds.

Danny thought about moving in there in spring, but it was pretty small. Then, at least, he could take off and go wherever he wanted and not have to listen to his mom bitchin' all the time. And he would change that dumb name on the boat: *Hell-In-Sails.* He smirked. It made no sense, and it was a stupid play on his mom's name: Helen.

After stowing the twelve pack in the fridge and setting down the bag of fish and chips from the drive-in at the end of the pier, Danny put his hand on the wheel and turned the key. The engines rumbled to life, and he throttled up to hear that roar that made him smile. He cranked it down, eased out of the slip, and idled over to the gas pump.

A beautiful day for November, he thought, as he swiped his almost-maxed-out credit card to fill up the tank. He hung up the hose. Now he was ready to head into open water and forget about parole agents, judges, and stupid-assed therapists.

If this was going to be his last ride of the year, he wanted to go big. Maybe get up to Agawa Bay along the Canadian side. It had been a long time since he'd pulled in to look at the Agawa pictographs. Not that he cared a fart about old Indian drawings, but it was a place Dad had liked to take him, and maybe it would be nice to go there and remember Dad and...and then, if it stayed this calm, he'd take a turn west into deep water—head out far enough to where he couldn't see land. Then maybe hit the casino at Bay Mills on the way back.

It took an hour and a half to navigate the Saint Mary's River channel, cruise along the east side of Whitefish Bay, and head into the big lake. Another hour and a half as he fooled around zig-zagging, guzzling beers, and racing; eventually he made it to Montreal Island in Agawa Bay. It was later than he had planned, and he was down to five beers. He had a decent buzz, an empty food bag, and Nickelback on the stereo. He decided to skip the pictographs. Picking up his phone, he changed the music to another middling rock band—Creed—as the boat made a wide arc to the west and headed into the horizon. *My kinda music*, he thought.

Just about every condition of Danny's parole had gone out the window with this little cruise: drinking, leaving the country. *Damn, if only I had my gun, I could plunk some seagulls or something.*

About ten miles more, Danny got bored with riding the easy swells, so he throttled down, cracked open another beer, and scuttled up top to kick back and watch the mid-afternoon sun on the water while listening to his music. Two swivel chairs and a low railing were up top. Fishing was an option, though he didn't have a fishing license for any country. *But what the hell? What's one more law?* But, *nah*, he didn't feel like messing with the tackle and all.

Offering his beer to the sky, Danny sang every word of "One Last Breath," oblivious to the intended meaning of the song and the mealy rock music. This song had been written for him.

He played one or two more Creed songs, getting more depressed and feeling more the victim of a world that didn't understand him and was out to get him. Another beer would probably dull the edge a bit and bring him out of this. Maybe time to switch to Skynyrd to chase away the blues. *Yeah. Skynyrd!*

Crouching down, holding the rail, Danny swayed over to the ladder. He looked somewhat like a circus act as he weaved down from step to step until he managed to make it back to the cabin. He tried to focus on his phone and punched in AC/DC because it was at the top of his playlist. He grabbed a beer––might as well get two—and went back up the ladder in step with the tolling of "Hell's Bells."

The chair swiveled away from Danny's grasp, and only the rail saved him from falling overboard. He set one of the beer cans in a holder and then fumbled and dropped the other can. He cursed as it rolled, and he reeled until he grasped the chrome rail with both hands. *Steady, steady. Deep breaths.* Head nodding to the music, he caught the can rolling back with his foot, picked it up carefully, and fell into the chair. He shook his head, laughed, and eased open the pop top to foam and fizz.

Slurping the rim of the can, he looked across sparkling water to... *an island? Wait. That's west, right? There's nothing west of here.* In still waters, far away near the horizon, the island sank even as he watched. *Weird.* Drunk, or whatever, he was pretty sure of what he was seeing. Slowly, the distant mound rose again, but.... *What the hell?* It looked closer, even though the boat should be drifting slowly the other way. East. After going down again, it reappeared, even closer. It sank out of sight. Rising, then dipping, it came closer and closer.

Danny stood, then leaned onto the forward rail while his head cleared, trying to figure out what he was seeing. The day was clear and calm with slight swells, but for some reason, here was this massive wave, or something, that could soon overtake the boat. "What the hell? An effing submarine right here in Lake Superior!" he slurred.

Frightened, Danny's head cleared enough for him to swing down the ladder. He stumbled into the cabin and punched off *AC/DC*, started the engine, and tried to see out the window to figure out which way to go.

A hundred yards away and closing, great spikes emerged like tree trunks pushing out of the wake, curved and sharp, twenty feet apart, rising from each side of a massive head.

"What the hell is that?" Danny yelled as he throttled up the twin screws and tore out, trying to angle away from whatever was out there.

Cursing and spitting, looking over his shoulder, Danny saw the thing was changing its course to follow the boat, rising and dipping. He pushed the throttle all the way up and swung south, but whatever was chasing him was able to keep within fifty yards. Now thirty yards and still closing. The swells grew larger as it gained speed. His only hope was to get to the harbor south of Whitefish Point or ditch the boat on the beach.

The monster backed off a little and kept its distance for another mile or two. It was only playing. A great swell formed again about fifty yards behind him, then vanished. Danny looked back to see the broad circle of ripples moving outward and dissipating. Even though he felt he was escaping, or that the creature had lost interest, he kept the boat throttled up and checked the gas gauge to see that the needle sat at one quarter tank. He could make it to the harbor. He was panting, mumbling, and scratching his head, wondering what had just happened. Suddenly, his stomach lurched, but he couldn't quite make it to the edge of the boat before an afternoon's worth of beer and fast food let loose all over the back of the cabin.

Stumbling to the wheel, Danny saw it out of the corner of his eye. He turned his head to face it: a great steady wake was now less than twenty-five yards behind the boat and gaining. It moved up and down, rising and sinking; a huge rushing wave sprouting massive horns, *and what the hell*? Sharp spines jutted from a back as broad as a whale. A shadow spread over the boat.

Danny collapsed over the steering wheel, causing the boat to veer wildly.

CHAPTER 19

A MEETING
PART II

"I'M SORRY IF THIS IS a little graphic." Ron looked from Maggie to Gracie. Gracie shrugged, indicating *continue.*

"Well, they found a Sea Ray that drifted onto shore near Paradise." He looked at each of their faces. "It was sheared off a couple of feet above the water line. Sharp and clean as a tin can," he sighed. "It was registered to Helen Sayles."

"Herman's boat," Maggie whispered.

Ron nodded while looking at the floor. "Just the lower half of a body was found there in the boat."

"Oh, Lord," Maggie said and turned away.

"Yeah. I talked to Sheriff Roy, and they have to do some toxicology and stuff, but they're pretty sure it was Danny." He waited. "They don't have a clue what happened. It was too clean. It hadn't run under a dock or under another boat. They don't know."

"Mishipezhu," Gracie said.

The room was silent.

"Yeah, well, I'm not sure if I'm ready to go there, yet, but in light of every other weird thing, I guess we have to wonder," Ron said as he turned to Adam, who was staring wide-eyed at the fire.

"You okay, Adam?" Ron reached over and grasped Adam's knee. "Your dream?"

"It c-can't be," Adam stammered. "I s-saw a beast, or whatever, in my dream."

"I know it's all very strange," Gracie said. "And we know so little. But there are those who believe the Great Lynx emerges from dreams. It enters into this world from dream."

"What the hell? Like, *I* did it? *I released this—thing*? What do you mean?" Adam looked at Gracie, confounded.

Gracie responded carefully. "Of course not, Adam. I didn't mean it that way, but this is why we're here. Whatever is happening, it is powerful. We have to be vigilant. We have to watch, in any way we can, with whatever abilities we have." She looked from Adam to Maggie.

"And I agree," Ron added. "There's a reason we're all here. Each one of us." He glanced at his book bag and scratched his beard thoughtfully. "Let me tell you how I see it—what I think is going on. I'll lay it out, and you guys can take it any way you want."

Unbuckling a clasp, untying frayed straps, Ron carefully folded open the trimmed flap. He slid out a tattered, leather-bound book, followed by two more books equally worn and ancient. Carefully, almost reverently, he set down the other two books and picked up the first one, laying it across his knees. He slowly traced the scrolling on the cover. Maggie smiled. She understood his reverence for his books. Adam looked from the book to Ron's face.

"Adam," said Ron, meeting his gaze, "I'm sorry you've been drawn into all this. Maybe it was just intuition when I called you. I don't know. We truly needed help at the agency. It wasn't just a ruse." Ron lowered his eyes to the book again. "All this stuff started happening. Then when I found out Gracie was back here, and that Graves was starting something, I.... Well, your name just came to mind. I'm not sure why, but I just felt you should be here." He paused. Adam nodded understanding, so Ron continued, "I'd been thinking of some of the dreams you used to tell me about. I don't think you even knew how they affected me, and I don't think you even realized how—what should I say?—how prophetic they were." Looking at Adam, Ron leaned in. "I needed you here not only as a friend, considering how crazy it was getting, but also as a compass, I guess. Yeah, that's it—a compass." Ron shifted back, looking at Gracie, while she nodded agreement.

"I'm not sure I understand everything you're telling me," Adam said, "but I've seen enough at this point to realize I probably just need to.... I just need to listen."

Ron softly brushed the book on his lap, then pointed at the other books on the table. "We *all* need to listen, and I think these books may speak to us about what's been going on." He opened the book to the title page.

"Jeez, is that Russian? Or what language is it?" Adam asked. "I didn't know you knew Russian."

"Good guess," Ron grinned. "It *is* Russian. And I *can* read a little Russian––very little. It's really tough."

Ron seemed a little self-conscious, hesitant, about sharing his insight. He was never willing to draw attention to himself. Despite his depth of understanding, he was more inclined to impart knowledge as tantalizing sips at just the right time. However, pointing to the other books, he continued, "This one is Spanish, and that one is English, but they're both really old, so the language is not much easier."

"What could they possibly tell us about a medicine man who's acting crazy and a bunch of Yoopers who think they're seeing ghosts?" Adam looked around at the other three.

Ron laughed. "Well, I'm not sure if I'm ready to jump to conclusions, but that's why I thought you three could help." He spread his hand, fingers apart, over the books. "These three books all have something in common. How do I put this?" He paused. "Each of these books documents horrendous war, strife, and suffering, but that's not essentially what they are about. They have something more mysterious in common."

He closed the book on his lap and set his finger on the cover. "This one is the newest, and it was written a hundred years ago. It chronicles the bloody devastation of revolution and war across Europe and Asia in the centuries leading up to World War I. That, in itself, does not make this book so special. We have lots of history books that document that era, right?"

Ron laid down the book and reached for another. "This one is older. It was written by a British officer more than fifty years earlier, and it documents the ghastly atrocities of the slavers in Africa. It also chronicles things like intertribal strife and social upheaval caused by slaving. It documents enormous suffering caused from disease as well."

"And this one," he said holding the third book, "was written in Spanish. It's even older. It concerns an area of South America in the late eighteenth century. It has less historical context, I think, because the extent of Mayan and Aztec civilizations was not understood at the time of the writing. It was only through later archaeological discoveries that we learned what we know now about these incredible cultures. The book still documents much of the genocide the indigenous populations suffered, and just how profoundly evil the conquering armies were in their lust for gold and territory."

Ron picked up the book off his lap.

"But like I said, there are lots of history books around, and many that probably do a better job, in light of what we know now, of documenting the history these books cover."

A tea kettle wailed down the hall from the kitchen and Maggie stood. "Sorry, Ron. Hold on a second; I'll be right back." She picked up the tray and empty pot from the coffee table. Her steps quickly receded down the long hall.

Gracie shuffled to the fireplace and stood with her back to the fire, spreading her hands behind her toward the hearth. She turned and slid back the screen, then reached over to the woodpile to get another log to throw on the fire. After she prodded the log in place with the poker, she faced the fire, rubbing her hands.

Adam looked at Ron and pointed at the books on the table. "Do you mind if I take a look?"

"No, of course not," Ron said.

Adam picked up the other books and carefully turned the pages while Ron followed with his finger the text in the book he was holding.

Gracie stayed by the fire. "It seems I'm always cold." She smiled.

"Maybe this will warm ya up." Maggie came in with a tray full of tall glass cups, tea bags, and a steaming carafe of cider next to an open pint of brandy. Gracie slipped back to her seat as Maggie set down the tray.

"So, you brought the hard stuff." Ron laughed. "I thought we were going to be serious here."

Maggie smiled. "I *am* serious," she said as she poured a dribble of brandy into a cup.

Gentle sounds of serving clinked and gurgled, amid a warm, spicy aroma, while Adam set the books back on the table and looked at Ron. "Okay, Ron, you have me hooked. What does it all mean?"

Ron set his cup down and looked at the book spread across his knees. He opened it to a page where a marker had been placed and held it so all three could see. He had to reposition it to catch the light. What they saw was an illustration—an irregular crescent with more Russian notations surrounding it.

"What is it?" Adam smiled and looked from face to face.

"Lake Baikal in Russia," Ron said. "It's the largest lake in the world by volume. It has about a third as much surface area as Lake Superior, and yet it has more than twice the volume because it is so deep. It was formed by ancient tectonic forces, and it could be millions of years old."

Ron took the next book off the table and opened it at a marker. "Lake Tanganyika in Africa. This lake is also larger than Lake Superior; it is actually one of the Great Lakes of Africa. Most people don't know that Africa has its own group of Great Lakes."

"And this one," he said as he slowly opened the third book to a roughly drawn map, "this is Lake Titicaca in South America, now bordered by Bolivia and Peru. It's not nearly as big as Lake Tanganyika or Superior, but it's the biggest lake in South America. This eighteenth century drawing makes it look much larger than it really is, but the location of the mountains and the old settlements are quite accurate.

"Sorry, Ron; still lost." Adam looked at Maggie and Gracie. "You two seem to know a little bit more about where he's going than I do."

Gracie patted her lips with a napkin and then cupped her drink in her hands. "He's only told us a little about this before—enough to whet our appetites. That's why we were getting together tonight—so he could go deeper." She looked from Ron to Adam. "We thought it might help you, and probably all of us, to know where this might be going."

"Yeah," Ron said. "*Might be going* is a good way to put it because we can't be sure. I'm kind of biased when it comes to lake stuff, so I don't want to jump to conclusions." He smiled. "I think I need you guys to keep me on track."

Adam raised his eyebrows, lifted the corner of his mouth. "All right, lead on."

"Okay," Ron said. "Here's what I think could be happening. Stay with me, 'cause it's pretty weird."

Ron poured a cup and shook his head when Maggie offered brandy. She shrugged and tipped a spot more into her cup.

"There's a lot here, and I can't take credit for its translation," Ron said. "I had help. There's a professor in Sault, Ontario—Dr. Brusilov—whom I've known for a long time, and he helped me."

"I remember him––Mikael," Maggie said. "He used to be a professor at Lake State and stayed here twice, I think. Once when he was working on a project and then again when the weather was bad. I had an arrangement for lodging with the university back then."

"Right, that's him," Ron said. "But even *he* had trouble with some of the text because of the dialect and style." He closed the book, laid his hand on the cover, and continued. "This Russian book was written by a Father Yasnoye Ozero. He writes about war and about some of the politics of his time. That part is okay, but it's not the best history book of the time. It's more a compilation or journal of his experiences than a history book." He tapped the book. "But the part of the book that was really interesting to me is when Father Ozero writes about the time he spent living among the Buryats in southern Siberia. His time on the mysterious island of Olkhon was especially intriguing. Even today, the area is known for the practice of ancient shamanism by the indigenous Buryats."

Ron scanned the group. "When Dr. Brusilov was working on the translation with me, he wondered how truthful the journal could be because he knew the priest's name was obviously an alias...."

"Oh, yes, *obviously!*" Adam laughed.

"No, really," said Ron, smiling, "the name Yasnoye Ozero means something like *clear lake*. About a third of the people living in the region at the time were exiles. It was the middle of the Russian Civil War. Battles between the White Army and the Red Army had spilled into the area. So, it may have been a good idea for him to keep his identity hidden if he was an exile. But that's another story."

Ron opened to the back of the book and took out a piece of lined paper with handwritten notes. "Like I said, my Russian is not good, but I wanted to get this right, so I wrote this out with Dr. Brusilov's help. Listen to this." He read from the paper as he followed the words with his finger.

> For weeks now, the people of the island have reported seeing spirits of the dead, some long passed, all long lost. To be sure, the high priests of their religion and the pagans who follow them, have always claimed to be acquainted with their dead ancestors. But now they are overwhelmed by the number of sightings. The sightings are also occurring in those villages on the shore just like they are occurring here on the island. Spirits leaving the lake. An exodus of the dead. Those drowned and never recovered are fleeing the lake.

"Drowned and never recovered," Adam said. He repeated softly to himself, "Those drowned and never recovered."

Adam shifted from leaning forward to sitting back on the couch. Gracie looked at Adam, rubbed her hands together, and got up to stand by the fire again. Maggie put her fingers to her lips as she glanced at Adam.

"I'm sorry, Adam; is it okay to continue?" Ron asked.

Adam drew in a breath and shook his head. "No, no, it's okay. Go ahead."

Ron paged farther in the book. "This is where it gets strange."

"Oh, it's not strange enough already?" Maggie asked.

Ron smiled, took a breath, raised his eyebrows quickly, and continued.

"One more quote, thanks to Mikael."

He turned over the piece of lined paper.

> Zhanzhima, the shaman, has told me many things; some I believe, some I cannot believe. He is the one who claims there is a spirit beast in the waters. A creature conjured in dreams. I do not believe this.
>
> But he claims that the evil of the wars, torture, and suffering that have afflicted this land have been swallowed by this great lake and that the lake is about to turn over, well up, and spew the evil into the skies and rid the world of it.

"Yeah, that's pretty strange," Maggie said with brows raised.

Gracie returned to her chair and leaned back. "I'm confused. You told me a little of this but...a beast? You mean like the Great Lynx or something? And the turning over of the lake. Do you think there is a parallel? Really?"

"I know, like I said, it's bizarre. But there's more."

Ron removed another piece of paper and unfolded it. "There was a cataclysmic event that he describes at the end of the book.

> In the midst of a warm November night, we witnessed a great event that caused all of us to fear for our lives. A great noise deeper than thunder with flashes of colored light brighter than lightning. The lake swept away from shore, but then rose up. It washed back, swallowing the pier. Finally, a great pillar of light shot into the sky, and the entire island shown as midday. As quickly as it had appeared, it vanished with a horrific report. All was black. All was as nothing. Then came the gray.

Ron looked up at each of them. "That's what was happening to Lake Baikal. And I'm not done, yet." There was silence as he continued. "Just hear me out. Stay with me, folks."

He picked up another book.

"Like I said, this other book was written by a British officer chronicling the devastation wrought by slavery in Africa and by horrible intertribal warfare. The officer focuses on several areas of the country, and one of the chapters involves the area around Lake Tanganyika. He says locals fled the area because they were seeing spirits migrating from the lake. It ends with a vague description of a turning over and eruption of that lake."

Ron picked up the next book.

"This one was written by another priest who was in South America. He wrote about some of the horrors caused by the conquistadors and the great suffering of the people of the South American continent. But this priest became fascinated by events around Lake Titicaca: spirits leaving the lake and a cataclysmic turning over of the lake."

Maggie looked confused. "Ron, are you saying that this is what's happening here? In Lake Superior? The dead are leaving in droves ahead of some great turning over?"

The others looked at her.

"What do you think, Maggie?" Ron replied. "This may be something we need you to answer."

"I think I already know the answer." She inhaled deeply. "That's why I'm here, right?"

Ron nodded.

Maggie touched the corner of her eye with her napkin. "Yes, of course it's true." She inhaled and let it out slowly. "The dead, the drowned, those never recovered *are* leaving the lake. I know this." She stopped.

"Go ahead, Maggie," Ron said.

"Spirits, apparitions, entities, or loops of existence. It doesn't matter. They are all leaving. Being pushed out or forced out of the lake from fear or ahead of some cataclysm. I've known this, and we've all heard about it and mentioned it in a roundabout way. I even talked about it with Cam. I'm sorry, Ron. I didn't want to be involved. But I know they are leaving. Something is happening to force them out."

She clutched the napkin with both hands in her lap. "Is that creature causing this?"

"We have to find out," said Ron. "That's why—"

"No. It's much bigger," Gracie interrupted. She looked at Maggie, then at Ron while tapping her chin with her index finger. "Mishipezhu is only a symptom, a sign of what's going on. The Great Lynx is riled up for the same reason the ghosts are leaving. And maybe we already know why this is happening. It's like you said, Ron; Lake Superior is like these other great lakes. It is the great repository of all the evil on the continent, and it's about to turn over and spew that evil into the sky."

"Wars? Revolutions?" Adam said. "I don't follow. There's nothing here, on this continent, on a scale like that. It's really interesting and all, but I think it might be a bit of a stretch."

"Maybe it doesn't have to be big disastrous events happening right now," Ron said.

"What do you mean?" Adam asked.

"Have there not been wars on this continent? Maybe it just reaches a tipping point. Think of that. There has certainly been death and devastation on this continent. There were centuries--millennia—of war among Native peoples before the Europeans even got here. And maybe there are undercurrents, things happening under the surface. What if you count the incredible violence and the disregard for life even today? I don't know." Ron turned his palms and shrugged. "I just noticed the similarities in these other lakes. I just think it's fascinating." He closed the books and brushed the covers. "Every continent has a big lake, and it seems as though it collects the evil of the continent over time and just sort of—"

"Turns over and cleanses itself," Adam finished. "Fascinating, Ron."

There was silence.

"This is a lot to absorb," said Gracie. She looked at her phone then cleared her throat. "I'm sorry, but I have to go."

"Now?" Ron and Maggie said at the same time.

"Yeah, I got a text from Duane. He's coming a little early to pick me up. It's getting scary with James Graves and all. Don't worry; he's parked right around the block, but he can't stop here because I think he's afraid we'll draw more attention to the inn."

"This is sudden, Gracie," Ron said.

She nodded.

"Where are you going?" Adam thought he sounded a little too desperate.

"Probably back to the rez at Keshena. It's time to leave it up to the FBI as far as Graves is concerned."

"The FBI? Really?" Ron said.

"Yeah," said Gracie. "There's more, but I really can't say right now. Graves is in pretty deep. He's got to be stopped. He will be stopped."

Ron looked at the floor, speaking as if to himself. "I know. He's got to be stopped."

Adam scratched his head and looked at Gracie. "Will you come back?"

She smiled at Ron and Maggie. "These guys know where to find me." She rested her hand on Adam's knee. "Hey, you know the Menominee could use some good psychologists, too, I think." She nodded at Ron. "If this guy will ever let you go."

Adam smiled.

Gracie thanked Maggie. They hugged briefly as they made their way to the door. Adam and Ron lifted their hands to wave as the door closed.

The three were returning to the sitting room when the front door burst open. "Guys, come see this!" Gracie said.

They went quickly out the door. Gracie led them onto the yard in front of the inn. From the west, the sky was molten with reds and blues as ribbons of violet danced and disappeared. Bolts of fluorescent green tore across the dome of sky above. Light washed the entire river and over the locks, while across the city, buildings were flooded in swirling color.

"What the...?" Adam said.

"Northern lights? It can't be. It's never looked like this," Ron said.

"I've never seen *anything* like this. Amazing." Maggie folded her arms and turned side to side as she looked at the sky over the broad Saint Mary's River toward Ontario.

A rumble, deeper and longer than thunder, crackled overhead and made the ground shake. They looked at each other. The street had been silent and empty, but now several porch lights came on and people came out to huddle, point, and stare.

After several minutes, the sky continued riled until the glow gradually faded behind streetlights and city glare.

"I guess this is a night to remember," Maggie said.

They nodded silently until finally Gracie said, "I have to go."

"Stay in touch. Text us as soon as Duane picks you up so we know you're okay!" Maggie said to Gracie.

"I will," Gracie said as she walked quickly, lifting her hand to wave behind her.

They watched the sky for a while, then ambled to the porch. Adam looked back at what was now a dim green aurora in the north.

They returned to the sitting room and sat in silence until Maggie cupped her hand around the teapot. "This is cold. Can I get you anything?"

"No, I'm fine," Ron said. Adam shook his head and looked at Ron.

"If this is all true, if this is what is really happening, how exactly does Graves fit in? What is he doing?" Adam asked. He drummed his fingers on the arm of the couch. "I'm worried."

"I don't know. I'm worried, too. It's about control--power. *Graves* doesn't know what he's dealing with. I'm not sure he even knows what he wants. It's very dangerous. He needs to be followed and stopped." Ron looked at the floor with his fingers on his forehead. "Look at what happened to Danny Sayles. And if Graves were to somehow mess with that? Well, I'm afraid of what could happen."

After a time, Adam inhaled and asked, "Ron, how about Gracie? How does *she* fit into all this? I mean, what does she do? What's her job? Is she with the FBI or what?"

"FBI? CIA? BIA?" Ron said. "She's part of an organization, but it is older than any of those alphabet groups. I don't think I'm free to say. Anyway, it's not like I really know that much about it. And she has never really told me much." He smiled while he looked at the floor and shook his head. "She's complicated."

Ron's phone chimed a text. He slipped it out of his pocket and read. "Ha! Speak of the devil.... It's her text. She must have met up with Duane." He swiped it, read the text, and raised his eyebrows. "But I guess it's more than that."

He slowly handed the phone to Adam who read it out loud. "*I'm with Duane. Talk soon. I think it's okay to tell them who Duane really is.*" Adam looked at Ron confused. "What does she mean?"

"Who is Duane, Ron?" Maggie asked.

Ron rubbed his hands and took a breath before saying. "Duane is Gracie's brother. He's not her husband, but he's very much in the FBI."

Adam knit his brows. "What do you mean? Why wouldn't she tell me—us that?"

Maggie nodded in agreement.

"Gracie is a very cautious woman. She takes care of herself. She has to. She manages her life, and her life is complicated." Ron smiled while looking at his phone. He texted a short note in reply and set the phone down. "She had to keep up the charade to protect herself from the likes of Harley. You met him; you know what he's like. And I have to believe she couldn't risk any *distractions* while she was here."

Adam was still confused.

"If that girl has to go to these extremes, and if the FBI has to be involved, then I'm even more worried about Graves. What kind of harm can he do by...?" Maggie stopped at the sound of the front door opening again. In her chair, she muttered, "Now what?" Then called out, "Gracie, is that you?"

A few steps were heard in the hallway, and there he stood in the sitting room doorway.

"Hey, guys," Cam said. "Ron! So good to see you!"

"Cam? What's going on?" Adam asked as he stood.

Maggie looked at Ron.

"Are you okay?" Ron asked as he walked to Cam, laid his hand on his shoulder, and shook his hand. "Wow, you're back. I heard about the trouble last night."

"Yeah. But I'm better. I saw Dr. Patel, and she said it was all right to leave. She discharged me. They really didn't have a diagnosis to keep me there or anything. It was like a twenty-three-hour release or whatever." Cam shuffled another step into the room. Maggie stood as he continued, "I don't have any insurance or anything, so I guess they were good to let me go with some Seroquel and Zoloft. I'm cool." He looked from person to person. "Really. Hey, did you see those weird northern lights and thunder or whatever?" He mimed an explosion with his hands.

The room was awkwardly silent.

"I'm sorry I interrupted. Really sorry," Cam said.

"It's okay." Maggie stood. "Uh, well...."

"Are you sure you're all right, Cam?" Adam asked. "Do you need to talk--more?"

Cam shook his head. "I'm good. I'm dealing with a lot, but I'm good, now."

Maggie looked at Ron, then to Adam. She spoke to Cam. "Well, your room is—"

"It's so nice of you," Cam said. "I—I feel like the Seroquel is sort of kicking in. If I could just go to my room, I think I'd be just peachy. Really. Thank you so much, Mrs. Stewart."

"Adam, I—" Ron began.

"I'm sorry, Ron," Cam interrupted, "but I guess I'll have to catch up tomorrow, or something. I'll have to curl up here on the couch if I don't get to bed pretty soon. Everything is happening so fast."

Ron stood there and said nothing more.

"Do you need anything? Anything at all?" Maggie asked.

"No, no, I'm fine. I will be good." Cam's voice trailed away as he walked down the hall.

They looked at each other. Ron shook his head tight-lipped. "I don't think I like this. I'll have to see if I can talk to Patel, and maybe I'll see what's going on, if Cam will give me permission."

Maggie stepped past Ron and called down the hall. "And please don't go in that old infirmary!" She looked at Adam. "It's not...safe."

CHAPTER 20

FLEE THE INN

H IS BOOK BAG HEFTED ON his shoulder, Ron gave Maggie a
quick hug at the door. "Are you going to be all right?" he
asked Maggie. Adam was standing at the sitting room door looking
dazed. "Adam? Is this going to be all right?" he repeated.

"I think so. I'll keep an eye on him," Adam said. "I'm not comfortable with his bubbly mood after what we saw last night."

"Text or call right away if you need anything," Ron said to them.
"I mean *anything*."

After Ron left, Maggie turned to Adam, her brow furrowed.
"What can I do?"

He looked up. "You've done everything," he said. "I'll watch him.
You can rest."

Maggie nodded, walked past Adam into the sitting room, and
headed for the pocket doors leading into the library. She said over

her shoulder, "I just need to take care of a few things on the computer and then I'm going upstairs. Good night, Adam. Take care."

"Good night, Maggie."

At the top of the servant's stairs, Adam turned down the short hallway to Cam's bedroom. Listening at the door, he heard heavy snoring. He felt reassured that whatever they had given Cam had knocked him out.

Adam read for a while, then scrolled through his phone. At a text, he stopped, and scrolled back up: Jean, the receptionist at the clinic in Indiana. It was brief and friendly, intending only to say *Hi* and see how Adam was doing. He felt embarrassed. He had not bothered to catch up with her, let her know how he was doing, or even ask how she was doing. He was probably not going back to Indiana, he realized, but it was not like him to be impolite. He replied with a few sentences and promised to give her a call. It was perfunctory—a formality. While writing the text, he was thinking about how far from Indiana his life had strayed in this short time. Now his life had become shuffled again—random and out of his control. "Just like when Julie died," he said to himself.

He hit *Send*, slid the phone onto the table beside the bed, turned out the light, and watched the shadow of branches crossing the window.

The tang of metallic taste and the smell of fresh air were hardly noticed, as he slipped away.

In the quiet dark, the sweet sounds and slow rhythm of waves softly swelled. The darkness was brushed away stroke by stroke, painted with yellow, blue, green, and white. He was on the beach again. Sand, sun, and a stiff onshore breeze swept away walls and windows.

Next to him, Julie sat on the blanket, just like before. Sand, whipped by the wind, stung his ankles and legs. The sun was strong; whitecaps far out in the bay chased all the way to shore. Adam and Julie sat close so they could hear what each other said, but they sat close mostly just to be near.

Something was different. She was not quite the same. This was not how he had remembered Julie when he had this same dream in Indiana.

He turned to her. "You're burning," he said. "Your shoulders are getting red."

She reached into the bag and handed him the sunscreen. "You can have it," she said. "I won't need it. I'm going in the water."

Adam smiled and continued as if he hadn't heard. "I thought Indians didn't burn. Hey, that's right, you're only half Ojibwe; it's the other side that's burning." He snatched the bottle and squirted a puddle of cream into the palm of his hand until the stream made a loud squishy fart sound. He laughed.

Julie made a weak smile.

"It's the beer. Pew! Stuff smells like coconuts," he said.

"You're drunk, Adam."

"It wasn't me; I swear. And I've only had one, uh, six pack."

"I will have to let it go, I guess."

"You'll let one go?" He snorted at the stupid joke. He started to spread the cream thick on her shoulders and back. She flinched at his touch. Her skin was like warm velvet. He swept slower across her upper back, then lower. "I'm afraid you'll have to take this off in order for me to do a proper job of it."

She slowly shook her head with her eyes closed. "Don't, Adam." She was serious. "You've been drinking too much." He wasn't listening.

Julie turned to see a family playing at the edge of the water about a half mile away. She took the bottle and put it back in the bag. But this time, she withdrew a folded piece of lined paper she kept hidden from him. She pushed him away, slid the paper under the cooler, and stood.

Adam watched her every move as she walked away. She sauntered toward the water, her suit riding lower than she would have allowed if anyone had been around. She was taut and maintained her gymnast's body from school, he thought. Her dark skin and hair were ravishing, contrasted with the white suit. She stopped to take in the blue-green water slashed by whitecaps. With her hands on her hips, she slowly turned to look back at the trees, the beach, and the sky, her expression flat and unreadable. She swung back, watching a particular spot in the tree line, then back to the water.

He drank in the brilliance of the shore: gleaming sand, the white waves in the bay, and her silhouette against the water. Even with the wind off the big lake, it was splendidly warm. She looked back and lifted her hand weakly to wave.

"Be careful!" he shouted.

She didn't hear above the roar, as another stiff gust tossed sand at his feet. She picked up one of the big black inner tubes from the sand while he emptied his beer and lay back. *Glorious,* he thought. *Perfect day.*

Julie watched the surf a while longer, then turned and tossed the tube back onto the beach. Looking down the beach and up to the sky once more, she stood there briefly. Walking into the water up to her knees, she dove headlong into a wave.

Adam lay for a long time, the waves, wind, sun, and beer kneading his mind into a happy mush. He was thinking of almost nothing. Slowly, the heat convinced him he needed another beer, and probably it was time to grab the other tube and follow her into the lake. He propped himself unsteadily on one elbow, reached over, and lifted a beer from the cooler. Looking around, he snapped open the can and pushed his sunglasses up on his nose. He sat up so he could see over the waves to find where she was floating. He couldn't see her.

Slowly, he stood, and their little world of blanket, cooler, towels, and trappings shrunk around his ankles as the great water seemed to swell with intimidation. It was only the waves obscuring his view, he convinced himself. That's why he couldn't see her. He looked far out where the whitecaps gamboled like lambs, and then near to the shore where the waves crashed like rams. On the beach were two tubes. She wasn't even in a tube, he realized, and spun to see where the beach met the wall of birch and spruce thirty yards from the shore. Panic simmered: she must have come out of the water and gone into the trees.

"Julie?"

Quickly, Adam walked a short way along the beach and looked across the water again. He searched the sand for footprints and then tramped up the sloping beach to the woods. He looked side to side to see around the trunks and into the shadowed depths. "Julie! Jules?" He spun and looked over the water, and called for her once more.

Garbled and liquid, Julie's voice came, emphatic but distant. "Adam! Cam! He's...." The voice trailed off, the dream slipping from his grasp.

Adam sat straight up and swung his legs out of bed. He rubbed his face with both hands. "Damn!" This is not how he had remembered that day. *Cam! He's.... What? What does it mean?*

Something's wrong. He would check on Cam, then head down to the kitchen. Maybe find a snack––sit and think. He pulled on a T-shirt and jeans, slipped into his shoes, and went into the hall. Cam's door was open, and he was not in his room.

In the hall, the bathroom door was open and dark. No one in there.

Adam hurried down the servants' stairs. At the bottom, he looked down the short, dark hall. The door to the infirmary was ajar, again, but he had not brought his phone. No light. *I'm not doing this again.*

A dim glow shown suddenly along the narrow opening to the infirmary. Adam pushed the great door all the way open. As he stepped into the ancient waiting room, the pearly glow and jagged violet opening drifted at the far side of the room. It did not alarm him, and he felt compelled to approach. Whispers and sweet, high-pitched melodies came from deep within. A murmuring voice rose as he approached the light, his hand outstretched.

The vision seemed out of sync with the room--out of rhythm. It was like a clock that's off by minutes or an anomaly cut and pasted into the room's ambience. Adam stopped and reached with fingers, nearly touching the whirling mist.

A delicate, rolling movement turned inside the glow like an embryo in an egg. Suddenly, a hand coalesced and moved to the surface, so near to Adam's outstretched fingertips. It wavered like a shadow that could not escape the light. Adam tried to speak; he tried to say her name.

Cam burst out of the door next to the spooled cashier's window, bounding across the room. Adam backed up, but Cam pushed past him and out the infirmary door, into the inn. He muttered erratically as he rushed down the hallway toward the front door.

Adam hurried to catch him, but paused and turned back into the infirmary. The vision was gone. He put both hands to his face, took a deep breath, and went back toward the inn.

"Cam! Stop! What the hell are you doing?" Cam was already out the front door.

Adam ran up the servants' stairs to his room, grabbed his phone, coat, and keys, and tore back down the stairs and out the door. Cam was already rumbling away in his old pickup. Adam was pretty sure he knew where Cam was going and what he intended to do to himself.

As Adam dashed for his car, he was stopped by a sizzling stream of lightning that thrust from west to east. Thunder followed, shaking the ground so hard that it nearly took him off his feet. After the lightning, a red glow remained in the western sky over the lake. The ground trembled again. Lights went on in windows up and down the street as the sky in the west turned from red to purple, then flashed blue.

Maggie's third story windows flickered as Adam was backing the car into the street. The sky split with another crackling blast of lightning.

CHAPTER 21

TURNING

"RON, WHAT THE HELL'S GOING on? Where *are* you?" Adam yelled into his phone, holding it away from his head, cringing at crackled static. "Cam's flipped out again. I'm following him...."

"Hell-o? Adam?" Ron replied. "It's Graves. I think he's going to Agawa. Can you believe this spectacle? I just got through customs... all hell broke loose. The—the lightning. Are you seeing this? Whoa! Another one! I can't..." The phone signal broke up. "Gotta stop him. It's the lake; Adam, it's the...." The connection was gone. No bars.

As Adam left town, the streets were filled with red lights and sirens. A wind was rising, throwing tree limbs like tumbleweed. It was after midnight, but the wild display of lights, the moaning wind, and the thunder brought people into the streets--strange people. Some were intent on getting home or were out to watch the sky, but many were simply scattered and milling around. In tatters, they looked lost and confused, not knowing what they were doing or where they were going. Adam thought of his discussion with Maggie: Were these just more fleeing wraiths in the middle of the night?

A back street out of town took Adam to the highway. The open road was dark and empty. Expecting to catch up to Cam's old pickup at any moment, he didn't slow through the little settlements along the bay, knowing police would be too busy to stop him on this harrowing night.

§ § §

Across the lake, water rolled, tormented and angry. It tore at islands and riled the shores. All freighters had gone to anchor; pilots, mumbling at dials, looked up with faces washed in deathly, green light to peer at a lake they could no longer recognize.

On rocky eastern shores, the black cliffs of a massive monolith appeared chiseled out of dark sky as restless waves foamed below. Near Agawa Rock, towering hemlocks swayed in restless anticipation against driving wind, while around the groaning trunks a small figure dressed in ceremonial garb had left the parking lot and shuffled determinedly toward the lake.

In his right hand, the figure carried a sage smudge like a huge green cigar, and in his other hand, he held feathers to fan the smoke. Headdress feathers spread like fingers, and necklaces swayed across his chest. A broad beaded sash lay over a ribbon shirt trimmed in black and purple. Several items were fastened to a belt that also served to hold up a pair of fringed and intricately beaded buckskin pants beneath his large belly. Moccasins with the namesake Ojibwa puckering along the top seam grated on the gravel path.

Myeengun disappeared down the deep alley riven through Agawa Rock. He followed steps into the dark, mossy depths that separated the great hill—barely a span across and several stories deep. He moved feathers and smudge to one hand and braced his other hand against the cold stone to feel the vibrating of this massive rock, which had been split by the tail of Mishipezhu before the time of The People.

Others were skulking in the darkness, watching and following somewhere in the deep crevasse. Either he didn't know they were there, or he chose to ignore them, confident in his power to control any entity that might appear.

§ § §

After Adam left the villages along the west side of the bay, an unquiet darkness closed around him. As the highway snaked near the restless lake, he began to feel as though the car were being pulled; if he were to take his foot off the pedal, the car would continue to accelerate. The forces reversed, the engine struggled, and now the car faced a headwind. Where the highway lay flat, it would suddenly distort and appear to wind downhill. He drove over rolling mounds and around curves that had not been there before, while veils of fog and spray poured over treetops. The sky was ablaze with stars and churning aurora—vibrating, electric, and alive.

A gust hit the car and nearly sent it skidding sideways; then another blast rocked it, sending branches and debris spinning across the twisting highway.

Sprays of driven water blew above treetops, drenching the windshield, causing Adam to momentarily lose sight of the road. The blizzard he had survived on the way from Indiana was still fresh in his mind. He felt panic growing. As wipers slapped, strange things skittered across the road. He slammed on the brakes. Too late, as a child stood gray and lost. He couldn't stop in time. But the vision merely washed over the car as spume and was gone before his tires screeched to a halt.

Stopped in the road, looking around frantically, buffeted by wind, Adam noticed two sets of silver eyes staring at him from cedars at the side of the road. They flashed at the edge of his headlight beams. He pulled slowly forward, lowering the side window. The eyes blinked, turned, and vanished. For only an instant, he saw small figures with bare backs and feathered headdresses.

He looked forward, took a deep breath, wiped his forehead, rolled up the window, and accelerated.

§ § §

Myeengun's feet slapped heavily down the deep stone alley. The churning sky above sent an eerie glow into the crevice of towering walls, damp stone, and pungent moss that pressed closer as the path deepened. A slippery path of steps had been cut into the rock floor and was scattered with shards from broken walls that funneled toward the lake.

The great cleft opened onto the lake along a narrow path. Emerging from the alley, Myeengun stopped to listen. Scree rattled behind him in a rhythm of footsteps, then paused. He smiled knowingly and continued along the short path that led to a broad ledge where waves rolled and splashed at his feet. A sharp rumble across the water startled him, so he had to catch his balance. He fanned the smudge with feathers, then lifted it high to avoid the spray. The spicy, rich smoke blended with the dank, deep aroma of lake and rock. He wiped his sweaty forehead with his forearm and looked warily from the path to the angry lake. He flinched and stooped in alarm when brilliant violet light flared and crackled from far out in the lake and sizzled overhead. Turning to look at the rim of cliff far above, he took a deep breath and trudged on.

The ledge was treacherous from the wash of waves. He stepped carefully until he reached the wall of ancient pictographs. Lightning seared the sky like a twisted yellow claw to reveal the blood red paintings: men in a canoe and writhing serpents drawn with a mixture of pigments whose formula had been forgotten ages ago. Above the serpents stood the Great Lynx: Mishipezhu, its horns and spiny back standing proud upon the wall. The healer prayed, wafted the smudge several times, and raised a talisman that was strung around his neck. He spread his hand flat against the image of the Great Lynx, bowed his head, and mumbled.

More light was erupting from the lake, pulsing in the sky: red, blue, and purple. The ground shook so that Myeengun briefly had to steady himself against the rock face.

He paused until the glow in the sky illuminated a hidden path that had been grown over with ferns and thorny, torturous, white rose vines. It lay open now. He picked his way up the narrow passage, panting. Under an arch of stone, he stepped onto a broad rock slab surrounded by the gnarled trunks of entwined cedars and thick-stemmed blackberry bushes. He had entered a clearing with the west side opening toward the simmering lake.

In the bushes was a sudden scrabbling and scattering. The cedar boughs rustled. The medicine man's face flashed momentary fear as he glanced quickly around, then walked warily ahead.

This secret lookout stood far above the lake and had been hidden from intruders for generations. Myeengun wiped his forehead again as sweat mixed with spray and ran down inside his shirt.

Dense spirea bushes surrounded a low altar at the edge of the cliff. Myeengun lifted his hands and chanted in a guttural, warbling mantra as he shuffled in rhythm toward the stone altar. Over the lake, an aurora seethed in a silent waltz of red and green that reflected across restless waters. It was difficult to tell if the lake reflected light from the sky or if the sky reflected the lake. Far away toward the horizon were more flashes. Thunder rolled from the west to the foot of the great cliffs rising above the Agawa shore. The wind blasted the cedars in repeated gusts as though huffing from massive bellows.

§ § §

A twisting whirlwind of leaves, sticks, and trash slid onto the highway and paused, spanning both lanes as it spun, lurched, and twisted to block the way for Adam. There was no way around it until suddenly a powerful gust rushed through the trees and slammed the wind devil, sending it crashing into the waving boughs of tall spruce.

Adam sped up again, but when he looked in the rearview mirror, things would appear to rush up behind him, then vanish. He kept his eyes ahead.

An ultra-blue horizontal flash spread across the lake and blazed overhead as quickly as a nuclear blast, washing every leaf and needle in blue brilliance. He could hear the thrumming, pounding. In the breaks between trees where he could see the lake, the tips of waves were phosphorescent and writhing.

As Adam crossed the bridge at the Tahquamenon River, the normally flat, sluggish stream was rushing under the bridge, sucked toward the lake in a roaring torrent.

Adam was worried that he had been wrong about Cam, that he wasn't headed to his cabin after all. But he had to stick with his hunch. He couldn't imagine anywhere else Cam would go, and he had to find him before he hurt himself.

Hurling north toward the village of Paradise, Adam looked at the speedometer; it had lurched to nearly a hundred. He took his foot off the pedal, but it didn't slow. The car weaved left, blown by another gust, and he tapped the brake again, narrowly avoiding a skid. The car began to decelerate.

Paradise had gone dark. Everyone had either left or hunkered down. Scraps of roofing and other debris blew across the road as Adam sped through town.

§ § §

On the broad, flat rock above the lake, the shaman raised his arms higher, his wavering voice growing as the pace of the deep incantation increased. He nodded and swayed to the cadence of his words while buffeted by relentless wind. The smoke from the smudge blew straight away from the lake. He bowed, he stood, he gestured with his arms as his voice rose and fell, growing in fervor, goaded by chaos.

Another voice. "Graves, stop! You have to stop!"

The medicine man stiffened, stood silently with arms raised, facing the lake.

"Graves. This is madness. You don't understand!"

Slowly, Graves turned to stare at the intruder and carefully lowered his arms. He dropped the smoldering smudge. The changing lights shone at his back while his voice carried above the clamor, clear with authority.

"Ronald––Jarvin: So, your name: *Great Counselor––Of-the-Lake* or is it *From-the-Lake*? Or will it be: *Back-in-the-Lake*?" He smiled cruelly. "Leave now. This has nothing to do with you, Jesuit slime. Leave now and you live. You have no idea what you are doing." Graves' face grew severe. He made fists and clutched them to his chest. "This is all beyond you!" He panted and grew furious shouting above the wind. "I am Myeengun! I…am…Myeengun!"

"You don't-know-what-you-are-doing, Graves! This is all beyond *you*! You will only make things worse!" Ron shouted back.

Graves glared at Ron. He looked down to see large beads and a crucifix dangling from the counselor's open coat. James tilted his head back and laughed aloud. "You…damned…fool! What are you doing here? I want…you…gone!"

§ § §

North of Paradise, Adam smelled burning engine oil and looked at his dash, but no warning lights were showing. He looked up just in time to avoid a tree that had fallen onto the road. Hitting the brakes sent the car into a skid; the back tires swung into the ditch, but the front tires had purchase and pulled back on the road. The car fishtailed to the other side, but he was able to swing it straight. Looking ahead, he saw a pair of taillights, flickering in smoke trailing from a moving vehicle far in the distance. It had to be Cam's old truck.

How can he keep going in that damned old truck? Adam thought. Just then, the taillights disappeared left and Adam slowed to take a sharp turn, following the red lights down a dirt two-track. As Adam pulled closer, the truck did nothing to evade him, as though the driver expected Adam to follow. Fumes rolled from the truck along the dirt road until, a few miles later, clattering and smoking, the truck suddenly veered right into a short parking space and skidded to a stop.

Cam jumped out of the truck and slammed the door, heading for the woods. Adam left his car and rushed past the truck as it smoked and sizzled.

"You wanna see? You wanna see?" Cam shouted as he disappeared into rustling shadows.

The sky glowed in shades of blue over the lake, lighting the pathway the short distance to the cabin. Beyond the clearing, through darkened forest, and across a pale beach, the lake lay shifting and troubled.

"Cam, stop. What are you doing? You don't have to do this!"

Cam burst into the cabin, the door crashing against the wall inside.

Adam caught up and reached the cabin, but Cam was already back outside and holding something cradled in his right arm.

"What is that? What are you doing?" Adam asked panting.

§ § §

Ron pushed the beads back into his coat and wrapped himself against the wind. He met the medicine man's gaze and set his bearded jaw, his hair tangled and wet with spray. "Don't do this, Graves. Just come back; this can't work. I *know* it can't! You don't have the power. You don't have the.... It's only the little people."

With a speed that defied the man's wasted body, James slipped the feathers into his belt and, in the same move, withdrew a large knife. He fiercely lunged at the huddled man. Ron lifted his right arm in clumsy defense as the knife slashed down through the sleeve and deep into his forearm. The returning swing clipped off fingers that spun into the darkness. Ron reached with his left hand, trying to grab the knife, but Graves angled back and slashed inside Ron's left arm.

Ron heard himself scream. Rage growing, he plunged ahead, flailing bleeding arms, flinging blood across rocks and onto his attacker. Graves charged, thrusting his shoulder into Ron's chest, and knocking him back several steps until he slipped on the rocks, which were damp with lake spray and blood. Able to regain his footing, he started toward Graves, but the medicine man had put his knife back in his belt and was just standing there with palms forward, silhouetted against the deep blue glow from the lake. Ron stopped, panting. Their eyes locked, but Ron saw no whites in the man's eyes, only a void of black hatred.

Graves smiled.

The twang of a bow was followed immediately by a sickening sharp crack. Ron looked startled, his eyes wide, the shaft of an arrow protruding from the back of his head. He fell face forward with a vicious smack on the cold, wet stone.

Graves looked up and nodded. Harley stood at the edge of the clearing, bare chested, wearing fringed buckskin pants, holding a bow.

§ § §

A brilliant red flash, the ground trembled. Cam held a ceramic container in the crimson light. He threw off the lid, fumbled inside, and pulled out a piece of lined paper.

"Adam, you have to read this. You have to see what it is!" he shouted.

"What is it? Tell me what it is!"

"Read it. Damn it. Read it!" Cam held the paper shaking in his outstretched hand while Adam stepped carefully near and took the note. He held it up in the dim light, but the light was not bright enough to read. While looking at Cam, he picked his phone out of his pocket to turn on the light. "Come on, Cam; what is it? What are you doing? Don't hurt yourself. What does the note say?"

Cam sobbed. "Just read! Damn it!"

A brilliant, purple sheet of laser light shot across the lake. A massive rumble shook the trees along the shore. Adam and Cam crouched and looked up, waiting, then stood again in wind that was swirling with sand and debris.

Leaving the note in Adam's hand, Cam turned suddenly and ran toward the lake, through birch and spruce to the edge of the beach. He stopped, his arm covering his face from the blast of sand. The wind blew straight in from the beach, neither gusting nor turning, but horizontal and steady. Above, the stars were canopied and seemed to undulate in the shifting colors that cast light across the water—an underworld scene of waves like huge, rolling snowbanks over black water that thundered toward shore and reflected the intermittent flashes of red, blue, and green.

§ § §

Graves turned toward the cliff and stepped forward with arms raised. He took up his wailing song to the lake in an ancient tongue. The lake replied in refrains of lightning, raging wind, and massive swells that rose and quivered without direction, like water shaken in a barrel. From the center of the lake, a brilliant burst of light flashed a sheet across the turbulent water and shown everything in deep violet, including Ron's bloodied body.

At cliff's edge, Graves found the smudge, withdrew the feathers from his belt, raised his arms, and resumed his incantation. But his passion had waned, and he was fumbling through ritual as he called over the lake. When the Jesuit had appeared, something in the shaman's mind had confirmed to him that he did not know the way, and he feared he was impotent to conjure the beast. All the pieces of the puzzle were not in place and, if he could admit it, he knew this even before he arrived at the lake. Tearing at the talisman that hung around his neck, he threw it to the waves. Pumping his arms and spreading his hands in supplication, he bent his head back and howled—empty, ravaged, and murderous.

At the edge of the clearing, Harley stood, unaware of Graves' growing anguish. With the bow slung on his back, his arms folded, and his chin tilted in serene satisfaction, Harley watched.

Suddenly, Harley's expression changed; his eyes widened and he looked past the healer and far out into the lake. He fell to his knees. His arms flapped uselessly at his sides while he tried to speak, but a hideous black, bloodied tongue had thrust between his teeth. As he tried to shake his head frantically, the mass protruded farther. He fell forward, a shaft protruding from the back of his head. Blood poured from his gaping mouth, running along the spearhead, and into the ground.

A small figure in white entered the clearing, swept past Ron's crumpled body, and approached the medicine man. A hand reached up, firmly grabbed a mat of hair and feathers, and yanked his head back while the other hand reached around his neck. A knife glinted as lightning flashed. Then blood gushed down the man's chest and pulsed as the blade slit through artery. Graves tried to gasp through the severed trachea, and gurgled blood. Staggering, his arms still raised and convulsing, he was pushed forward to the edge of the cliff. He buckled and leaned forward. Far below, the waters were frenzied, and two waves surged and parted like massive jaws while great horns, like masts, thrust from the water. The limp body fell forward, crashed on a lower ledge; ceremonial bones and beads rattled. The body turned as it hit, head garishly thrust back and neck gaping. Graves rolled into the mouth of the beast and was gone.

The small figure, clothed in white buckskin dress and moccasins, stood briefly on the edge of the cliff looking down, then turned and walked toward Ron's body, bloodied and still, lying on the rock. A white moccasin braced itself carefully on Ron's head, and with one smooth motion, the arrow was yanked out and flung over the cliff.

The woman stood upright, reached around her head, untied her long black hair, and shook it loose. She looked down at the body at her feet, knelt, rolled him carefully onto his back, felt his neck for a pulse, and then stroked his hair.

"I'm here, Ron," Gracie said.

§ § §

Adam caught up to Cam on the beach just as a great flash of purple light sliced across the entire lake, broad and flat. A laser show from horizon to horizon, intense at the center, it spread to wash everything in electric violet. Giants wrestled underground.

A red blast followed, boiling far out in the lake, mounding. The rising edge of the mass shifted serpentine and sizzling like the sun's surface, as though a dragon planet were rising from the lake. As the great dome rose, they turned their faces upward as if watching a rocket launch.

The waves were swept silent. The water went flat and began to recede farther from shore.

"What...is...this?" Cam screamed.

The red dome burst wide with a searing roar and they ran for cover, diving behind a tangled tree that had fallen along the bank.

When the dome split, out came--nothing.

Black nothing.

Molten blackness poured from the receding red dome to obliterate everything. It flowed toward them, causing the stars to disappear, the horizon to vanish, and the lake's surface to become enveloped as it spread outward. Nothingness. The black rolled over them, and they could see nothing, feel nothing, or hear nothing for minutes. Cam tried to speak, but it was like drowning in oil—a horrible, whispering thickness that clawed into their souls and caused them to feel hollow, fearful, and empty.

They lost all sense of themselves, all sense of time and consciousness. It may have been minutes, it may have been hours, but gradually, darkness turned gray and left the air dense and nitrous.

In the fallen tree's roots, they found themselves enveloped in silence. The smoky veil covered all; it was unbroken and smooth like volcanic ash. Everything lay in the same dead light without shadow, because everything was shadow.

§ § §

The slate sky was turning to the first hint of a flat, bleak dawn when Cam finally stood. Morose and overwhelmed, he shuffled through the sand back to the cabin.

Adam remained within the branches of the deadfall and looked over the lake's charcoal black surface. He felt confused, numb, and detached. He realized he was still holding the piece of paper Cam had forced him to take. He turned it slowly in the bleak light, not really comprehending what it was, and only vaguely remembering how it got there. Minutes passed before he unfolded it and turned it toward the dim light forming in the east. He read it slowly; the words were not taking form on the page and not registering in his head. He swallowed, his mouth dry, and rubbed his scratchy eyes.

As he read it again, he felt a panic of grief build within him and fill his throat.

> Dear Adam,
>
> I can't fix myself. I cannot live with myself, and I cannot look at you because of what we did to you. It was so

stupid. You were always the only one, but what we did to you destroyed it all.

No, I destroyed it all. I did it. I'm so sorry.

Goodbye.

I Love YOU.

Julie

Adam read it again, then sat a long time in the sand with his legs pulled up, his head resting on his knees, and his hand lying in the sand at his side, holding the note. With his other hand, he pounded his leg while he sobbed.

"I'm sorry, Adam," he heard behind him.

He looked up to see Cam. "I'm so sorry, Adam."

"I…don't…want…to…know." Adam put his head down.

"It's my fault. We were—"

"Don't say *one…damned…word* or I swear to God I'll kill you!" With his forehead on his knee, Adam shook his head slowly. His voice was low and steady as he looked down at the sand. "I'm this close to…."

Cam shuffled toward the cabin, then turned. "You have to hear this, Adam. You have to." Adam looked up and across the water. Cam continued, "It was an impulse. Stupid. We were both drinking." His voice faltered. "Then after I heard that she went missing, I was afraid that she'd…. I couldn't stand it. I went to the beach that evening. Maybe I thought I could save her, or find her body or something. I don't know. What the hell."

Without looking back, Adam just lifted the note in reply.

Cam forced out the words. "I found that note when I came back to the beach. The cops were milling around; most of them were down by the landing, and your stuff was still there. It was right under your cooler. Nobody had moved it." He covered his face with his hands. "I'm nothing but a coward. I couldn't bear to show you the note so you would see what we had done. I couldn't face you." He looked up. "I was such a coward that I couldn't even kill myself--*like she did.* After a time, all I could do was hide away in this damn cabin. I couldn't stay in my life. I'd ruined two other lives, and I couldn't bear it."

There was no response from Adam. Cam walked past the cabin, and after several tries, and some tinkering under the hood, his truck started and he chugged away.

Over Adam, a ghost of dawn lifted the slate ceiling above still black water.

CHAPTER 22

RETURNING

ADAM DID NOT RECALL LEAVING the beach, getting in his car, or driving down the two-track to the highway and through Paradise.

He remembered burning the cabin.

His mind was blank as he drove along the shoreline past the beach where his best summers were spent and where Julie had been lost. He refused to feel anything, or even turn his head as he drove by. Nothing. The lake was taciturn and void. *Nothing to see here. Move along.*

He continued through Bay Mills, past the casino, slowing as a TV news van pulled from the lot onto the street. Another news van was turning into the parking lot, while one or two more were parked in front of the casino.

Nothing to see here. Move along. Show's over.

§ § §

When Adam had left the beach and walked to Cam's cabin, he had been holding the note. He had kicked the cabin door off its hinges, found a lighter near the stove, lit the note, and tossed it on the bed. With papers and clothing that were laying around the room, he had stoked the fire until smoke filled the room. He had thought about staying—about throwing himself on the bed, feeling the flames as they seared the anguish, stupidity, and anger. Anger at what? At whom? Anger at himself. Relish the pain of his stupidity.

The smoke had forced him out. He had stumbled from the cabin, hacking and spitting, leaning against a tree with his forehead against his arm. He had wept until smoke curled around the eaves. Flames had appeared behind glass, quickly consumed the interior, and twisted from the open door. The heat had pushed him back. With elbows flaring, he had placed his hands on the sides of his head and looked up as several pine branches sizzled and smoked above the cabin. Tears had wet his cheeks, but there was no comfort in what he'd done—no satisfaction, no relief.

Like an open mouth, fire had screamed from the door and long fingers of flame had cupped the ragged eaves. Smoke and heat had lifted the roof's shingles and seeped between the stacked logs.

Whoosh! Something had ignited inside and blown out the windows and coughed through the door. The entire cabin had become wrapped in flame that reached to the top of pines and spruce. Tendrils of smoke had risen from the ground, and tree trunks had simmered.

Adam had covered his face with both hands and taken unsteady, backward steps, shielding his eyes from the inferno. Turning to the sky, he had felt as though his soul had been yanked out, emptied, and turned to ash. *Nothing's left. Nothing to see here. Move along. Show's over.*

§ § §

Adam followed the TV news van as it crawled ahead, lost on an unfamiliar rural highway. He sank deeper inside himself, feeling more foolish than angry. Beyond angry--used and foolish.

When Adam reached the inn, the sky was brightening through a gray skin of thin clouds. It was an ordinary cool day in late November. Maggie's car was gone.

He entered the front door. The unlit house was shadowy in flat light. The hall was silent in a vague luster that filtered from windows off side rooms. No fire burned in the cold sitting room, and the library sat in darkness, curtains drawn.

The hall creaked as Adam walked past the darkened main stairs. At the end of the hall, the kitchen seemed strange in the empty quiet. With many windows, it seemed bright in comparison to the rest of the house. Standing outside the kitchen, Adam paused at the servants' stairs and looked the other way into the darkness that was the short hall. The great door to the infirmary was narrowly open. He brushed his hand across his forehead, stood for a full minute, then shuffled to the door and grasped the handle of the oak door, holding it a long while. He began to close the door, but stopped, looked at the ceiling, and sighed. The door whimpered as he opened it fully and entered the infirmary's waiting area.

As Adam crossed the room, his shoes crunched and popped on bits of plaster and glass. The door on the far side of the room was closed, but he opened it without hesitating. He turned the corner past the tall windows and started up the steps. He felt nothing: just a big, empty, decaying building cast in gray light.

On the second floor, Adam faced the windows and paused. He walked up to the one in the middle, which looked out onto the yard behind the inn. He saw the bay window of his room. Many times, he had stood and looked at the infirmary from that perspective, and now he was looking back. It was deathly silent in the infirmary with only the rare tick or rasp in the dying infirmary.

"Julie, I…." He did not realize that he'd begun speaking.

"Julie, I…." He wiped a tear off his cheek.

"I forgive you," he whispered as he traced aimlessly on the window. He cleared his throat and looked behind him, and then out the window again. "We shared the best years. Our best years. I will hold on to that." He sniffled. "But I am here. I have a life." He paused. "I have to make a life."

Adam stepped back and looked at the windows, down the narrow hall, at the ceiling, and spoke aloud. "You may go. You may go in peace. I release you." He closed his eyes. "As you release me." He wiped his eyes and did not notice his feeble smile. "It's finished. Let's both be glad." He shrugged. "Let's find a way to be happy."

CHAPTER 23

THANKSGIVING

R ON STOOD IN THE DOORWAY, staring absently, transfixed
by the flame and remembering. His head ached. The fire
snapped. He blinked.

Sitting in one of the big chairs, Maggie fidgeted with the edge
of her apron, looking at Ron. "Do you think he'll come down?" she
asked.

"What? Oh, I don't know. It was quiet, so I didn't even knock."

"I heard him rustle a little last night, but otherwise, he hasn't
moved. Like I said before, I haven't talked with him in two days, and
that was only mumbles." She leaned forward as though starting to
stand. "Why don't you sit down, Ron? You need to rest, for goodness
sakes! You're more sliced up than that turkey's gonna be."

He laughed cautiously as he walked slowly to the couch. Easing
himself onto the seat, he held his head with his left hand while he
rested the casted right arm on his lap.

Maggie tsked, lowering back in the chair. "You're just lucky that at least one Indian doesn't know a practice arrow from a hunting arrow."

He rolled his eyes and looked into the fire.

"I was just thinking," Maggie continued. "Where do you suppose our little Gracie Bird flew off to? Where did she say she was going? I wish I could've had her and her brother here for Thanksgiving. I really liked that girl."

"Not sure about Gracie. I...." He paused as a voice from that horrific night whispered through his memory. Then he nodded slowly and continued. "Yeah, I—I suspect somebody in Keshina knows; back in Wisconsin."

She grinned and raised a brow. "Do you think Adam will be taking a trip to Wisconsin any time soon?" She waved her hand. "Never mind; that's just nosey talk."

Ron smiled while watching the fire.

Maggie looked over at him, concerned. "Are you sure I can't get you something else for the pain?"

"No. That prescription is starting to work, and it's settling things very nicely for the moment. I can manage. It was worse overnight. My right hand...and my arm...and my head...and my back. Other than that, everything else is pretty good."

Maggie shook her head. "I can't believe they only kept you a couple of days."

"After they sewed everything up and did the CT on my head, what else were they supposed to do? Bring in the highland pipers? Dance a jig?" Ron opened his eyes wide. "Whew. This pain med *is* kicking in."

Maggie laughed. "You know they had pipers at the fort back in the day, so maybe some spirits—"

"Don't even go there. Hopefully, all the ghosts have gone to rest for a long, long time."

"Yes, they have. I feel certain they have." Maggie looked thoughtfully at the floor a long while. She looked at Ron. "May they all find peace wherever they've scattered—a home."

The foghorn of a doorbell sounded and Ron jumped. "Ouch!"

Before Maggie could get up, the front door opened and someone hurried to the sitting room.

"Uncle Ron! Oh, my God. Are you okay?" Samantha burst into the room followed by her father, Jan. "Don't stand up!"

"I'll be fine as long you don't hug me, I guess!" Ron said. "I'm glad you two made it down here."

"When Dad called, he said he'd told you I would've gotten here yesterday, but he thought you needed another day to sleep. Oh, my God, look at all the bandages. You look like a mummy!"

Maggie stood and gave quick hugs. "So good to see you again. It's been too long."

"You, too, Maggie. Thanks for having us," Jan said.

Samantha sat on the couch near Ron while Jan and Maggie sat in the chairs. "You look awful!" Samantha said.

"You're just full of compliments, aren't ya?" Ron shifted on the couch and winced.

Samantha laughed and reached to touch his arm but stopped. "I only have bits of the story from Dad. Oops." She covered her laugh. "I didn't mean to say *bits*. Ha, I know—your fingers!" Jan and Ron rolled their eyes and laughed, sharing a family's dark sense of humor. She continued. "I heard about Mr. Graves and what those guys did to you. But how did they ever find you? The paramedics, I mean." She looked at Jan and back at Ron. "Dad said some woman called it in?"

"They don't know who it was," Ron said. "It was on the nephew's, Harley's, phone. They don't know if it was some girlfriend who had come there with Harley or a passerby who didn't want to be identified."

"Where's Graves, and who do they think killed the nephew, then?" Jan asked.

"I talked with Sheriff Roy again this morning, and he was trying to get what he could from the Mounties in Canada," Ron said.

"It's sounds bizarre. Well, what about this *isn't* bizarre? But they don't know if Graves made some kind of sacrifice of Harley and then escaped, or if he committed *hari-kari* and fell over the edge of the cliff. There was lots of blood near the cliff and—"

"Oh, dear," said Maggie, standing. "I have some things I have to take care of. Dinner should be ready in about twenty minutes."

Ron looked up. "Sorry, Maggie."

"Do you need help?" Jan asked.

"Hey, I can help." Samantha stood. "I'll catch up after dinner, Uncle Ron. Maggie and I haven't talked in a long time."

The brothers sat in silence, watching the fire. After a couple of minutes, they heard Adam's voice near the kitchen down the hall, talking quietly to Maggie and Samantha. Ron looked at Jan.

"Jan," Ron said in a hushed tone, "before Adam comes in here—I don't know what happened between Adam and Cam Jourdain, yet. I remember talking with him on the phone on the way up to Agawa before the lake blew up. He was chasing Cam to his cabin at Vermillion because he thought Cam was going to kill himself, I think."

"Where's Cam now?" Jan asked, keeping his voice low.

"The sheriff said they found him walking on Highway 28—nearly got run over. His truck was broken down near the intersection there, like he was going to head west. Who knows where? He's in the Marquette hospital now and will hopefully be there for a while."

"Does Adam know?" Jan asked.

"I don't think so. That's why I want to go easy. I still don't know what happened with them."

They were silent. Jan stirred the fire, added a log, and sat down again.

"Jan, there's something else. I don't know who else I'd want to say this to, but with all the weird stuff that's gone on, I have to tell you."

"Sure. What is it?"

"Well, it was the darnedest thing out there, at Agawa Rock. While I started to come around, I think I heard a woman speak. I knew I needed help, but whoever she was, it seemed that she'd left. So I just lay there--helpless. I couldn't move and I couldn't speak." He adjusted the bandage over his right fingers. "I was pretty sure at least a couple of my fingers were gone, and I didn't know how bad I might be cut up. My head hurt like hell. I thought I was probably dying."

"They found your fingers, and you said they were able to—"

"No, wait." Ron held up his left hand. "There's more."

"I'm sorry; go ahead."

"After a while, like I said, I thought the woman had gone away. I was sort of in and out of it. I was scared. I didn't know where Graves was, and the wind and thunder and flashes of light were terrible. Incredible." He stopped. Jan waited for him to continue.

Ron took a deep breath. "This is so crazy. I don't know how to say this." He wiped a tear from his cheek and his voice was hoarse as he continued. "Little hands; I swear that I felt little hands on my back, and from the glow of the sky and the flashes of lightning, I saw pairs of little bare feet next to me." He laughed thinly. "I thought they were a bunch of kids. Weird. I figured I must be hallucinating."

Ron sighed. "Whatever they were, they rolled me over, and touched my head, my chest, and the cuts on my left arm and hands." His voice wavered. "They were bare chested, despite the terrible weather. And they had long feather headdresses that whipped in the wind." He paused. "Did you know? Did I tell you where the paramedics found my two fingers?"

"I wondered how they found them, in the dark and all," Jan began to say.

Ron said, just above a whisper as he pointed at his chest, "They found them on my chest!" He shook his head slowly. "On my chest."

"What? Who did that?" Jan said.

"And I think that's why I got out of the hospital in only two days. The doctors couldn't believe it. The ortho surgeon said he'd never seen anything like it. His explanation was a little more graphic, but after they reattached the fingers, they pinked right up and everything worked perfectly. I know I won't have much feeling in them, but I'm not going to complain. Even the divot in the back of my head was good. It didn't penetrate the dura, just the scalp and outer bone. So I needed some patching up and now some time to heal, and I hope that's it. I have to see the doctor tomorrow and start therapy next week. It's…it's like a miracle. I don't know what happened."

"I just thought of something. Look at this." Jan was scrolling rapidly through photos on his phone. "I was working on this, doing research, and carving this set for the past year or so. I think I showed you one or two of them when you were up there at my place. I'm done with it now." Jan handed Ron the phone. Ron scrolled through photos of the carvings Jan had been working on the night he saw the visitors from the French ship—a small woman with a headdress, long braided hair, and a breast plate. He had other photos of the other woman and the three men who made up the set.

"That's amazing. That's it!" said Ron. "I only saw flashes, but I…. That's why I thought I was hallucinating. I never told you about the dream Adam told me about when he was in a forest, did I?"

"Hey, guys," Adam said quietly as he walked into the sitting room. Ron turned slowly, still holding the phone, and Jan stood and quickly shook Adam's hand. Adam stepped behind Ron and patted his shoulder. "Don't get up. *Please*, don't get up." He walked around the couch and sat next to Ron. "How are you?"

With his good hand, Ron grabbed Adam's knee and smiled. He stared at Adam. "It's so good to see you. So good." He looked at Jan. "We were just talking about you."

"I heard," Adam said.

The three men sat quietly for a time.

"When are you going to tell me about it? About everything that happened up there at Vermillion?" Ron asked.

"Mmm...." Adam thought about it. "Not yet. It will come. There is so much...to sort out." He looked down. "God, Ron. I'm so glad you're okay. I've only heard a little, and Maggie was talking about it out in the kitchen. I was so scared when you told me you were following Graves up there to Agawa. When are you going to tell *me* about what happened up there?"

"Mmm, not yet. It will come. There is so much to sort out." Ron smiled.

A brief time passed until Adam cleared his throat and broke the silence. "What were you guys looking at on the phone?"

§ § §

Seated at the oak table in the formal dining room, they were a subdued, but happy circle. Extra leaves in the table were not needed this year. A rich glow, enhanced by candlelight, reflected off cherry woodwork and polished furniture; it shown on a meticulous setting of antique dishes and elaborate silverware, and lit their faces. At the center of the table stood a perfectly browned turkey surrounded by a bowl of steaming mashed potatoes, a pan of dressing, and other dishes.

Maggie reached out her hands. "Do you mind if we hold hands, uh, wrists?" She smiled at Ron. "And pray?"

She gently held Ron's right wrist, and each in the circle followed her lead as they took hands and bowed their heads.

EPILOGUE

No gift bestowed by the Creator is more precious than early spring in the north. In March, the woodchuck burrows up through mud and snow to emerge on sun-hardened crust. It ventures out for dead leaves, peeled bark, and green twigs that were left by the snowshoe hare—food that is now exposed by the cycle of melt and freeze paring away layers of snow.

By May, the delicate spring beauty and trillium are painted across silent forest floors and wreathe dark trunks held in slanting light. The glade opens to the serene blue-green of broad water that murmurs and rocks like a new mother.

At midday, beaches along the south shore are washed clean by white light and foam, and to the east, the tall rock cliffs, jagged against deep blue sky, are warming. Small subterranean creatures edge onto the surface, blessed by sun.

Agawa Rock rises in full light, gleaming. Ancient pictographs flare red in silent parade: the canoes, the horse with four moons, the hunter and deer. And the Great Lynx above two serpents with strange scrabbling legs.

But new characters are scrawled on the rock for future centuries to ponder. Above Mishipezhu, figures are still drying in the sun, drawn with a mixture of pigments, the formula for which has long been forgotten: two new images. The lower image is a small broken man, falling, bent at the waist, arms wide. Above the man, in warm sun on gray rock, stands the image of a white doe.

ACKNOWLEDGMENTS

I'D LIKE TO THANK MY wife, Sally, for her exceptional reading and insight. Writers are a dime a dozen, but great readers are rare. She is a great reader in every sense. Because of her dedication and advice, she deserves credit for half this book, maybe more.

My family has been a supportive and tolerant sounding board through all my discussions. They were brave readers of early drafts and provided precious correction and direction. Thanks to my son, Jonah, for so much creative input and two complete readings. My daughter, Sarah Bertolini, more than paid off her journalism degree with her laser focus and good comments. My daughter-in-law Amie did a valuable reading of a late draft and helped me roll it up. Makai-ya Griffin cleaned up my French references and offered wonderful tips. Naomi Griffin reviewed a chapter for college-girl accuracy.

I know I will miss listing some friends. Den and Nan Nordstrum: Friends for life. Nan, you still need to think about being an editor.

Your thoroughness and insight challenged me to work harder. Den, your reading, encouragement, and great photos of the moody ambience of Lake Superior have been an inspiration.

I'm grateful to Robin Keith for reading through a very early draft and saying, "You did it!" Your experience in the field gave me the assurance that I could bring this in for a landing.

Gayle Hazelbaker smashed stereotypes of libraries and librarians. You've given us good stuff: encouragement, books, and lots of laughter.

My Yooper readers are precious:

Kate VanHouten (fellow ex-pat) for early editing and insight—I'll say it again, you need to pursue your enormous writing talent. Wanda and Mike Perron, your enthusiasm (you read the whole thing aloud on the way home from Kate's!) and Wanda's expertise on Native language, culture, and lore is outstanding. Thanks for the word "Akudo."

Skip Parish offered early insights into navigation, boats, and research vessels. He is someone who can genuinely say he's lived his life on Lake Superior.

Steve Parish, from a long line of Native fisherman and Rock gods, is an inspiration and gave me insight on Native casinos.

There are always those who've played small roles, whom I may have bounced stuff off of, and whom I forgot to mention. I'm sorry.

Thank you Superior Book Productions. Tyler Tichelaar is a fastidious editor and a kind teacher. Larry Alexander is a patient and friendly formatter. They are true professionals and have been instrumental in carrying this book to publication.

ABOUT THE AUTHOR

CRAIG A. BROCKMAN HAS LIVED near the Great Lakes all his life, and he has worked along the shores of Lake Superior for much of that time. Employed in The Indian Health Service and at Lake Superior State University, he came to know the rich fabric of the Upper Peninsula.

The Upper Peninsula's lakes, forests, and mountains will always be a frequent destination for Craig and his family. In 2017, an article in the *Ontonagon Herald* chronicled the final 140-mile leg of his hike across the entire U.P. from the Drummond Island Ferry Dock in DeTour Village to a sandbar at the mouth of the Montreal River on the Wisconsin border.

Craig currently lives with his wife in Tecumseh, Michigan. In 2007, he published *Marty and the Far Woodchuck*, a middle-grade novel. *Dead of November* is his first novel for adults.

Made in the USA
Middletown, DE
31 October 2022